THE SILK R

Volume 4 of The Silk Tales

A NOVEL

BY

JOHN M. BURTON QC

EDITED BY KATHERINE BURTON

This book is sold subject to the condition that it shall not, by way of trade or otherwise, be lent, resold, hired out, or otherwise circulated without the author's prior consent in any form (including digital form) other than this in which it is published and without a similar condition being imposed on the subsequent purchaser.

TEXT COPYRIGHT © JOHN M BURTON, 2016

ALL RIGHTS RESERVED

John M. Burton has asserted his right under the Copyright, Designs and Patents Act, 1988 to be identified as the author of this work.

This novel is a work of fiction. Names and Characters are the product of the author's imagination and any resemblance to actual persons, living or dead, is entirely coincidental.

First Edition 2016.

FOR MY MOTHER, WHO LOVES A COURTROOM DRAMA.

Books by John M. Burton

The Silk Brief, Volume 1 of The Silk Tales

The Silk Head, Volume 2 of The Silk Tales

The Silk Returns, Volume 3 of the Silk Tales

The Silk Ribbon, Volume 4 of the Silk Tales

The Silk's Child, Volume 5 of the Silk Tales

Parricide, Volume 1 of The Murder Trials of Cicero

The Myth of Sparta, Volume 1 of The Chronicles of Sparta

The Return of the Spartans, Volume 2 of The Chronicles of Sparta

The Trial of Admiral Byng, Pour Encourager Les Autres, Volume 1 of the Historical Trials Series

Treachery, The Princes in the Tower.

Table of Contents

CHAPTER 1
THE PUPIL 11
CHAPTER 2
THE SILK RIBBON 22
CHAPTER 3
THE NEIGHBOURS 30
CHAPTER 4
DEATH OF A LOVER 36
CHAPTER 5
THE INTERVIEW 42
CHAPTER 6
THE NEW BRIEF 54
CHAPTER 7
THE CONSULTATION 61
CHAPTER 8
THE JUNIOR 68
CHAPTER 9
THE CHANNEL 74
CHAPTER 10
FIRM GROUND? 82
CHAPTER 11
THE RUSSIAN INTERPRETER 88

CHAPTER 12
A BARRISTER'S STRIKE?... 93
CHAPTER 13
THE BROTHER 99
CHAPTER 14
ACCIDENT OR MURDER?....................................... 107
CHAPTER 15
A VISIT TO NEWCASTLE 112
CHAPTER 16
THE LOVING HUSBAND... 123
CHAPTER 17
COSTA SMERALDA 132
CHAPTER 18
BACK TO REALITY... 138
CHAPTER 19
THE TRIAL COMMENCES....................................... 145
CHAPTER 20
THE PROSECUTION OPENING 156
CHAPTER 21
THE NEIGHBOURS 169
CHAPTER 22
MORE NEIGHBOURS 179
CHAPTER 23
SEVERAL SHADES OF RED................................... 198

CHAPTER 24	
THE FRIEND	215
CHAPTER 25	
THE EMERGENCY SERVICES	225
CHAPTER 26	
THE TASER	247
CHAPTER 27	
THE NOTEBOOK	265
CHAPTER 28	
THE SEARCH	275
CHAPTER 29	
THE PATHOLOGIST	284
CHAPTER 30	
THE FIREARMS EXPERT	290
CHAPTER 31	
CHALLENGING THE FIREARMS EXPERT	299
CHAPTER 32	
FURTHER EVIDENCE	306
CHAPTER 33	
A NEW CASE?	316
CHAPTER 34	
THE DEFENCE CASE	321
CHAPTER 35	
A TESTING TIME FOR HUGH	341

CHAPTER 36
THE DEFENCE WITNESSES 359

CHAPTER 37
THE DEFENCE EXPERT 370

CHAPTER 38
THE PROSECUTION CLOSING SPEECH 378

CHAPTER 39
THE DEFENCE CLOSING SPEECH 390

CHAPTER 40
THE JURY DELIBERATIONS 406

CHAPTER 41
THE VERDICT 412

CHAPTER 42
THE SILK RIBBON 420

CHAPTER 1

THE PUPIL

Sara Petford-Williams took one look at her client and she knew it was going to be one of those days again!

It was Monday, 8th June 2015 and she was in Highbury and Islington Magistrates Court in North London. She was now formally referred to as a 'second six' pupil, which meant she had finished her schooling with outstanding 'A' levels, obtained an upper second class degree in Law at Bailliol College at Oxford university, and secured an upper second with distinction in her bar exams. She had then completed her first six months of pupillage following an experienced barrister around watching how he conducted cases. Now, finally, she was permitted by the Bar Standards Board to take on cases of her own, to earn a proper living and represent those wrongly accused in anything from simple theft to murder cases.

In practice of course, things were very different. Like many pupil barristers she was completely broke. She came from the Jesmond area in Newcastle. Despite her hyphenated name, her family was not wealthy. Her father, Geoffrey Petford-Williams, was the second son of an old family whose fortune had been frittered away by previous generations and the considerable efforts of the Inland Revenue. She had an uncle, Hugh Petford-Williams, who had inherited what was left of the family fortune, but he was an alcoholic and the family rarely saw him, despite the fact that he lived in the same area. It was a fact that caused much consternation amongst the rest of the family that he had been forced to divide the substantial family home to turn it into flats so that he could maintain a certain standard of living and slowly drink away the remains of the family fortune.

Her father was a senior accountant in a company in Newcastle that manufactured computer parts. Her mother worked as a personal assistant to a rich business man in a financial company and although the family was not poor, they were not rich by the standards of their previous generations.

However, because their finances were only poor and not appalling, Sara had not been eligible for a grant at University and, although her parents had helped her a little financially, the tuition fees in Oxford and then the bar course, added to the cost of living whilst she studied, had been prohibitive. She was now in debt to the tune of £57,000, and the payment of £15,000 per annum which she received from James Wontner QC's chambers, as a pupil, only just covered her rent and some of her travel into London. Eating, drinking and purchasing clothes had become a luxury.

Nevertheless, she was happy to be a barrister and she was grateful to her father, who had studied mathematics at Oxford and had met James Wontner QC there. She was sure that had assisted her entry into chambers despite the so-called 'transparent and fair' recruitment policy.

It was the career she had always wanted. To appear in the Old Bailey, under the statue of justice, securing acquittals for her innocent clients after a devastating cross examination of a lying witness, intent on fooling everyone with his perjured testimony. However, the reality was very different. She started pupillage on Monday, 27th October 2014 and Graham Martin was appointed her 'Pupil Supervisor.' It had not taken her long to realise that Graham's practice was a poor one and she had seen only a few, low quality, Crown Court trials with him. The highlight had been the trial of an amateur rugby player accused of stealing a policeman's helmet after a match. He was obviously guilty but the jury had been generous and acquitted him, probably because they found the whole case silly, rather than because of Graham's advocacy skills.

She was allowed to follow the silks around court in a few cases and see some better quality work, but that accounted for very little of her time and, for the most part her first six months in chambers had been very dull. She had looked forward to her second six months where she could conduct her own cases and demonstrate her own advocacy skills in court.

She began practising 'on her feet' in April 2015 and soon realised that it was not what she had expected. She had spent six weeks now, representing her own clients, but she had not seen the inside of a Crown Court once, never mind conducted a trial in one. Her court diary had been filled with a large number of 'first appearances', where all criminal cases begin their long or short journey. She had travelled to many magistrates' courts, filled in endless pages of legal aid application forms and waited hours for her cases to be called on in court, behind a long list of many others that had all been listed for 10 am. Finally, when the moment arrived for her to stand up in court for her client, the hearings would frequently last no more than five minutes. The cases were then adjourned for someone else to conduct in the future. This had been her daily grind and it was no consolation that it was the same for most pupil barristers.

Upon joining chambers, Graham told her that she would be paid for every case she conducted personally and this would be in addition to the £7,500 she was receiving from chambers for her second six months of pupillage. However, in practice she had only received £50 for the cases she had conducted to date and that did not pay for the considerable amount of coffee she needed to stay awake at court, waiting for her cases to be dealt with, never mind the horrendous travel expenses she had accumulated getting to courts in and around London and elsewhere.

Now she was looking through the cell bars in Highbury and Islington Magistrates Court, at Mr Erguvan, a Turkish defendant, arrested for beating his wife.

Sara had completed all the forms and passed them to him through a small gap in his cell. She passed her pen through to him for him to sign the forms but, as she did so, she noticed scars up and down his arms and along his wrists. Had he tried to take his own life in the past? Did he self-harm? Suddenly a dreadful possibility struck her, what if he uses my pen to harm himself? He looked at her and noted her observe his injuries. He suddenly grabbed the pen and with a violent movement forced it towards his neck. Sara's mouth dropped in abject horror as her thoughts played out in front of her. However, before the pen pierced his jugular vein, Mr Erguvan stopped and he looked at Sara and laughed, "Me have fun with you!"

Sara exhaled in relief and laughed nervously at her client, throwing her hand out to retrieve the pen, but not before he signed those all-important forms that would ensure she could get paid for this dreadful morning. When she had fully regained her composure she excused herself telling her loathsome client she would she him upstairs where she would be applying for his bail. She sought to hide her true feelings for him by offering a smile through slightly gritted teeth.

She had joined the Criminal Bar to protect the innocent and the oppressed. What did it say over the doors of the Old Bailey, 'Defend the children of the poor'? She had already noted Mr Erguvan's list of offending history. He had been arrested seven times previously for beating his wife. On all occasions except the first, the charges had been dropped as his wife had formally withdrawn the allegations and refused to give evidence against him, no doubt on the usual promises from him that he would change. Sara also noted that he had one previous conviction for dealing in heroin. He had received eight years for this offence, and served four of them, so at least his wife got some respite from him during that period.

As she left, Mr Erguvan gave her a lascivious grin, clearly assuming it was the one that would charm any woman and reassure her that he would make a truly wonderful lover. Sara turned away quickly to hide a mixture of amusement and disdain and tried unsuccessfully to comfort herself with the thought that at least this afternoon she had the delights of travelling to

South Western Magistrates Court in Clapham, South London. There she was to conduct a sentence representing two Albanians convicted of pickpocketing. Things were really looking up for her!

A tube journey and one stop on the overground train later and Sara was at Clapham Junction, having shot across London, consuming three cups of coffee and one tasteless ham and wilted salad sandwich along the way to fortify her. Sadly, the afternoon was not proving to be any easier than the morning. She discovered that the Albanian clients did not have the benefit of legal aid. She dutifully phoned the solicitors to discover what had happened and they told her they had instructed a tenant in her chambers on the first appearance in court but had not had any further involvement in the case as legal aid had been refused. They insisted they had told her clerks not to send anyone today. She immediately phoned her clerk, Asif, who told her there must be some mistake, he claimed he had spoken to the solicitors on the phone the previous day and they had instructed chambers to send someone.

She had been around long enough to know that the clerks at Temple Lane Chambers never admitted mistakes so she assumed either the solicitor or Asif was lying. It was not easy to work out which one as both had sounded equally convincing. It made no difference, there was nothing she could do. She had prepared the case, she might as well conduct it even though she would not be paid. After all she must 'defend the children of the poor.'

At 1:40pm, she tracked down the Albanian interpreter Ms Ljena Manjola and they went to the cells to see her clients, the brothers Driton and Enjell Valmir

After a brief discussion with both, she went upstairs to court three to await her turn in the long list of 2 PM cases. The Usher, Julie, was friendly and informed her there might be a little wait as the bench of magistrates had not dealt with their morning list yet. Typical, she thought to herself.

At 3:10pm, the clerk of the court, a man from South Wales called Redvers Evans, announced to Sara in front of the magistrates, "We're moving the case of Valmir and Valmir to court four, you will probably get on quicker there."

Sara smiled and made her way to court four. There she found that the magistrates were not in court. All was quiet as she looked quizzically at a Crown Prosecution representative, Charles Adams. She had come across him before on a number of similar occasions., He was seated in the advocates' bench at the front of the court.

He nodded to her and enquired, "Have you been sent from court three? Don't worry, the

18

magistrates have just gone out to consider their decision in a shop-lifting trial."

He looked at the shabbily dressed, unrepresented, defendant who sat slumped miserably in the dock, and then glanced back at Sara and winked, quietly adding, "I don't think they will be long, it's an overwhelming case. He was caught with a couple of pork chops inside a carrier bag, hidden under some newspapers."

Sara looked towards the dock and saw the greyish features of an emaciated seventy-four-year-old man. Forty-five minutes later the Magistrates returned into court and announced, "Considering the burden and standard of proof, we are not satisfied that this defendant is guilty and so we acquit him. Mr Wilson, you are free to go."

Charles Adams' mouth dropped and Sara hid a smile as she thought, that's what an acquittal looks like in the magistrates' court. She had yet to experience one herself. For a brief moment she wondered if defendants would be better off representing themselves but she quickly dismissed such a foolish notion.

Her case was called on shortly afterwards and the prosecutor outlined the circumstances and drew the court's attention to the fact that both defendants had four previous convictions over the past year for exactly the same type of conduct. He also pointed out that they had only been in the country 14 months. Sara spent fifteen minutes mitigating, explaining; the terrible social and family background from which the pickpocketers had come, the fact they had to flee Albania in order to save their lives from dangerous street gangs and that they had only started pickpocketing purely through abject poverty and the need to buy food to survive.

She reserved her best point in mitigation for last. By a miraculous coincidence both of them had been offered their first ever job with an uncle in the building trade. It was due to start on the following Monday and both defendants had decided there was no future in further criminality and now they would have the means to lead honest lives in the future.

The Magistrates left the court to confer and did not take long before returning and imposing a sentence of four month's imprisonment on each. Sara was happy, it was actually a good result, they could have sent them to the Crown Court for sentencing where their sentences could have been measured in years, not months.

Feeling quite proud of herself, she went downstairs to the cells to see them, only to find that they were both shouting and spitting at the interpreter, apparently complaining about being represented by a woman!

Sara left shortly afterwards taking a look at her watch. She was glad to see it was still attached to her wrist as Driton had held onto her hand a little too long when he had shaken her hand before the case. It was now 4:55pm. What a day. Maybe she had earned £50 since 9:30am - less than the minimum wage for an unqualified school-leaver! Surely things would get better soon?

CHAPTER 2

THE SILK RIBBON

"I'll see you later."

Hugh Petford-Williams said goodbye and closed the front door of his flat behind him, pulling it hard to ensure the dodgy lock had caught properly.

It was around 9pm on Thursday 18th June 2015. He had left his wife Rosemary in the kitchen, drinking with the next-door neighbour, William Johns. Johns could be a bit facetious and even obnoxious when drunk, but Hugh had learnt to enjoy their heated discussions.

Johns had been an RAF Harrier pilot in the Falklands War and Hugh's father had been a Battle of Britain pilot, so they enjoyed sharing war stories. They both appreciated the absurdities of war, how apparently little or trivial things could make such a big difference to the outcome of a battle or campaign.

Hugh fastened his coat, it was rather cold for a June evening. He smiled as he remembered their discussion of a few minutes ago. They had been celebrating the fact that it was two hundred years to the day since the Battle of Waterloo had been fought. Johns had toasted the victory, adding that it had little to do with the Duke of Wellington, and more to do with the weather! It had rained heavily that June in Belgium and Johns maintained it was the rain and mud that had defeated Napoleon, not Wellington nor the Prussian army under General Blucher.

Johns was full of such crazy anecdotes and what made them interesting was there was a grain of truth in some, though Hugh thought his last one sounded ridiculous. All sensible people knew that Napoleon lost because he was beaten by the superior defensive tactics of Wellington. Napoleon also probably had an off day. As Hugh had told Johns, Napoleon spent more time on the loo that day than at Waterloo! It happens to the best of us, he thought with a smile.

He made his way to his club, which was only five hundred yards from his flat. As he had been drinking, he decided he would not take the car. He could manage the short walk even in his condition.

As he hobbled down the gravel pathway, he noticed the curtains twitching in the upstairs bedroom of the neighbouring flat. It was probably that nosey neighbour, Dr Richard Jeffries, or his equally prying wife. They always seemed to be spying on him. He actually wished he had never sold them the flat.

Hugh lived in a two-bedroom flat in his old family home. The house had been in his family for several generations and he had lived in the original eight bedroomed house almost all his life, save for when he went to study Philosophy at Oxford University.

He had been a mature student as he had gone straight into the family business after school. After a few years, his father, probably unimpressed with Hugh's lack of business acumen, had persuaded him to go to university and he had begun his three year course in 1975, aged 24. His father helped him obtain a place through some of his contacts.

A university education in Philosophy had been a complete waste of his time, but it was one of the few courses available to him. He would have preferred to study history but failed to obtain sufficient grades at A-level. He freely admitted that academia was not his strong point. The one thing he was grateful for from his university education was that he had met Rosemary there and they had married three years later after obtaining their respective degrees.

They had returned to his family home in 1978. Hugh had secured only a third class honours degree but Rosemary had proved brighter and obtained an upper second class honours degree in Biology. Both worked in the family business and found that their degrees proved of no use to them whatsoever in the work they did. Hugh worked as a Manager alongside his father and

Rosemary worked as his father's Personal Assistant.

Hugh's family ran a clothing firm that was started by his father after the Second World War. It was relatively successful until his father retired due to ill health in the early eighties. Unfortunately, the business finally collapsed in the late eighties. Hugh was adamant that it was due to the looming recession and not the manner in which he ran the company. Thereafter he had toyed with a number of business ventures, sadly none had been successful.

Hugh's father died in late 1992 and Hugh and Rosemary continued to live with his mother in the family home. His mother had continued to finance his business ventures with increasing reluctance and pay all the household bills until her death in 2011. Hugh had then inherited the house and the remains of the family fortune. However, the inheritance tax had been crippling and he had to borrow money from a reluctant bank to convert the house into four flats. The idea was to keep one for himself and Rosemary and sell three in order to pay the tax and put aside sufficient money for he and Rosemary to live on.

Hugh acknowledged, to just about anyone who would listen, that throughout his life he had not been good with money and had frittered away large sums enjoying himself and speculating on unsuccessful business ventures. He also admitted that Rosemary had been of great assistance dwindling away the family fortune.

They sold all three flats within six months of them being completed. He and Rosemary retained one flat in the centre of the house where the old main entrance had been and which they retained to preserve the feeling of grandeur which made them feel as if they still owned the whole house.

As one entered the flat from outside, there was a lavatory on the left, opposite to a stairway that led to the first floor. There was a downstairs bedroom next to the lavatory and opposite that was the kitchen which led to the garden. Upstairs, his flat had a bedroom, living room and bathroom.

If guests stayed at his flat, Hugh liked to put some distance between them and himself which is why he had designed his flat with his spare bedroom on the ground floor. All the other flats in the former family home were tastefully designed on two floors, all containing two bedrooms on the top floor with a bathroom and the living room and kitchen/dining room downstairs.

Dr Jeffries and his wife were the first purchasers and had bought the flat next to his own. Jeffries was a Doctor of Philosophy, not Medicine, and apparently worked with computers. Hugh had thought they might become friends with their shared academic background but Jeffries had been dismissive of Hugh's knowledge and instead, was always complaining about something or other. Hugh had quickly grown to detest both the man and his wife.

Hugh sold the next flat situated on the other side to Jeffries to a quiet couple, Gerry and Clare Payne. He understood they both worked in the centre of Newcastle, in the financial sector. They were in their thirties and had a young child. They rarely chatted to Hugh, and he was content with that. He sold the final flat, next to his own, to William Johns in early 2013.

At first, Johns had kept to himself but then Hugh had bumped into him in the Black Badger, a local public house, and they started chatting and discovered they had a shared interest in military history. It had not taken long before Johns was a regular visitor to his flat.

Hugh's wife, Rosemary, had immediately taken to Johns. They were all roughly the same age. Rosemary and Johns were now both 59, Hugh was just a few years older at 64. They had all got along well until an unfortunate incident last October, although that was a distant memory now.

Hugh had to accept that throughout his life he had enjoyed a drink. Alcohol had proved his support in difficult times and he had never wished to rid himself of what some people unwisely called his addiction, but which he called his crutch. His doctor foolishly claimed it was alcohol that led to his obesity and diabetes. He disagreed. These conditions were undoubtedly a result of age and were probably hereditary. He thought. about his father, also a heavy drinker, who had suffered from the same conditions. Definitely hereditary he thought, and nothing he could do about it other than console himself with a drink or two.

Sadly, the diabetes had slowed him down in a number of important areas. Firstly, he had to reduce his sugar in-take, which had not been easy. Secondly, he found he was increasingly unsteady on his feet and, more concerning to Rosemary than to himself, he was now impotent.

He had tried all the remedies out there including prescription Viagra. That had only resulted in him being nauseous and coming out in rashes. Obviously, Rosemary still had her needs and that led to that unfortunate incident in October last year.

Hugh smiled for a second as he recalled Johns' face when Hugh had pointed a rifle at him, if his shots had hit three inches to the right, he would have permanently wiped Johns' smile off his face!

As Hugh approached the door of his club, he momentarily thought about Johns and Rosemary alone in his home. They were shamelessly flirting. Hugh dismissed the thought and entered the club. He would enjoy a few drinks with his friends and put those thoughts out of his head.

CHAPTER 3

THE NEIGHBOURS

Dr Richard Jeffries let the bedroom curtain drop back into place and turned to his wife, "I just saw the old man go out again. I suspect his wife and Johns will be at it again soon. At least they'll be downstairs, but these walls are paper thin and I cannot stand that woman's constant groaning!"

His wife Janet just politely smiled at him, wishing that someone would make her groan like that occasionally. She said nothing but increased the volume on the television. Richard thanked her and continued watching the documentary on Artificial Intelligence, which he had waited all night to see, whilst she continued reading her historical romance novel, 'The Thrusting Rapier and The Royal Maid.'

Richard was 57 and Janet 55. They had met at Cambridge University in their late teens and married five years later. Richard had continued his education and obtained his Doctorate in Philosophy. He had wanted to lecture and become a professor at the university but the posts were not available and eventually he had accepted a job in computing. As far as he was concerned he had become something of an expert now and was annoyed that his talents were not being properly recognised by his bosses!

Richard and Janet had one son who they had named Robert after a distant relative. He was now aged 27 and had left home to study at London University. Robert liked London so much that he had moved down there permanently and they rarely saw him now. In 2012, they had seen this flat for sale and moved here out of the family home, deciding they no longer needed a three bedroomed house.

Although Richard had welcomed the move, he soon become unhappy as he could not stand Hugh. To him, the man was an alcoholic who rambled on. At one stage, Hugh had tried to engage Richard in a discussion on philosophy as if he had the requisite knowledge to discuss such matters with Richard!

Richard had also become annoyed at the constant noise that came from next door. The Petford-Williams had become 'very friendly' with their neighbour, William Johns, and could often be heard through the walls engaged in loud discussions about some battle or other boring topic. Richard and Janet had also become aware that Rosemary and Johns' relationship was a lot closer than it should be. Frequently when Hugh left the house, they could hear Rosemary and Johns engaging in noisy sex in their spare bedroom, which was unfortunately situated right next door to the Jeffries' living room.

It had become intolerable and Richard wanted to complain, but Janet prevented him on the basis that Hugh may not know about the relationship and they may not be thanked by anyone for being the source of that revelation.

An hour later, the documentary was just finishing as both Richard and Janet heard loud noises coming from the Petford-Williams' flat. They were both startled when they heard someone shout in a high-pitched voice, "I'm going to kill you, you bastard." A few seconds later, they heard a loud bang.

"Good God Janet! I'm sure that was a gun shot, you don't think he's finally killed her do you?"

Janet was equally shocked at the noise but quickly gathered her thoughts and replied, "Don't be silly Richard, no one goes around shooting anybody in Jesmond. This isn't Manchester!"

He nodded, "I suppose not, but nothing would surprise me in that household!"

"Anyway," she continued, "it sounded like a woman's voice to me so it was probably her shooting his lordship!"

Richard's look of fear changed to one of amusement at the nickname his wife had given their eccentric neighbour. He added jokingly, "You never know, we could be lucky, they might have shot each other!"

They laughed at their own malice. Janet glanced at the clock before she continued reading. Her novel had reached a climactic scene with the hero ripping off his shirt and advancing towards the heroine with a thumping breast and passion in his heart and clearly in other parts of his anatomy. Rosemary was desperate to get back into the book before her own excitement faded.

Their neighbours, Clare and Gerry Payne, were in the front room of their flat when they also heard a loud bang. The Richards' flat was between them and the Petford-Williams' home so they had not heard any conversation but the loud bang was audible over the sound of their television.

"What do you think that was?" Clare asked her husband.

Gerry shrugged, "No idea, I suppose it could be a car backfiring."

Clare frowned at him, "It didn't sound like that to me. I'd swear it was a gunshot!"

Gerry laughed, "Don't be silly, who would be firing a gun at this time of night?"

Clare was not happy with his dismissive comments. He had been the same back in

October last year when she was sure she heard two gunshots fired from the Petford-Williams' flat. She looked out of the front room window to try and find the source of these latest disturbances. She pulled aside her curtains a little. It was still light outside but she could not see anything clearly. Wait, she thought, isn't that Mr Petford-Williams entering his flat through the main door?

It was difficult to see from her angle but she was sure it was him. Perhaps he had been using his car. It was an old one, it probably did backfire. She closed the curtains and sat down. She realised she was being silly. Who would be firing guns in this area at this time of night.

Richard Jeffries was now watching a documentary on Astronomy whilst Janet was absorbed by the hero who had now fully disrobed and was lying exhausted and panting heavily next to the equally satisfied Royal Maid who lay languidly amongst the folds of satin sheets which adorned the four poster bed of the Tudor Inn. He had just declared to her that he was in fact a Royal Prince but despite their respective stations in life he would ....

"What's that?" Richard exclaimed, "I'm sure that was another shot."

Janet put her book down with a frown. She was beginning to think Richard was deliberately trying to ruin the story for her. There was no

34

passion in their own relationship anymore, why did he have to ruin it when she was trying to find a harmless substitute. She dutifully listened but could hear nothing.

"It's nothing Richard, now will you let me get back to my book!"

Janet picked her novel up from the bed and placed earplugs in her ears. She then covered herself in the bedclothes whilst re-reading the last couple of paragraphs. This was an important time for Esmerelda, her whole future depended on whether Rupert now declared his undying love and Janet did not want any more interruptions before the thrilling climax.

CHAPTER 4

DEATH OF A LOVER

Hugh closed the kitchen door behind him and, gripping the rifle tightly, looked at the mess in the downstairs lavatory that had just moments before been William Johns. Blood was flowing freely from a gaping wound on the right side of his neck. Hugh had ordered Rosemary to press a large towel against the wound, but the blood was still gushing out and it did not look like it would stop. He took the house phone and dialled 999 getting through to the operator immediately. The call was logged at 10:08pm.

"Which service do you require?" asked the female voice.

Hugh raised his voice as if that might speed up matters. "I require the ambulance service and I require it quickly." He paused before adding reluctantly, "The police better come as well."

The operator was not fazed, she had dealt with countless such calls, "What is the nature of the emergency and what is your address?"

Hugh's impatience was getting the better off him as he answered tersely, "My neighbour has been shot and is bleeding to death. My address is Flat 1, the Elms, Manor House Road, Jesmond. Get an ambulance here quickly or he will bleed to death."

There were a few seconds silence before the operator responded, "I've dispatched an ambulance and the police will be following shortly. Can you tell me how your neighbour got shot?"

Hugh hesitated before answering. "Yes, I shot him." Again, he paused before adding, "It was an accident. My rifle went off and shot him through a lavatory door. I didn't mean to shoot him. Now I'm worried that he might die and it will be my fault."

"Where's the rifle now?"

"I've got it. Don't worry though, it's safe, I've removed the remaining cartridges and I will put it safely away."

"Is the victim still alive?"

"Yes he is, but he won't be much longer if you don't get a bloody ambulance here quickly!"

"Where is he wounded?"

Hugh looked at the receiver with uncontrolled annoyance, "In the neck, now will you stop asking any more damn fool questions and get someone here quickly."

"Sir, I have to ask these questions so the ambulance crew know exactly what they face when they arrive. Is he still bleeding?"

"He was shot in the neck, of course he's still bleeding."

"Have you got a bandage or a clean towel that you can apply to the wound to staunch the flow of blood?"

Hugh raised his eyes to the ceiling, "My wife is already applying a towel to the wound. Please get the ambulance here soon."

"Is there anyone else with you?"

Hugh was about to lose his temper entirely, "No there bloody well is not. I'm not going to answer any more of these damn questions, when will the ambulance be here?"

"Their normal response time is eight minutes but they may have to wait for the police so it might be longer."

Hugh shouted down the receiver, "Why for God's sake will they have to wait for police?"

"You mentioned there was a rifle and they will want to wait for the police for their own safety."

Hugh was apoplectic now, "For God's sake, I told you it was an accident!"

"Yes but the police still have to check there is no danger to the ambulance crew. Hello, hello?" the voice asked in vain.

There was no reply. Hugh had slammed the receiver down.

Within seven minutes of the call being made, an ambulance, driven by Paul Holland, pulled up outside Hugh's address. He was accompanied by James Marshall, a paramedic. Both remained seated in the vehicle waiting for the police to arrive. As they waited, they saw a silver-haired portly man waving at them from the address and shouting, "Come in here! There's a man dying!"

They both looked at each other, shrugged their shoulders and got out of the vehicle. In situations like this they knew the protocol was to wait until the police arrived to make sure that they were safe. However, they both had the same thought. If he was going to shoot them he could have done so already.

They followed Hugh into the flat and immediately came across the tragic scene. William Johns was lying on the floor in front of the downstairs lavatory, looking mortally pale. Rosemary was kneeling by his right side pressing a blood-soaked towel against the right side of his neck. She was covered in blood and was clearly drunk, muttering and shaking her head, "He's dead! ... It's my fault."

James moved her gently to one side and took over applying pressure to the wound whilst Paul assembled an intravenous drip. Both knew they would have to work fast if they were to have any chance of saving him.

Hugh stood over them, calmly watching the whole procedure. Occasionally, he looked over at his sobbing wife. He was fascinated by the scene and watched dispassionately as if he was watching a late night film.

He thought of the absurdity of it all. Johns had fought in the Falkland Islands, going daily on bombing missions to destroy Argentinian positions around Port Stanley. The Argentines had thrown everything they could at him. Fighter aircraft from the Argentinian mainland, anti-aircraft missiles, cannon fire and bullets from the ground and apparently not one of these had ever come close to hitting him. Yet here he lay on a lavatory floor in Hugh's flat, dying from a single .22 bullet fired through a thick toilet door.

He was brought back to reality when suddenly two large policemen came crashing through his front door. One was pointing a Taser at him and screaming something at him. He turned around to look at the officers, astonished at the manner of their arrival in his home. He was about to remonstrate when the officer with the Taser gun quickly approached him and applied it to his

40

right side, just above his hip. Within a split second he felt himself thrown to the floor as an excruciating pain pulsed through his body, accompanied by a loud crackling sound. The last thing he recalled was a feeling that his heart was going to burst and the smell of burning when suddenly, everything went quiet and a dark mist descended over his eyes.

CHAPTER 5

THE INTERVIEW

Detective Sergeant Charles Bull took a gulp of his tea before addressing Hugh, "This interview is being recorded, your legal rights have been explained to you and you have been cautioned and told you do not have to say anything, but it may harm your defence if you do not mention when questioned something which you later rely on in court. Anything you do say may be given in evidence. Do you understand that caution?"

Hugh looked at him with growing impatience. It was midday on Friday 19th June. He had been in police custody since about 10:20pm the previous night. He was annoyed at the treatment he had received. Some burly policeman had rushed into his home, said something about getting on the floor and before Hugh had a chance to do anything, the officer pounced on him and electrocuted him, almost giving him a heart attack. He had passed out and must have fallen heavily because he had bruised his knees badly. He awoke only to find his hands had been forced behind his back and handcuffed before he had a chance to say a single word. Not satisfied with that, the police had forced him out of the flat and he had passed the obnoxious Dr Jeffries' who grinned at him in pleasure. He was then manhandled into the back of a waiting police car. He had been taken to this police station where he was placed in a small cell and had been detained for the best part of thirteen hours before being questioned.

Admittedly, he had received cups of tea and some greasy mess that was supposed to pass for breakfast, but the worse thing for him was that he was not being allowed to go home and see Rosemary and he was now being asked a lot of damn fool questions.

"Of course I understand it, I'm not a half-wit," he protested in response to the standard caution.

Charles nodded, "And you don't want a solicitor?"

"No I do not, I have nothing to hide."

Charles put his most serious expression on his face, "You are sure sir, as you've been told Mr Johns died at three this morning, this is now a murder investigation. Are you sure you don't want a solicitor?"

Hugh closed his eyes and sighed, "How many times do I have to say it, I have nothing to hide. I will answer your questions. I would like to get out of here as soon as possible."

Charles nodded, he was conscious this interview was being video and tape recorded, so not only would every word be caught, so would every gesture. He had done enough in his own mind to appear to be fair and given Hugh a chance to have a solicitor, now he would start probing.

"Very well sir, I just need to let you know that your release will have nothing to do with me, that will be a decision of the Custody Sergeant."

Hugh nodded so Charles continued, "Let me start by asking you a few background questions."

Over the next fifteen minutes he covered a short history of Hugh's life; when he was born, where he had lived, when he got married, when he had inherited the house, when it was converted and finally when he first met William Johns. He had already obtained statements from the neighbours so he was aware that Johns and Rosemary were lovers, now he needed to have Hugh confirm that he was aware of the relationship. A little gentle probing was required.

"Can I call you Hugh, Mr Petford-Williams is a bit of a mouthful?"

"Of course," Hugh replied impatiently.

"Thank you. Now can you tell me what your relationship with Mr Johns was like?"

Hugh looked at him as if to say these were damn silly questions but he thought the sooner he answered the sooner he would get home.

"I liked Johns, he was a good conversationalist. He could be a little obnoxious after a few drinks, but generally I enjoyed his company."

"What was Rosemary's relationship with him like?"

Hugh prickled a little and hesitated before answering, "Rosemary liked him a lot."

Charles sensed he had hit a raw nerve so he continued, "Were they lovers?"

All pretence at subtlety had left the room. Hugh shifted uncomfortably in his seat before answering, "I would not say lovers. They were very close and my wife has certain needs that Johns satisfied."

Charles eyes widened slightly, "Can you tell me what you mean by 'certain needs'?"

Hugh sighed before continuing, "Officer, I have suffered from diabetes for a number of years now. Sadly, one of the effects has been to render me impotent.

I have tried a large number of remedies including prescription Viagra, but none have worked. Viagra for example made me particularly ill.

Rosemary loves me dearly and I love her. She has her sexual needs like every woman and I cannot supply them. Johns stepped in to provide that service."

"What do you mean, 'that service'?"

Hugh looked at him as if he was a complete idiot. "I mean that on certain occasions, with my permission of course, Johns and my wife would engage in sexual intercourse."

Charles could not hide the look of surprise on his face, "With your permission? Were you present?"

"Of course not! I didn't enjoy the idea of him having sexual intercourse with my wife. I just accepted that her natural desires needed to be fulfilled and it was better that I knew who was fulfilling them than she go off with some complete stranger."

"When did this first start?"

"Last October."

Charles looked through his notes of the statements taken from the neighbours and smiled when he noted a comment by Clare

46

Payne. "Was there a similar incident to this one in October last year?"

Hugh looked at him suspiciously, "What do you mean, 'a similar incident'?"

Charles read out part of Clare Payne's statement and then asked, "Did you use your rifle to fire any shots at Mr Johns in October last year."

Hugh nodded, "Oh that. Well, yes and no."

"What do you mean, 'yes and no'?"

"Well, we had all been drinking heavily one night towards the end of October. I recall that we were celebrating the fact that my niece had just been given a training contract as a barrister in a London chambers. I think barristers call it something damn silly like a 'pupillage'. We invited Johns over to celebrate with us.

Anyway after about six litre bottles of wine between us, I went out to my club for a couple of double whiskeys. Unfortunately, whilst I was away, Rosemary's needs got the better of her. I came back to find them both in the spare room having sex."

Hugh looked down at the table before continuing, "I am sure you can appreciate it was not a pleasant sight, seeing Johns' naked backside going up and down on top of my wife's naked body. I was obviously angry and I went to my room to get my rifle."

He quickly added, "Solely in order to scare Johns of course, not to injure him."

"Did you scare him?"

"Oh yes, not at first though, I burst into the spare bedroom and they were still in bed giggling like a pair of naughty school children. I pointed the gun at Johns but he just laughed and made some cutting remark, 'Excellent Hugh, you've finally found something you can get up.' I remember Rosemary giggling when he said it. Of course that angered me more and I fired a couple of rounds into the pillow next to his head. I had no intention of hurting him and he wasn't hurt, but he did shut up!"

Hugh allowed himself a brief smile at the memory. Charles noticed the smile and looked up at the camera to check the red light was still on to indicate it was recording. Seeing that it was, he continued, "Tell me about the rifle, where did you get it from?"

"I've had it a few years now. I bought it from an antiques dealer. It's an old Victorian fairground rifle, a Model 62A, 1890 Winchester pump action .22 rimfire rifle."

Charles scribbled a note of the name before asking, "I'm not an expert on rifles, but I thought you could only buy them from registered firearms dealers, not in antique shops?"

"Well it wasn't in working order when I purchased it and was an antique. Over time I got the necessary parts and renovated it and got it to work again. I purchased some rimfire cartridges and used it in my back garden to fire at targets in a target range I set up."

Hugh smiled, "I did quite a good job if I say so myself. I purchased several bales of hay and surrounded an area in my garden with them. I doubled them up at the back so no shots would accidentally leave the property or hurt anyone."

Charles looked at him sternly, "You do realise it is illegal to possess firearms without a firearms certificate, even for target shooting?"

Hugh nodded, "I do, but I thought there was an exemption for antiques and this was clearly an antique. It was well over a hundred years old when I bought it! Anyway, as I said it was more of a target gun than anything else. I never thought it would be able to kill anything other than rats!"

Charles made a quick note of that comment before continuing, "Well you must have thought Mr Johns was a bit of a rat. You had invited him into your home, shared your drink with him and now he was taking liberties with your wife?"

Hugh laughed, "I didn't mean that sort of rat! It's only a .22 rimfire rifle, it's not that powerful."

"It killed Mr Johns though, didn't it?"

Hugh did not answer so Charles continued. "What happened after you fired those shots into the pillow?"

"Everything calmed down and we all chatted over a few more glasses of wine. Rosemary made it clear she loved me, but still had her sexual desires. I eventually agreed with them that they could have the odd session together but they must not rub my nose in it, nor should anyone outside the three of us be made aware of the arrangement.

It was agreed that I would leave a sign when I was going out for long time. Rosemary, who has always been a little theatrical, came up with the idea that I should tie a red silk ribbon on the handle of the door of the spare bedroom. That would be the sign that I was out for a long time and they could engage in sexual intercourse if they wished. However, if I did not place the ribbon it would mean I would be back soon. It was a simple rule, no red silk ribbon, no sex."

Charles took a full note of these comments before asking, "Did you place a red silk ribbon on the bedroom door last night?"

Hugh hesitated, "No, I wasn't going out for that long."

"So tell me what happened?"

"We all had a pleasant evening. We consumed a few bottles of wine together. Johns and I were discussing the Battle of Waterloo and arguing about why Napoleon lost."

Charles scribbled the word 'argument' on his notepad which Hugh saw and immediately said, "It wasn't a serious argument, it was more of a debate! Anyway, then I went to my club and had a couple of drinks before setting off home again.

As soon as I opened the front door, I heard giggling from the spare bedroom. I knew they were at it again. I admit I was annoyed. Johns had breached our agreement. I wanted to scare him so he never made the same mistake again.

I went upstairs to get the rifle. It wasn't loaded, so I loaded it. I pumped it and put a bullet into the barrel ready to fire. I was going to shout at him, threaten him and probably fire a shot into the headboard or something like that to make the point. I had no intention of hurting him."

"But you did?"

Hugh frowned, "Yes, but not intentionally."

"Did you make any threats to him?"

"No, I didn't have time. I don't know if you know anyone with diabetes? It affects you in a number of ways. I have told you it has caused me to be impotent, another side effect is that I have grown increasingly unsteady on my feet.

I was coming down the stairs when I tripped. I was holding the rifle in my right hand with my forefinger on the trigger. As I stumbled on the stairs I accidentally pulled the trigger and put a bullet through the lavatory door. I didn't even know Johns was in there at the time. I thought he was still in the spare bedroom with Rosemary."

He looked down and shook his head slowly from side to side.

Charles nodded but continued, "We have taken a statement from two neighbours of yours who say that they heard someone say, 'I'm going to kill you, you bastard.' Did you say that?"

Hugh hesitated, "I don't recall saying that, I told you I was only trying to frighten him. If I did say it, I didn't mean it."

"Could anyone else have said that?"

"No, I suppose I must have said it, but this was most likely when I first entered the house, not when I was on the stairs."

"What happened after the rifle went off?"

52

"I remember hearing a muffled cry and then I saw a trickle of blood coming from under the lavatory door. It soon became a stream. I kicked the door in and saw Johns had collapsed onto the floor. I immediately told Rosemary to get a towel to stem the flow of blood. I made the rifle safe by ejecting the remaining cartridges and placed it by the stairs. Then I phoned for an ambulance and the police. I even waited outside for them to arrive to save some time and direct them to Johns!"

He paused before looking Charles in the eyes, "It should be obvious, officer, that I wouldn't have done any of those things if I wanted to kill him. It was a terrible, tragic accident. I never intended to kill him or even to hurt him, I only wanted to scare him."

CHAPTER 6

THE NEW BRIEF

David Brant rose from his desk as Tim Adams walked into the room. David feigned politeness but he still could not stand the man for reasons he had never really fathomed. Nevertheless, he saw no advantage in being unfriendly and greeted him, "Hello Tim, how is Lewes Crown Court these days?"

Tim gave a beaming smile in return, "Same as ever David. Since I won the Paul Morris case, I seem to have a never-ending stream of prosecution work down there."

David nodded gracefully, noting with irritation Tim's constant references to winning the one case they had both appeared in as opponents.

Tim did not appear to notice as he continued, "I'm thinking of asking the clerks to give you and James some of my returns so that I can practice elsewhere occasionally. You wouldn't mind prosecuting now and again would you David?"

David would not mind at all but the last thing he wanted was to be constantly doing Tim's rejected cases. He could not handle much more of Tim's condescending sneer.

"That's kind of you Tim, but I'm quite busy at the moment and, anyway, I'm more of a defence lawyer. I'm sure our Head of Chambers would be happy to help you out."

Tim looked puzzled, "Really? The clerks told me you were quiet at the moment, I thought you might appreciate a few silk cases?"

David continued smiling, with increasing difficulty, "Typical clerks, they don't think we're busy unless we are working 24 hours a day, 7 days a week, 365 days a year, except in a leap year of course! No, thanks though Tim, I'm busy enough at the moment."

The reality was very different however. David's diary was indeed quiet at the moment and his practice was once again in decline. James Wontner QC had returned as Head of Chambers and was busy again, with the clerks focussing on building up his practice, by sending cases to him that would have previously come David's way. David had willingly stepped down as Head of Chambers upon James' return last year, although he was beginning to wonder whether it had been the right decision. James had insisted that chambers appoint David as Deputy Head of Chambers. David knew it was an almost meaningless title, carrying with it a number of responsibilities but no benefits. Still, it had the advantage that when things went wrong in the day to day running of the set, as they frequently did, tenants would approach him and say they wished he was still Head. It gave him some feeling of comfort, but not much.

David left the room, pretending he had somewhere to go. In truth, he just wanted to get away from Tim, a common feeling these days. He had earlier heard Tim's voice approaching their room, which is why he had risen from his desk. Tim wondered if it was just a coincidence that every time he entered, David was leaving, and he could not resist commenting, "You must be busy, David, whenever I come into the room you are off out somewhere!"

David made his way slowly to the clerks' room. It was Thursday, 25th June, and he had not conducted a single case this month and there was nothing in his diary until mid-July when he had a case listed in the Court of Appeal for a single day. He needed to speak to his senior clerk about this!

As he walked into the clerks' room, he saw all the clerks busily answering phones or entering data enthusiastically into their computers. He looked towards his senior clerk, John Winston, who was busy on the phone. "I'll have a word with him. He's very busy at the moment but he does have a small gap in his diary next week and he may be willing to do you a favour as a goodwill gesture."

David smiled, wondering what poor tenant in chambers was going to be sent hundreds of miles from London and told the usual, 'It's a favour for a good firm, it's an excellent contact, they have plenty of work, treat it as a loss leader and they will send you all their work!'

John put the phone down and looked up at David, "Hello sir, I was just talking about you to a solicitor."

David's smile quickly left his face but John continued, "It's a murder brief sir. I know you like those, something to get your teeth into."

David's smile began to re-appear as John said, "It should be good for a couple of weeks, estimated to be tried in mid-October this year."

David's diary was empty from October onwards so his smile grew bigger as he gratefully replied, "Good news John, thanks."

"It's a shooting, sir, it's not your usual stabbings."

David moved further into the room, far more interested now as John gave more details. "The defendant is a relative of that new pupil of ours. He insists she gets the junior brief. She has checked with the Bar Standards Board and they have said if she feels capable enough of conducting such a case, they have no problems with her acting. No conflict of interest."

David thought for a moment that it did not sound right to him that a pupil should be conducting a murder case, even with an experienced leader. The whole purpose of having a silk and a junior on a case was so that the junior could take over if the silk was taken ill or had to go elsewhere. Also he did not like the fact that the defendant was related, but he decided he would worry about these matters after the brief arrived. He looked at John's beaming face and asked, "What stage has the case reached?"

John looked at the note he had made on his computer, "It's only just at the preliminary stage. The case has already been transferred from the magistrates' court to the crown court and there is a preliminary hearing this coming Monday. The solicitors asked if you would attend even though there's no legal aid in place for Queen's Counsel yet."

David nodded in agreement, it made little difference to him as there was no fee for a preliminary hearing on legal aid anyway. It was included in the brief fee so it made no difference to him whether legal aid was granted now or not, provided he conducted the trial he would get paid. In addition, he knew that preliminary hearings did not take long. It would be a quick journey to the Old Bailey in the City, and then he would probably be out in time for a decent lunch. "No problem John, I'm happy to assist."

John beamed back at him, "Glad to hear that sir, I knew you would help out and it sounds like a good case. You'll enjoy it I am sure."

"No problem John, just give me the case details."

"Yes sir, it's the case of Regina against Hugh Petford-Williams. He is charged with murder, you will be leading Sara Petford-Williams. The instructing solicitor is called Nicholas Mark, from the firm is Mark, Wright and Rogers."

David nodded, "I've not heard of them. Could you provide me with a back sheet with all the details, so I don't have to try and memorise them?"

John smiled, "No problem sir, I'll get Asif to print one out for you and stick it in your pigeon hole."

David thanked him and was just leaving the clerks' room when John added, a little too innocently it seemed to David, "I'm not sure I mentioned this earlier Mr Brand, but the case is in Newcastle."

David immediately stopped in his tracks, his smile having turned upside down. "Newcastle! That's practically Scotland!"

John quickly responded, "I believe so, sir, your geography is probably better than mine. Still, it's an excellent brief and things are a bit quiet at

59

the moment. I'm not sure where the next silk brief is coming from these days."

David looked at him coldly, realising he had been too quick to accept the case without asking where it was. He should have realised because he recalled now that the new pupil said she came from Newcastle. He knew he had no choice but to take the case, so he added ironically, "All right, John, I'll do it as a favour for a good firm. It's probably an excellent contact, I'm sure they will have plenty of silk work and I'll treat it as a loss leader. Who knows they might send me all their silk work in the future!"

John smiled knowingly at David, "You never know, sir, you never know."

CHAPTER 7

THE CONSULTATION

David strolled into Newcastle Crown Court at 9am on Monday morning. He queued up waiting with a number of others to go through the metal detector at the entrance to the building. Once inside, he made his way to the lifts only to find that two out of three were not working. A frustrated security guard told him they had to get parts from Germany and it was taking months.

It did not promise to be a good day for David. He was not being paid for this hearing, legal aid had not even been extended to cover Queen's Counsel and there was always the possibility it never would be. The case had been listed at 10:00am, making it virtually impossible for him to travel from London in the morning by rail, so he had had to come up the night before, on Sunday evening. He had stayed in a hotel near to the court, hoping that would make his journey easier.

Unfortunately, when he arrived at the hotel he was told that the restaurant was closed on Sundays and he had to walk the streets, only to find a Chinese restaurant that did not serve alcohol on Sundays! Further, with the cost of train, hotel and dining expenses taken into account, he was already out of pocket in excess of £300. Things were not looking up this morning when he had to walk up the stairs hauling a heavy suitcase containing his overnight clothes, robes and papers! Life as a silk used to be so much more civilised.

On the bright side, the robing room was on the second floor so the climb was not too hard. He pulled his suitcase up the four flights of stairs and then made his way to the robing room, only slightly out of breath.

As he entered the room he saw a number of the local counsel looking at him suspiciously, no doubt wondering who this London barrister was coming up here taking the local bar's work away from them. His mood did not improve when he went down to the cells to discover that the prison van bringing his client the relatively short journey from Durham prison had not even arrived yet. At least there is one good thing, he thought, things could surely only get better from here on!

At 9:40am, he was finally allowed into the cell area to see Hugh. Introductions were made by the solicitor, Nicholas Mark. "Hugh, this is Mr David Brant QC who has come all the way from London to represent you today. He will be your Queen's Counsel at the trial, leading your niece, Sara…", he quickly added, "…as you requested."

Hugh looked at David coldly but shook his proffered hand as David offered the compulsory greetings, "Good morning Mr Petford-Williams. I'll call you Hugh, if that's ok?"

Hugh still assumed a cold indifferent manner, but nodded at his counsel.

"Good. Hugh, today's hearing is what is called a 'preliminary hearing', very little will happen although the judge is likely to set a date for your trial and a timetable for steps to be taken by both the prosecution and defence. I've read the few papers that have been served to date, and I understand you will be fighting the case."

Hugh intervened forcefully, "Of course I will, it was an accident as I have already told Nick here."

David smiled with relief, after all, it was a long way to come for a plea of guilty.

"I understand that Hugh. Can we deal with a few issues before we go into court?"

Hugh nodded, "Certainly, but I want to know whether you can get me bail today?"

Nick immediately intervened, "Hugh, as I have told you before, we have not listed the case for a bail application today. We have to give the prosecution proper notice and, quite frankly, it's not worth applying for bail in your case. You will

63

have to plead guilty to the firearms offences in due course and those will undoubtedly carry an immediate sentence of imprisonment. In any event, it is rare to be granted bail on a murder charge before a judge has had the time to consider the strength of the evidence against you and he is not going to be able to do that until the prosecution have served all their papers. This will not happen for about another six weeks."

Nick turned to David, "Do you agree Mr Brant?"

David nodded, thinking how helpful it was to have a solicitor who knew what he was talking about. If Jimmy Short had been involved in this case, he would have been telling the client, 'Of course you can apply for bail, you'll get bail no worries, and you'll get off the murder, there's no evidence against you!'

David looked at Hugh and was about to speak when Hugh asked, "I don't understand why I have to plead to the firearms charges. As I've pointed out, this was an antique rifle and I thought there was an exemption for antiques."

David decided he ought to answer this question, "You are right that there is an exemption for antique firearms under section 58(2) of the Firearms Act 1968. Although 'antique' is not defined under the act, the Government has issued recent guidance and in any event, the exemption for antique firearms only applies if the antique is possessed as a 'curiosity or ornament'. If you possess the rifle and ammunition for it, it is usually not considered that it is possessed as a 'curiosity or ornament'. Also, the fact that you fired the rifle into a pillow to scare Johns in the past will also prevent it being exempted in this case."

Hugh was clearly grateful someone had explained the law to him. He was about to speak when David added, "In any event, ammunition does not fall within the exemption and there is a separate charge for that offence. My advice is to plead guilty to the firearms charges once an indictment is served and then we can concentrate on the more serious murder charge."

Hugh agreed and David continued with the consultation. "Tell me Hugh, your defence is one of accident, you never intended to kill Mr Johns or to cause him really serious harm. It was simply an accident."

Hugh raised his voice slightly, "I've said this a number of times but no one is listening!"

David shook his head, "We are listening but I need to ask you a number of questions. Can you explain to me how the accident happened?"

Hugh took him briefly through the details of the incident whilst David asked a few questions, all

65

of which Hugh answered quickly and confidently.

After Hugh had finished, David asked one last question. "It's early days yet, so we will not know what witnesses the prosecution will rely on. It is likely they will call your neighbours, a pathologist, the police officers who arrested and interviewed you and a firearms expert to give evidence as to whether this could have occurred as a result of an accident. We will probably need to obtain our own expert report as well. The prosecution is unlikely to call your wife to give evidence because, according to the case summary, she told them she could not remember a great deal because of the amount of alcohol she had to drink that night. She also said she did not want to say anything. In law, she is not a 'compellable witness' for the prosecution, in other words the prosecution cannot force her to testify against you because she is your wife.

Hugh nodded as David carried on, "However, she was present during the incident and undoubtedly witnessed something and possibly could confirm your account. Do you wish us to contact her and obtain a statement with a view to calling her as a witness at your trial?"

Hugh looked ashen as he replied immediately, "Under no circumstances are you to approach my wife. She has been through enough and I do

66

not want anyone to pester her. No one should speak to her and if anyone does I shall sack you all and get new lawyers. I hope that is crystal clear!"

CHAPTER 8

THE JUNIOR

David travelled back from Newcastle to London King's Cross rail station, arriving just after 4pm. The Preliminary Hearing had taken place in front of Mr Justice George Bright QC. Mr Justice Bright normally sat in the High Court in London but was 'on circuit' sitting in Newcastle Crown Court for four weeks. Nothing of importance occurred at the hearing, save that the judge announced that he would be returning to Newcastle in October and would try the case then, provided that the parties would be ready. More importantly to David, he had announced that, if an application was served to extend legal aid to cover Queen's Counsel and a junior barrister, he would grant it, so the trip had not been a wasted one after all.

Mr Justice Bright, like most High Court Judges, had a background in civil law, but from comments he had made in court, he seemed to understand that criminal practitioners were facing difficult times financially and he did what he could to assist with timetabling and listing for their convenience. Although David had never come across him before, he had heard that the judge lived up to his name and was also fair minded in trials. He expected that Hugh would receive a fair trial as a result.

After leaving the station, David crossed the road to catch another train from St Pancras station to Blackfriars station, where he then walked the short distance to his chambers.

As soon as he arrived, he noticed that the clerks room was unusually quiet. Normally, even if they had no work, the clerks would look busy, but not today.

His senior clerk, John was looking out of the window when David walked through the door. He immediately turned round and asked, "Hello sir, how was Newcastle?"

David went to his pigeonhole, looking to see if anything had arrived for him. It was empty, as usual, "Fine thanks, Mr Justice Bright said he will grant a certificate for silk and junior and the case is listed for 19th October with a two-week time estimate."

John smiled, "Excellent news sir, we need the work at the moment." Turning to Nick he said, "Nick, put that in Mr Brant's and Ms Petford-Williams' diaries please."

He turned back to David, "I understand Mr Adams wants to see you, he's thinking about organising a boating trip across the channel and wants to know if you would like to go. A few of us have said yes, but space is limited."

David gave a half-hearted smile. The idea of being cooped up on board a boat in the Channel for any period of time did not inspire him, but the thought of being cooped up with 'Captain' Tim Adams was an anathema to him. It would probably just be slightly preferable to a few years of negotiating the nine circles of Dante's Inferno.

As he wandered towards his own room he came across Sara and asked her to join him. She sat down and once she had made herself comfortable, he asked politely, "How are things going for you in chambers?"

She beamed back at him, "Very well thanks. I'm enjoying the work even though it can be frustrating at times. Most of my cases would be poorly paid, if it wasn't for the fact I'm not getting paid at all!"

David laughed, "Welcome to the Criminal Bar, I'm afraid it doesn't get much better. Anyway I called you in just to say I represented your uncle today. The trial date is set for Monday 19th October with a time estimate of ten days. He is very keen that you be the junior barrister. I'm going to assume that I owe it to you that I was instructed?"

Sara blushed a little. She had watched David in court a few times during her pupillage and as a result she had recommended that he represent her uncle. However, she did not want anyone else in chambers to know that, just in case it alienated other silks who might be considering her tenancy application in the future.

David saw that she was uncomfortable, "Don't worry I won't tell anyone and if somebody asks me, I shall just say my 'fame' has spread to the distant wilds of Newcastle."

She gave him an ironic thanks as he moved on to discuss the future of the case.

"Sara, as I said, your uncle is adamant he wants you as the junior. I have two concerns about that. Firstly, I don't know how close you are to him, but representing a relative can be very difficult, particularly on a serious criminal charge. It's difficult to be objective and if you are not, you are not serving your client's best interests. Secondly, the junior should be able to take over from the silk if he is taken ill or has another professional engagement and it therefore follows that a junior should not take a case that is beyond his or her ability. Now I don't intend to be ill and have no other cases listed in October and the case does seem relatively straight-forward, but I do need to know you understand the difficulties you might face."

Sara nodded, "I do David. I have thought about whether I should take this case on. In fact, I'm not close to my uncle at all. We have rarely even met. My father never got on with his older brother, so I have seen him only a few times over the years. I have no doubt I can be objective in his case. Secondly, I have yet to conduct a Crown Court trial, never mind a murder but I do want to conduct this case and conduct it with you. I feel I will learn a great deal and I'm looking forward to the opportunity."

David smiled, Sara might not have much experience at the Bar, but she was an expert in diplomacy. He thought for a moment before asking, "You say you're not close to your uncle but he apparently said in his interview with the police that in October last year he was celebrating the fact that you had obtained a pupillage?"

Sara smiled, "I sent a global email to everyone on my contact list to tell them I had been offered a place here. My Aunt probably got the message and told him. To be quite frank he may have been celebrating my getting a pupillage but I suspect that if he hadn't been, he would have found another reason to celebrate that night."

David nodded, it was undoubtedly the truth. It had seemed to him that Hugh probably 'celebrated' something every night of the week. He was concerned at Sara's lack of experience but then he had worked with very experienced junior barristers and solicitors on cases who had not contributed a single thought to a case when he was leading them and had avoided conducting any advocacy.

David pondered for a few seconds before saying anything, then he announced, "Sara, I will be happy to work with you. You are at that stage of your career where, although you don't have the experience you certainly have the enthusiasm to work hard and that is a great quality. I am sure you will be willing and able to deal with any task I set you. Let me set you your first one ... can you make me a coffee, milk no sugar?"

Sara looked at him aghast but before she could say anything David laughed, "Don't worry, I was only joking. I'll make the coffee. You will have to get use to my appalling sense of humour!

Now there is one matter I would like you to help me with. I note in this case that the police used a Taser on your uncle. I have never been involved in a case where a Taser was actually used. Could you do some research and find out all you can about Tasers and when they should be used. Meanwhile, how do you take your coffee?"

CHAPTER 9

THE CHANNEL

Despite being noon on Saturday 11th July, it was quite cold in the middle of the English Channel. David was on the deck of a sixty-foot yacht called 'The Dolphin', grasping the handrail keenly. Tim had hired the yacht for the weekend. They had collected it from Portsmouth on Friday night and berthed in the Solent, just off the Isle of Wight that night, where they had had a party and enjoyed many bottles of Champagne. Now they were headed out to sea, past the Isle of Wight, across the Channel and in the direction of Cherbourg. They expected to get there in about ten hours, at about 6pm, make their way ashore through Customs, have an evening meal and then go back to the yacht to make an early start on Sunday morning back to Portsmouth.

David had not wanted to go on the trip at all but when he mentioned it to Wendy in a rather dismissive manner the week before, he was surprised that she was thrilled at the idea and he had felt he had little choice but to go along.

There were ten of them on board in five cabins with ten berths. As well as David and Wendy, there was Tim and his wife Rachel, James Wontner and his wife Virginia, John Winston and his wife Sally and Sean McConnel and his latest girlfriend, Tatiana Volkov.

Friday night had not been as bad as David had feared. In fact, he had quite enjoyed the evening. Now though he was suffering from a headache which he put down to the motion of the boat but which Wendy had uncharitably attributed to the amount of Champagne he had consumed the previous night.

Tim and his wife were avid sailors and both had obtained various levels of sailing qualifications. Tim had a yacht skippers' qualification and Rachel had a yacht crew certificate, which meant they were allowed to hire this yacht boat without having to hire anyone to sail it for them.

However, the downside was that both Tim and Rachel had bored them with tales of their yachting trips. Although David had heard several references to scuppers and spinnakers, he had no idea what they were and even less interest in finding out. He had amused himself the previous evening by chatting to Tatiana, a 33-year-old Russian interpreter who Sean had met during one of his Russian fraud cases and asked out to dinner and the rest was history. They had been together for three months now.

David was interested in her story about moving to London following her brother who worked for a Russian bank in central London. She had not found it easy to obtain employment and finally

75

accepted a job as a court translator because of her near perfect English. She told him that her salary had recently been heavily cut due to austerity cuts and a general reduction in payments to interpreters, but she loved the work and continued with the job anyway.

She had regaled him with stories of mistranslations in court and they had laughed at each other's jokes. Wendy had not seemed to care about all the attention he gave Tatiana. She had seemed quite happy chatting to Virginia about her art work. Sean had not seemed concerned either. He appeared more interested in listening to Tim than in spending any time with his girlfriend.

David's headache had significantly improved as the day wore on, but the motion of the sea was making his stomach feel like there was a violent storm brewing inside. There were very large waves in the Channel that day and the yacht seemed to ride high out of the water and then suddenly crash down with alarming frequency. He had always considered himself a good sailor but, then again, spending time on massive cruise ships in the Mediterranean probably did not count as sailing. He was finding this a very different experience.

Wendy stood next to him, holding firmly onto the handrail but seemed to enjoy the wind and sea spray on her face and hair and the rhythmic motion of the sea under them. His stomach was now beginning to feel awful with biting cramps making him double up in pain. He turned to Wendy and moaned, "I wish I'd brought some sea sickness tablets."

Wendy looked at him casually and replied, "You ought to ask your little Russian friend, I bet she'd be more than willing to help you out!"

Perhaps his assessment of her mood the night before had been a bit off. He did not respond though as he had other priorities at that moment and he moved quickly to the rear of the boat to see to them. After a few minutes bent double over the handrail, he felt a little better and started to wobble back towards Wendy.

Over the loud-speaker, Tim announced that they were now roughly in the middle of the Channel, making excellent progress and that they would be in good time for their meal in Cherbourg. He told them he had booked one of the best sea food restaurants in town, where lobster and crab were cooked in a special sauce made of cream, Bretagne cider and spices. David immediately turned round and ran to the back of the boat again.

Four hours later, David was lying on his berth below deck. He was beginning to feel better again and decided to visit the galley for a cup of tea. When he arrived, he saw that Wendy was chatting and laughing with Sean and Tatiana. As he came in, she asked him in a much more caring voice, "How do you feel now David?"

He looked at the sympathetic faces and replied, "Much better thanks, I'm getting ready for that meal tonight."

They all smiled at him and carried on in conversation. He raised his eyebrows slightly as he heard Wendy announce, "The four of us must have dinner together in London sometime in the next few weeks."

She turned to David and asked sweetly, "Don't you think that will be nice David?"

He was not sure what expression to adopt, and he made sure he did not look in Tatiana's direction when he replied, hopefully safely, "I'm sure it will be."

They all started to chat together and were all getting on quite well when Tim suddenly rushed into the galley and announced nervously, "We've got a problem."

David looked at him sternly, "What problem?"

"It's not my fault, but it seems the navigation system is off on this yacht. I was expecting to see land by now but I can't see any. I've checked the navigation charts and done some hasty calculations. I think we're about forty miles off course."

Sean quickly responded, "That doesn't sound that bad."

Tim nodded, "It's not terrible but we are only travelling at about nine knots. Even if I switch the engines on we are unlikely to get more than ten knots out of them. It means, even if I am able to navigate without using the defective on-board system, we will arrive three or four hours later than planned. We'll be too late to dine in Cherbourg and then there's the risk that tomorrow we will have difficulty getting back to Portsmouth!"

There was complete silence in the galley as Tim's words sunk in. David was the first to speak, "How can the navigation system not work, this is an expensive boat and the GPS on an average mobile phone could probably get us there?"

Tim flushed a little, "I suppose it's possible that I may have made a slight mistake in setting it when I originally entered our course. I wanted to ensure we didn't spend too long in the shipping lanes. Anyway, I don't think over-analysing it will help us, the point is what do we do now? Do we try and make our way to Cherbourg or do we turn round and I'll try and navigate back to Portsmouth? We have some food on board and plenty to drink. We could have another pleasant evening like last night."

David's stomach had settled and become used to the motion of the ship, he was also hungry and looking forward to excellent French cuisine in Cherbourg and the thought of eating last night's leftovers did not appeal to him, any more than relying on Tim's dubious navigational skills to get them back to Portsmouth during the night.

"We were due to arrive in Cherbourg at 6pm, if we head in the right direction what time will we arrive now?"

Tim responded quickly, "Sometime between 9 and 10pm, but the problem is the Port's not the easiest to navigate in the dark. I really think we are better off aiming towards the coast and staying in a cove until early morning when we can make the trip back to Portsmouth. at least that way we will have the benefit of light to guide us."

The others were consulted and although Tim's standing as a sailor had fallen somewhat in their eyes, much to David's unspoken delight, they all agreed he still knew better than they did and agreed with his last suggestion.

Five hours later, just after 9pm, they were anchored in a bay about twenty miles to the east of Cherbourg. They had all gathered in the galley sharing out the remains of last night's meal with the addition of a number of items that had been intended for breakfast. Tim had broken out the 'emergency' supplies of Champagne and David thought it strange that they all seemed to be enjoying themselves more than if they had managed to dine in an expensive fish restaurant in Cherbourg.

David sat between Wendy and Virginia in the galley. He had arranged it so he was as far away from Tatiana as he could be in the small space, just to prevent any further acerbic comments from Wendy. He did notice that Tatiana glanced across the table quite frequently at him, but he avoided making further eye contact with her. Instead, he was deep in conversation with Virginia who was telling him, in remarkable detail, about the plans she had for her next piece of artwork, based on a nautical theme, it would be called, 'Dolphin Discovery', or something like that.

David feigned interest as they discussed the type of canvas she would use, the different paints, the style, the particular sea creatures she would include in the design and where she would exhibit her final masterpiece. As he grinned and nodded at her, he could not help thinking what awful sacrifices he had to make for his love of Wendy!

CHAPTER 10

FIRM GROUND?

David was now back in his element, standing on terra firma and arguing a case in the Court of Appeal. It was a murder case involving the concept of 'loss of control'.

For years, juries had been presented with the concept of 'provocation' as a limited defence to murder. It was limited in the sense that if it was successful, it could only reduce a murder charge to manslaughter. However, Parliament had decided the concept was too wide and ended in a lot of deaths of spouses. In order to reduce the occasions it was available as a defence and in order to bring some certainty in the law, Parliament abolished the defence of provocation and replaced it with the more limited 'loss of control' defence under the Coroners and Justice Act 2009.

If successful, it still reduced murder to manslaughter but Parliament introduced a further few steps in the concept making it more difficult to rely on. A trial judge would have to decide whether to leave the issue to the jury and had to decide whether there was a 'qualifying trigger' before it could apply. Infidelity could not be a qualifying trigger.

Needless to say, David's case involved infidelity. His client, Geoffrey Thomas was a hardworking man. He thought his marriage was secure and his wife was loving and doting. His employment in railway maintenance involved some shift work and one third of the time he had to work nights. During those periods he had established a routine. He would leave his house just before 10pm and rarely get home before 6am. Unbeknown to him, on some of those nights, his wife Daphne would invite her lover Jim round to the house. Jim would always leave around 4am in order to avoid any unfortunate meetings with Geoffrey. Unfortunately, on one such night, both Daphne and Jim fell asleep in the matrimonial bed, and only awoke to the sounds of Geoffrey entering the room. Naturally, Geoffrey had been somewhat unhappy at seeing his wife naked in bed with another man, both only partially wrapped in a blanket.

He went straight to the kitchen and picked up a knife, and having returned to the bedroom, forcefully told Jim to leave. Jim did not leave immediately. Geoffrey's wife had given evidence during the trial, even though she was not, by law compelled to do so, as she was married to Geoffrey.

She claimed that Geoffrey had screamed, "You bastard!", and then plunged the knife into Jim's heart. According to Geoffrey, Jim had got up from the bed, picked up an empty bottle of wine that they had consumed that evening and brandished it, telling Geoffrey to leave his own home, as he was going to move in permanently.

In these circumstances, the Judge had not left 'loss of control' as a potential defence to the jury and they had not accepted David's submission that Geoffrey was acting in self- defence. They convicted Geoffrey of murder and he received a life sentence, with a minimum term of 16 years before he could apply for parole. David appealed the conviction on the basis that the Judge should have left the defence of loss of control for the jury to decide as he might have been acting in self-defence but lost control and over-reacted.

The case was listed on Friday, 17th July, but, because of other cases listed in the same court, it was not until the afternoon that David addressed the court. He received a grilling from the Court of Appeal judges and had almost been thrown by the senior Law Lord's first comment, "But there was no evidence of loss of control in your case!"

David stared blankly for a split second, before quickly responding with, "With respect, My Lord, it's clear from the words his wife stated he used at the time, that he was angry and out of control."

Lord Chief Justice Waller immediately responded, "Anger does not equate with loss of control, nor do a few expletives. If they did, judges would probably have to leave loss of control to the jury as a possible defence in every single murder case that appeared before them."

These exchanges continued for the next forty-five minutes and it was no surprise to David that the Court dismissed his appeal. Nevertheless, although the experience had reminded him of Sunday's journey back from France when the waves had tossed him about the boat relentlessly, he had enjoyed it far more than sailing on the open sea.

He left the court and crossed Fleet Street and returned to his chambers. As usual, he popped his head into the Clerks' Room and said 'Hello' to the clerks. As he was about to turn and leave the doorway of the Clerks' Room, John shouted out, "You've had a call sir whilst you were in court. It's from a Ms Tatiana Volkov, she left a number." He paused before adding, "That's Mr McConnel's friend isn't it?"

David looked at him coldly, knowing that John was no doubt assuming some scandalous relationship was brewing and was revelling in the prospect of spreading the gossip around a chosen few in chambers. He decided to act quickly, "It's probably about a potential case she mentioned the other day when we were all together in the Channel."

85

John gave him a smirk to suggest it was no such thing. David just shrugged his shoulders dismissively and ignored him.

He returned to his room clutching the post-it note with Tatiana's number on it. He wondered whether the safest course to take was to screw it up and forget about it. Tatiana had not mentioned any potential silk case to him on the yacht and he wondered what she wanted and, more importantly, what Wendy might think she wanted!

However, his interest was aroused and, five minutes later he dialled the number. Tatiana answered immediately, "David, thank you so much for calling me back, I hope you don't mind me phoning you, I was going to call Sean and ask for your number, but he is in court today and I could not get through to him."

David's interest was increasingly aroused, wondering why she would ask her boyfriend for his number? He presumed the call must be about a professional concern, maybe a new case?

"My pleasure, how can I help?"

"I'm in my office at the moment and it is a personal matter, I wondered if we could meet for a drink tonight?"

David was now unsure of what she wanted. His feeling of discomfort was now balanced by a feeling of pride that an attractive young woman wanted to meet him for a drink. Nevertheless, he had to think of Wendy.

"It might be difficult tonight as I'm meeting my partner, Wendy, tonight."

There was a pause at the other end of the line.

"I understand, could we meet earlier, it won't take long. I would like to see you. I could come to your Chambers, if you prefer."

Wendy was her usual busy self and would be coming back from Luton Crown Court later today. He had arranged to meet her in the Temple for a drink at 7pm before going for dinner. It could not hurt to meet Tatiana first, though meeting her in chambers did not seem like a good idea.

"I could meet you in a wine bar called 'Briefs' at say 6pm, it's in Fleet Street, near to chambers and it's easy to find."

"Ok, I'll see you there. I look forward to seeing you again. Thank you so much David."

CHAPTER 11

THE RUSSIAN INTERPRETER

David was seated at a table in Briefs at just before 6pm, sipping from a small glass of the house claret. He had decided not to buy a bottle as it might give the wrong signal.

At exactly 6pm Tatiana walked through the door. She looked stunning in her fitted business suit, perfect makeup and wavy blonde hair worn long. Heads turned as she walked into the bar and followed her as she acknowledged David and approached his table. He could not help feeling good as a few male members of the Bar looked in his direction enviously.

He rose from his seat graciously to greet her and she kissed him on both cheeks. He blushed a little as he asked her, "What can I get you to drink?"

"Thank you, I'll have a glass of Champagne."

Rather surprised, he asked, "Any particular one?"

"Anything but the house, they can taste so metallic."

David continued smiling, regretting that he asked the question which kind, just to impress her. He ordered an expensive glass of Champagne, wondering at the same time how a junior member of the Bar like Sean could afford a girlfriend with such expensive taste! Maybe he couldn't?

He returned to the table with the drink and immediately asked her how he could help. One glass of that would be quite enough, he thought to himself!

She sipped at the champagne, looked into his eyes and slowly and seductively reached across the table to touch his right hand. "When we first met, I knew I could trust you. I sensed that you care about people and we have a great deal in common."

David smiled but quickly withdrew his hand as he noticed Tim Adams walk into the Bar and look across at them with a beaming smile. David felt distinctly uncomfortable as Tim came over to their table and said, "Hello David, hello Tatiana. I just wanted to say hello, I won't stay as it looks like you are in the middle of a private conversation."

He beamed at them as he added, "How's Sean, Tatiana? I haven't seen him since our trip."

She returned his beaming smile before answering dismissively, "Neither have I".

Tim went and joined a group of barristers who were standing at the Bar, but turned to look at them a few times during their meeting.

"I don't really like that man," Tatiana said as she watched him leave their table and join his friends.

David could not help himself as he said quietly, "That's something else we have in common!"

She looked at him with a puzzled expression, "Pardon?"

He smiled, "Nothing, carry on, you were telling me why you wanted to meet me."

He looked into her eyes and guessed what she wanted, He knew he would have to let her down easily, after all he was in a relationship with Wendy.

She returned his smile. "I can trust you David, I'm sure I can. I was desperate to meet you again."

He kept smiling thinking this was becoming a little embarrassing. He sipped at his claret as Tatiana carried on, "Even though we only met for such a short amount of time, I feel that you are someone I have known all my life. Someone who would help a person in need."

David began to wonder where this was going. She did not want a loan did she? She had certainly come to the wrong person if she did.

Tatiana looked around to make sure no one was listening and grabbed both his hands this time, "David, I really need your help. It's my brother."

David had felt embarrassed at the attention she had given him but now he felt a little deflated. He pulled his hands away slowly, "Your brother?"

"I told you he worked for a bank in London. Today he phoned me in a panic. The bank has started an investigation into certain transactions carried out by him. They say there is a shortfall in accounting of over a million pounds and they believe he has stolen it. He is adamant he is innocent. I know Sean is a barrister but I don't think he can help me with Ivanov's problem. It is too big. You are a very senior man, very old and experienced, you must have a great deal of experience of cases like this?"

David had heard little after the expression, 'very old' and was very much regretting this meeting. His ego had been massively inflated by Tatiana's earlier attention and then it had been burst like a balloon, all in the space of a few seconds. Still, he did not want anyone around him to realise this. He nodded at Tatiana and reached across the table to put his hand on hers, all for the

91

benefit of the spectators and whispered, "I suspected it was something like this. Of course I will assist your brother in any way I can."

CHAPTER 12

A BARRISTERS' STRIKE?

The meeting with Tatiana had not lasted much longer, although she had accepted his offer of another glass of expensive Champagne. He reminded himself as he bought it that he must check his credit card limit this month. Very little money had come in for him recently and there was a real risk he would be reaching his limit. At least he had a reserve card to be used when his main card was rendered useless.

He agreed to suggest good solicitors for Tatiana's brother to contact and further agreed to take the case on as silk should her brother want it. He also agreed to see the brother on a pro bono basis in chambers to give some basic guidance should he need it.

David's diary was empty at the moment. His next case was the Hugh Petford-Williams case, which was not listed for trial until October. That was three months away. He hoped he would be instructed on another case in that time. At least there was a chance that he might receive a return from another barrister in the next three months, even if it was the obnoxious Tim Adams!

However, on Tuesday 21st July, an emergency chambers meeting was called by James Wontner.

The issue was the annual one about legal aid cuts. The Government had announced that it would not cut advocates' legal aid fees but they were going ahead with an 8.75% reduction in litigation fees for solicitors in addition to the 8.75% cut there had been the year before. Solicitors went on strike, refusing to accept any new cases at the reduced rate. A number of barrister's chambers had agreed to support them by also refusing to take these cases and refusing to conduct returns from other barristers expecting this joint force to put pressure on the Government to negotiate. James had called the meeting, wanting to know whether chambers should similarly support the solicitors' action.

The meeting was held at 6pm and it was not long before there were polarised positions divided roughly along the lines of seniority. The juniors were almost all in favour of the action, the senior barristers were equally against it.

Tim Adams was one of the first to voice his opinion. "I should say at the beginning that my opinion is not influenced by how busy my practice currently is. I am booked up with work until January 2016, so I am not looking for any returns. Also, I am conducting mainly prosecution work at the moment and no one is suggesting that we don't accept prosecution returns as they are not affected by these fee cuts.

In my opinion, it is pointless supporting this strike. We all know solicitors cannot afford to strike for long. They have large monthly staff and other bills to pay. Inevitably, the strike will end within a month or two at the very most. I doubt solicitors will actually lose out. No doubt they will be telling their clients to wait before submitting applications for legal aid. Then when the strike is over they will submit them and be paid exactly the same amount. However, the junior bar will suffer greatly financially by not taking on new work and by refusing to conduct returns.

This is the wrong fight. As we all know, in January the Government are going to change legal aid rules again and reduce the number of solicitors who can conduct legal aid. That will certainly affect the Bar and that is what we should be striking about, not the current reduction in solicitors' fees."

Most of the senior members of chambers agreed with him, but the juniors were more vociferous in their opposition.

Wendy quickly spoke up, "I don't agree with Tim at all. If this cut goes ahead, solicitors will look for other areas to make profits. If the Criminal Bar does not support them now, they will have every reason to seek to do more of our advocacy work by keeping the briefs within their firms and refusing to brief the Bar. We need to go on strike now or it will be the end of the Criminal Bar."

There were several loud voices of support from the juniors and even one or two senior members made sympathetic sounds in support.

James Wontner noticed how numerous members of chambers were trying to speak at once so he interrupted them, "Can we have some order in the meeting? We cannot all speak at once. Clearly this is an emotive issue and whatever decision we take tonight will undoubtedly affect our livelihoods. Let us hear from the Deputy Head of Chambers who has not said anything yet. I am sure we would all appreciate his wise counsel."

David glared at James, he had not wanted to address the meeting. He tended to agree with Tim's opinion, although he was loath to say so. It was also difficult for him to express his true opinion because, unlike Tim, he needed return work at the moment. It was also difficult to take the opposite stance to Wendy in the meeting, that could have more worrying repercussions at home!

He gathered his thoughts before addressing the now silent meeting. "Unlike Tim, my diary is not full of work so this action will have a direct effect upon my practice, although it is fair to say that there are not so many returns for silks at this time of year, so the effects may not be that great. As we all know, the courts are reluctant to list serious cases during the summer holidays.

That being so, on the whole, even though they give seemingly opposite opinions, I tend to agree with both Tim and Wendy."

There were a few unfavourable comments round the room, some suggesting David was sitting on the fence. He waited until they were quiet before continuing, "I agree with Tim that this is the wrong fight, but I also agree with Wendy that we need to support our solicitor colleagues because if we do not, they are not likely to support us in the future. Like Tim I doubt this strike will last long and I doubt it will be successful. I also tend to agree that solicitors' firms will not lose much whereas the junior Bar may suffer greatly. Nevertheless, I question whether we can afford not to be seen to support the solicitors who instruct us? I think not. So even though I think it the wrong issue, it is unlikely to last long and it is unlikely to be successful, I am in favour of supporting the solicitors."

The meeting carried on for another hour with most members of chambers wanting to express some opinion. In the end, it was clear that the vast majority of chambers was in favour of striking. James announced that was the decision and from the following day, no member of chambers would be accepting new work under the new legal aid orders, nor would anyone be accepting returns.

David left the meeting with Wendy reflecting that he had probably just voted to be unemployed for three months!

CHAPTER 13

THE BROTHER

David did not go into chambers on Wednesday or Thursday. There did not seem much point, but on Friday he had arranged to meet Anton Volkov, Tatiana's brother.

At 4pm, Anton was shown into David's room for a brief discussion. After introductions were made, Anton immediately dealt with the reason he was there.

"Mr Brant thank you so much for seeing me. People in my bank have made very serious allegations against me. They allege that I am guilty of a very serious offence. I am not guilty Mr Brant, I am completely innocent but I don't know what to do. Tatiana said you may be able to help me. She is very fond of you and has highly recommended you."

"Thank you, Tatiana is very kind. I know a little about your case from what she told me, but it is very sketchy. Let me ask you a few questions about the allegations and then I may be able to give you a preliminary advice."

"Of course, Mr Brant."

"Firstly, I would like to know just how far the investigation has gone. Have the police become involved yet?"

"No, the bank does not believe in bringing them in until they have done their own investigative work. They believe that bringing the police in may introduce too much media attention, so they will only contact them if they believe there is a case against me."

David nodded and moved on to ask the next question. "Are you the only one being investigated or are there others?"

"I haven't been told the answer to that, although the questions put to me suggest they are not looking for anyone else. They went into some detail with me."

David made a note in his blue Counsels' note book before asking, "What are the bank alleging?"

"I'm employed by the MAFEAE Bank, you will have heard of them. 'The Middle And Far East And European Bank. We are based in London but our trades cover just about everywhere in the World. I am employed in the International Investment division with a specific interest in the Middle East."

He hesitated, "Well, I suppose I should say that I was employed!"

David nodded whilst taking a note of the names. Anton continued, "Difficulties arose with investments made in the Middle East. I was mainly responsible for them. It was genuinely believed that some countries had settled down after the turmoil over the last few years and were ripe with investment opportunities. However, the belief was misplaced in a number of areas and massive losses were made. I was responsible for making a number of what proved to be very risky investments and a relatively large amount was lost."

David looked up from his notes, "What do you count as a 'relatively large amount'?"

"About ten million pounds."

David's eyes widened slightly.

Anton did not appear to notice and carried on, "I was reprimanded for taking unnecessary risks and told my bonus was jeopardised."

David smiled, "Only in banking could you lose ten million pounds and be told your bonus would be 'jeopardised'!"

Anton just stared at him before continuing, "Due to the losses that were made, the bank had to transfer about eight million pounds from the reserve assets' division of the company to the Middle East division to cover those losses."

"Why only eight million pounds?"

"Because the Middle East section had made large profits in the past and had large assets that were remaining in the account, so they did not need to transfer the full ten million."

Anton smiled to himself and then added, "You would not think we had made such profits considering the poor bonus I received!"

David nodded as he wrote a big 'PM' in the margin of his notebook, standing for 'Potential Motive'.

Anton continued unaware of David's line of thought, "I was primarily responsible for dividing that money into a number of accounts to cover those trading losses. The Bank is now investigating one of those accounts which they say was actually in profit but had funds transferred into it when there was no need and then those funds were fraudulently transferred out to a company called Speculative Emergency Acquisitions Limited.

The Bank are saying that I was responsible for those fraudulent transfers and that I have some undefined interest in that company!

At first about £1 million was transferred over a three-month period earlier this year, but about two months ago a further £2 million was transferred over a period of four working days.

The following week Speculative Emergency Acquisitions Limited went into liquidation and no one can trace the assets or the Registered Directors of the company."

"Did you have any dealings with the Directors?"

"Not directly, I remember the Managing Director was called Ms T. Luckov, because I saw it on documents, but I never spoke to her."

David looked at him sympathetically, "So why are they saying you had anything to do with this fraud?"

"Well, they are speculating because they have no one else to blame. Admittedly, I made the initial transfers to this company as they came up on my computer screen as requiring immediate transfers. That covered about £500,000. I did make subsequent transfers amounting to just under that amount. Unfortunately, when I did there was a red flag on the computer screen. The red flags are created by a software programme created specifically for our company identifying that a transaction may be fraudulent and extra checks should be carried out. Nevertheless, I went ahead with the transfer because I was told to do so in the past by my section leader. I was told always to ignore the first red flag as often there's a glitch in the system."

"So others ignore these red flags as well?"

"Well that's a problem for me. Although many have told me they have in the past, they now all say they never have, nor would they, nor has anyone ever told them to. I think they are just protecting themselves by lying."

David nodded, that was not unheard of in any business, never mind when fraud is alleged. He continued, "Are they alleging anything else against you?"

Anton hesitated, "Yes. It is purely circumstantial, they have investigated the computers involving the transactions and they say that my personal home laptop has an IP address that is the same as one that was used by Speculative Emergency Acquisition Limited for one transaction! It is ridiculous, the transaction was for a payment of less than fifty thousand pounds. There is no link between my laptop or any computer linked to me and the rest of the three million that has gone missing."

David had dealt with many cases involving computer IP (Internet Protocol) addresses. From his experience this was a far more worrying aspect of the case.

"How did a bank get your personal IP address?"

"Oh, it's the bank's laptop. They provide them to us so we can take work home. I did log into it at home, I suppose they got it from there."

David looked at the briefcase that Anton had brought with him and was clutching at now. He pointed to it, "Does your briefcase contain any papers relating to this allegation?"

"Yes, I have brought a few documents to show you."

Anton placed the case on David's desk and opened the contents. Half an hour later after pouring over a number of documents, David had reached his own conclusion. Anton was not guilty of stealing a million pounds.

He had probably stolen a great deal more!

However, he was not going to turn down the brief if it arrived on his desk. After all, he could be wrong, he had not seen all the relevant material.

He provided Anton with the names of a few good quality solicitors who dealt with serious fraud cases. Needless to say, Jimmy Short and Rooney Williams LLP were not amongst them!

Anton left chambers seemingly happier than when he first arrived. His final comment was to say that Tatiana had asked him to remind David that Wendy had suggested they meet up for a meal and she was hoping it could be arranged soon. David told him he would remind Wendy. He personally doubted the meal would ever materialise. It probably had not helped that

105

David had told Wendy about Tatiana's contacting him and him meeting her, 'to discuss her brother's legal problems.' Wendy's questioning look when he mentioned meeting Tatiana in a wine bar and buying her expensive Champagne had the desired effect of making him feel distinctively uncomfortable. He had toyed with the idea of not saying anything but then he thought that if he did not, she would undoubtedly have heard about it from another obvious source.

He looked across the room to Tim Adams empty desk and then tried with some difficulty to put the image of a smirking Tim out of his head.

CHAPTER 14

ACCIDENT OR MURDER?

Outside his chambers the Temple Gardens were bathed in a mid-August Sun but David was at his desk with his reading light on. The Sun never seemed to light his desk whatever time of day or year it was. He was busy looking at the Hugh Petford-Williams' brief which had just arrived. He pulled at the silk ribbon which tied the papers together and delved into them. He was pleasantly surprised to find that the solicitors had done a great deal of work on the case. There were already some detailed instructions, a proof of evidence from the lay client, and a document headed, 'Defendant's comments on the prosecution witnesses' statements'. It was good to be working for a decent solicitor again, unlike his experiences over the last few years with Jimmy Short.

He noted that there had already been a Pleas and Case Management Hearing in the case, which Sara had attended. Hugh had been asked to formally enter his plea and certain directions had been given ensure the case was ready in time for the October trial date. Hugh had pleaded guilty to possessing the rifle and to possessing the ammunition, but not guilty to the murder. Happily, David had been able to avoid a further trip to Newcastle to attend that hearing.

The case appeared relatively straight forward. There was just one issue, was it an accident or not?

Hugh claimed it was, whereas the prosecution maintained it was a deliberate attempt to kill, or at least to cause serious injury and as Johns had died, it therefore amounted to murder.

There were a number of witnesses to be called by the prosecution. There were four neighbours who all heard the fatal shot that must have killed Johns. Dr Jeffries also stated he thought he heard another shot as well but he said he was not sure now. The prosecution clearly thought that he was mistaken as the second shot did not fit the prosecution theory of one shot through the lavatory door. Also Hugh was adamant there was only one shot fired. There was support for that from the fact that only one spent cartridge was found on the stairs near the lavatory, where it had been ejected from the rifle. Another spent cartridge was found in the garden, but this was near the target range that Hugh had set up and was consistent with his claims that he used the rifle for target shooting.

The neighbour, Clare Payne, also stated that she had heard shots fired in October last year, which Hugh confirmed in his proof of evidence was when he discharged the rifle into the pillow Johns was resting on.

David read through the police officers' statements. Two of those who first attended the house in response to the 999 call, had given statements. They stated that they had crashed through the front door in case the paramedics were in danger from a gun-wielding maniac in the house. Both were clear that Hugh made a sudden move when they told him politely to get to the floor. They said he was still carrying the rifle and they believed it might be loaded. They both claimed that they jumped on him and the Taser was used to protect the paramedics as well as themselves.

Detective Sergeant Bull provided a statement dealing with the interview and produced as exhibits the video and audio tapes that were used that day. He also provided a statement saying that when Hugh was charged with murder, he responded, "It was not murder, it was an accident."

There was a statement from Dr Henry Roper, a Pathologist, who examined the body of Johns. None of his findings were particularly contentious. He noted that Johns had signs of an advanced stage of liver disease that suggested that he consumed far too much alcohol in his life.

On reading this, David thought he felt a slight pain in back, on the left hand side in the area of his kidney. Was it psychosomatic? He made a quick decision, he would abstain from red wine for a few days.

He read on and noted that a blood sample had been taken at the hospital on Johns' admission and revealed a reading of 245 mg per 100 ml of blood. That suggested that he was over three times the drink driving limit in England and Wales at the time he was shot.

Dr Roper examined the wound to the neck which was in a 'teardrop' shape as the bullet had been deflected by the door and hit Johns' neck at an angle slicing through the jugular vein before exiting leaving a larger wound. The wound had some traces of small wood splinters from the door. Dr Roper had no doubt that Johns' death was the result of a single gunshot wound to the right side of the neck which cut through the jugular vein causing severe haemorrhaging from which Johns bled to death. Dr Roper pointed out that the paramedics and hospital staff had worked 'magnificently', Johns had received transfusions at hospital amounting to three times his own blood volume, but the injuries were too severe, he did not recover consciousness and was pronounced dead at 3am.

The final prosecution witness was Dr Christopher Brown, a firearms expert. He gave a detailed history of the Winchester Model 62A, 1890 rimfire rifle used, detailing; its power and accuracy.

He had visited Hugh's home and noted the angle at which the bullet had hit the door. He produced a series of photos showing long steel rods in place to demonstrate the trajectory of the bullet and possible areas from where the fatal shot was fired.

He concluded that the lavatory door had deflected the bullet slightly upwards and to the left. If it had not, Johns would have probably been hit roughly in the centre of the chest about 15 cm below and 10 cm to the right of where the bullet actually hit as you look at him. In his opinion, although he could not completely rule out the possibility of an accident, the most probable scenario was that the bullet was fired from the second or third step on the stairs by Hugh aiming downwards at the centre of the lavatory door.

That was where you would expect Johns' heart to be if he was seated on the toilet.

CHAPTER 15

A VISIT TO NEWCASTLE

By Friday 21st August, the Bar's strike was over. The larger firms of solicitors had stated they were no longer continuing to strike, in order to show 'goodwill' towards the Government. Clearly there was no point in the Bar continuing its own strike in those circumstances. It made no difference to David. He had not been offered any new work during the strike and none afterwards. At least it gave him plenty of time to concentrate on the Petford-Williams' case.

It did not take long for him to master the papers and discuss them with Sara and their solicitor, Nick. The evidence was not overwhelming but certainly Hugh faced a number of problems. There was no issue that on his own admission, he fired the fatal shot and had been reckless carrying a loaded rifle down the stairs, even if the killing had been an accident. Of major concern was the prosecution expert's opinion of the most probable scenario. As David explained to Sara, juries tended to like experts and it was abundantly plain that Hugh needed his own expert to consider the evidence and hopefully support Hugh's account of how the accident occurred.

David asked her to write an advice to obtain an extension of legal aid to instruct a firearms' expert. Within 48 hours Sara produced the advice and four weeks later legal aid was extended. The solicitors then instructed Dr Francis Macdonald, an expert on all manner of firearms. He soon prepared a draft report, basically agreeing with Dr Brown's findings, although it did refer to the fact that Dr Brown had used rods, measurements and photographs, rather than newer 3D laser scanning equipment and computer software.

Having read the report David and Sara travelled to Jesmond to the solicitors' offices to discuss it with the expert. They arranged to see him on Thursday 17th September at 10:30am and then to see Hugh in Durham prison in the afternoon in order to reduce the number of trips they had to make to Newcastle before the trial commenced.

Although they travelled together on Wednesday afternoon, Sara stayed with her parents and David stayed in the same hotel as last time. This time he was happy to find the restaurant open and he enjoyed a sirloin steak and a large glass of Argentinian Malbec whilst overlooking the River Tyne. The evening was somewhat more enjoyable than his last visit.

In the morning, David made his way to the solicitor's offices after a large cooked buffet breakfast at the hotel. He turned down the offer of extra toast, there had to be some limits.

He caught a cab from his hotel to Jesmond arriving at 10:00am. On arrival he was shown into a reception room by Julie, the receptionist, and provided with a coffee. He had already consumed two but he felt it churlish to refuse a third one. Within minutes his coffee arrived just as Nick and Sara came through the door. After mutual greetings, Nick ushered them into a large conference room. David noted that Nick had a set of the court papers already open on the table. He was suitably impressed. The conference room looked like those in barrister's chambers in the Temple. The walls were lined with legal books and law reports and there was a large oak conference table in the middle of the room with eight solid oak chairs around it. It was clearly designed to impress clients. The legal books all looked in pristine condition, as indeed they were. Few lawyers relied on them these days, preferring to use online resources for research. Nick had managed to purchase them cheaply as a result and they were there, functioning as expensive legal wallpaper.

Nick waited until they were seated before commenting, "I thought we may as well meet half an hour before the conference just to discuss the case and any thoughts you have. Is there anything either of you want to raise with me?"

Sara looked at David, she was not going to volunteer anything whilst he was there. David sat upright and shuffled a few papers before answering, "Obviously I've met Hugh once for only a short period. I wasn't really able to make a proper assessment of him. You've met him several times, can you tell us what you think?"

Nick pondered the question, looking at Sara before answering, "I understand he is your uncle but I trust that I can speak candidly?"

Sara nodded, "Don't worry, I've seen very little of him over the years. Anyway, you have instructed me in the case as a junior advocate and I intend to look at the case like I would any other, with an objective eye."

Nick smiled at her, not bothering to question how objective she really was. Hugh wanted her in the case and he was not going to risk losing his large fee by putting any obstacles in her way.

"Good! Well Hugh can be very challenging. At first he came across as someone who simply did not trust me. He refused to supply any real instructions and just kept quiet on visits moaning that we had not obtained bail for him. However, after a time he mellowed and began to listen to questions and answer them in detail. Sometimes a little too much detail! I had never heard of some of the devices he had used to try to obtain an erection!"

David's eyes raised slightly as he added, "Well I suspect we won't need to go into too much detail about that. What do you make of him as a potential witness? Does his account sound plausible?"

Nick looked directly at David, "As you know, that's always a difficult question. Sometimes he appears completely honest when he gives me instructions about that night. Other times, he seems to be telling me what he thinks I want to hear or what will sound best to a jury. Generally though, I think his account sounds plausible. He is quite a raconteur so I believe he will make a good witness."

David made notes on his computer during the meeting which he had set up for the consultation. He then asked, "He has been in custody sometime now, has he asked for a bail application to be made?"

Nick shook his head. "No, at first he was very keen that we should apply for bail but I suggested we wait until we had seen the prosecution papers. Then when they arrived he changed his mind. He said he was getting used to prison. He has become quite a celebrity in there and he finds that his opinion is much sought after. He accepted that he had no defence to the firearms charges and that's why he pleaded guilty. He knows he will have to serve some time in custody whatever happens, and, as he points out, he might as well start serving his sentence now rather than be released on bail and then returned to prison."

David nodded, he could see the sense in that. Nick reached for some papers and passed copies over to David and Sara. "This came in today, it's further prosecution unused material. I don't think there is anything important although they have served a statement from Hugh's wife, Rosemary."

David and Sara read through the statement. Rosemary had made a statement to police a few days after Hugh's arrest. She stated that she had no intention of giving evidence against Hugh and would not attend court. In relation to the incident on 18th June, she could recall very little. She believed she consumed close to two litres of red wine that night and her recollection was very hazy. She remembered them all drinking together and recalled that they were having a good time. However, she did get bored when Hugh and William started talking about the battle of Waterloo. That was when she switched off and started drinking a lot more.

She vaguely remembered Hugh leaving and then going to bed with William, but, after that, everything was a blank until the police and ambulance arrived.

The police had also asked her about the previous incident. She remembered that well. They had all been drinking but she had not drunk as much on that occasion. this time. Again, Hugh had left to go to his club.

She had found William Johns to be amusing, good looking and ultimately desirable and had succumbed to his advances. She had sexual intercourse with him in the downstairs bedroom. She remembered Hugh coming into the room brandishing the rifle and saying he was going to kill William. She had been terrified but William had treated it as a joke and made some crude reference to Hugh's impotence. She had seen how Hugh reacted to it. She had seen something she had never seen before, a look of pure hatred as Hugh raised the rifle and fired directly at William just missing his head by a few inches, the bullets hitting the pillow his head was on. She had been terrified. She thought Hugh had intended to kill William, but in his anger had missed him.

They finished reading the statement, and Nick commented, "It's a good job she's not giving evidence for the prosecution and its put paid to any idea we might have of calling her. I don't think any of us would want the prosecution putting that statement to her in cross-examination!"

They continued discussing the case for half an hour and then, shortly after 10:30am, Dr Macdonald was led into the conference room carrying a large bag. He had brought with him the stock and firing mechanism of a Winchester rimfire rifle and was about to explain how it operated. After accepting the offer of a coffee from Julie he opened the bag and showed them the contents.

"As you see, I haven't brought the whole rifle, I didn't see the need. I suspected you wouldn't want me to be firing live rounds in your office!"

Nick laughed and looked at Julie as she was leaving the room, "Not unless you were aiming at one of my staff."

Julie gave him a sarcastic frown and Dr Macdonald smiled as he pulled out the cut down rifle from his bag. "I'm afraid I couldn't get hold of an 1890 model but I obtained a 1906 model that was only slightly modernised. They have roughly the same firing qualities."

He produced a tube with a triangular hole cut in one end. "This is the same type of magazine that Mr Petford-Williams had. It can take 16 of the bullets that are placed in the rifle here." He pointed to the stock of the rifle he had brought.

"The bullet is then put into the breach by pumping this wooden part, situated under the barrel. As it is pumped, a bullet is taken from the magazine and placed in the breach. The same action then cocks the hammer which you see is rather prominent and just in front of the stock of the rifle. The pumping action also pushes the trigger forward making it ready to fire, like this."

He used his forefinger to apply pressure on the trigger, the hammer hit forward and would have hit the rim of a cartridge, expelling a bullet, if one had been present.

David nodded and asked to examine the mechanism. After pumping it he gently touched the trigger and the hammer snapped down. He looked at Dr Macdonald, "As we can see from your draft report, you examined the original rifle."

"Of course, my secretary made the necessary arrangements with the prosecution and I went to Dr Brown's laboratory where he showed me the rifle and we did some test firing."

David nodded, "Yes, thanks for that. What we really want to know is, is it possible to cause this action by accident as our client states? He states he had already loaded and then pumped the rifle so a bullet would have been in the breach, the hammer would be cocked and the trigger forward in the firing position. In your draft report you do not deal with that aspect, is there a reason?"

Dr Macdonald smiled at David, "I examined the original rifle and found the trigger required a greater amount of pressure than this rifle, before it would fire. I suspect it is because Mr Petford-Williams adapted it and used none standard parts to make it function. As for your question, the answer is, yes, it is possible. If he carried a loaded rifle downstairs, it is possible he stumbled and grabbed the trigger applying the right amount of pressure just at the moment the rifle was pointing at the centre of the lavatory door."

David nodded again, "So it's possible, but is it likely?"

Dr Macdonald returned the nod with a knowing smirk, lawyers always tried to pin him down on such questions. "Unexpected accidents can occur around firearms. It's quite possible that he was angry, pumped the rifle upstairs, came downstairs, stumbled, and shot through the door. I wouldn't like to say whether it's likely or not as that requires an assessment of the Defendant that I'm not in a position to make.

I can say that it was remarkably foolish to walk down stairs with a loaded rifle with no safety catch in place. It was also a remarkably unlucky, or, I suppose, a lucky shot, depending upon which way you look at it. As the prosecution expert states, the bullet just happened to hit the centre of the door just in front of where Mr Johns' heart would have been located.

That would usually take quite an assessment by the shooter and an aimed shot."

David was slightly concerned at the answer. "If you are asked by the prosecution which scenario is more likely, accident or aimed shot, what will you say?"

Dr MacDonald contemplated the question for a few seconds before answering, "I shall say truthfully that I am not qualified to say. That is definitely a matter for the jury and either scenario is equally possible."

CHAPTER 16

THE LOVING HUSBAND

Dr Macdonald declined an offer of lunch with the lawyers, telling them he had to travel to Manchester to examine an Italian-made Olympic .380 BBM starter pistol to determine whether it had been converted to fire real ammunition and he simply did not have the time.

As David, Nick and Sara were all travelling to Durham prison that day, they decided to travel straight there and have lunch in a local restaurant.

Nick drove the team along the A1(M) to Durham in his brand new Mercedes C220 CDI. The conversation predictably fell upon the recent strike action of criminal barristers and solicitors, and the questionable future of the profession as a result. As they chatted, David could not help appreciate the irony of Nick discussing their impending poverty whilst driving such an expensive vehicle.

The journey took them 40 minutes to the prison. A further 10 minutes later and they were enjoying the cuisine in a local Chinese restaurant near to the prison. An hour later at 2:20pm they were allowed into a prison conference room and a few minutes later Hugh was brought in.

After the initial greeting, David moved on to deal with the case. "Hugh, there are two recent developments we need to deal with. Firstly, the prosecution have served a statement from your wife Rosemary. It's served as 'unused material' so they are not going to rely upon it in court and they are not going to call her as a witness."

Hugh looked concerned at the mention of his wife's name, but he said nothing and let David continue. "Also, this morning we had a consultation with Dr Macdonald, the firearms' expert and he gave us an opinion about the rifle and the accident. There is little to say about that. He dealt with the rimfire rifle and told us all how it operates, but you know that anyway. In relation to the accident, he confirmed he will give evidence that it is feasible that the accident occurred in the way you have told us. However, he will not be drawn on whether it was likely or not."

Hugh jumped to his own defence, "Well it's not only possible, it's the way it happened!"

David looked at him closely, "When we get to trial, the prosecution may ask you to demonstrate how it happened. I'm reluctant to ask you to do so as, in my experience, it is difficult to recreate accidents in a courtroom. I will undoubtedly object if the prosecution asks, but I suspect the judge will allow it. Do you think you can recreate it?"

Hugh looked at them one by one before answering, "Definitely. I will be keen to show them how this tragedy occurred."

David moved on to deal with Rosemary's statement. He produced a copy for Hugh to read before he asked him any questions. Hugh read it and put it down. Tears were forming in his eyes and he wiped them with the back of his hand when he realised he did not have his handkerchief. Before David could say anything Hugh asked, "Are you married Mr Brant?"

David did not reveal his personal circumstances to clients as a rule, but he decided to reply this time, "I was, but I'm divorced now."

Hugh nodded, "That must have been very difficult for you whatever the circumstances."

"It was, but let's deal with your case."

Hugh let out an audible sigh. "I love my wife Mr Brant. I have loved her from the moment we first met at Oxford and I will love her for the rest of my life. I would do anything for her."

David smiled, hoping this was not going to get too sentimental as they had a lot of ground to cover but he knew better than to interrupt. Hugh obviously wanted to get this off his chest.

"You see, Mr Brant, we were studying different subjects at Oxford and, at first, I only saw Rosemary from afar. I tried all manner of tricks to 'accidentally' bump into her, but she never seemed to notice me. She was stunningly attractive, she still is, and she was always surrounded by attentive men."

He paused for a few moments, sinking deeply into his memories before taking another deep breath and continuing, "Then one day, I found her sitting alone on a bench in the grounds of the college. She was crying. I sat next to her and handed her my handkerchief. I was glad at the time that it was a clean one! At first, she looked at me as though I was mad but she took it and then, after I expressed some sympathy, she unburdened herself to me.

She had been in a relationship with another student, an absolute swine, I can't recall his name now. They had been together from within a few weeks of her arriving at Oxford.

That day we spoke, she had gone to visit him and found him fornicating with a female student from her own study group. A close friend of hers. She had even introduced them, trusting him completely. Anyway, I took the opportunity to get close to her, I thought I might not get another. I offered to teach him a lesson."

David gave him a warning look as this story could prove troubling to their defence, but he remained silent as Hugh continued, "She told me he wasn't worth it and she would move on once she'd recovered. She's a strong woman Mr Brant. I have always felt she can deal with any tragedy or triumph with equal determination. She has always reminded me of that Kipling poem, how does it go?"

He paused for a few seconds as he tried to recall a distant memory, "Ah, I remember now,

'If you can meet with Triumph and Disaster

And treat those two impostors just the same;'

That sums up Rosemary to me. Anyway, I digress, she accepted my invite for a coffee, then for a drink, then for a meal and the rest is history."

David looked at him sympathetically, "I can understand all that Hugh, but of course, we do need to concentrate on the issues for trial."

Hugh looked at him perplexed, "But this is relevant to my trial. I am demonstrating how much I loved my wife. That explains why I would do anything for her, even permit another man to take her to bed!"

Nick decided to intervene, "I think we all understand that Hugh, but we have a very limited time. As you know we only get two hours on these conferences and it takes twenty minutes of that time to get through prison security."

Hugh looked at him, "I consider this very relevant and I need to tell you. Rosemary and I continued to see each other throughout our time at University. We parted a few times, always at her instigation, not mine, but we always got back together and eventually, after University, we married and went to live at my family home. We made no use of our respective degrees but worked in the family clothing firm."

A degree of pride entered his voice, "You may have heard of 'Petford-Williams Bespoke Suits?"

Nobody but Sara had heard of them and that was only because her father had mentioned the firm to her. Hugh looked a little crest-fallen but he continued, "Anyway, I worked as a manager with my father. Rosemary worked as our personal assistant. Father absolutely doted on her. I don't think he was ever really happy with my mother, nor her with him and he probably liked having a young woman around.

Eventually father retired. We continued with the business and it looked like it was going to be a great success, but then one of this country's regular recessions hit the business and we had to fold."

Hugh looked at them all to ensure they were all listening to his tale, "Rosemary and I were happy but we had one regret, that we could not have children. I had a low sperm count and Rosemary had certain problems that I will not go into. Nevertheless, we had a wonderful and fulfilling sex life."

He paused and frowned, "Then I was diagnosed with diabetes and after that I found it increasingly difficult to obtain, never mind maintain, an erection."

David glanced at Sara to see how she was reacting to this abundance of family history, but she was taking a note and looked unaffected by it all.

Hugh noticed the look and also glanced towards Sara, giving her an understanding smile before continuing.

"The real problems came when my mother died. It was a very stressful time. We had to find the money to pay the death duties, or whatever they call them these days.

We could have sold the house and moved into something smaller but we decided to convert the house into flats and sell them off. I managed to get a loan from the bank. That was no easy thing but the bank manager was a member of my local club and a fellow mason, so it proved a little less difficult than it might normally have.

The conversion works to the house, the pressing tax man, our increasing debts, none of these problems helped my condition. Of course Rosemary still had her needs and I tried everything to satisfy her, oral sex, scrotal rings to ensure an erection, even Viagra, but nothing worked."

It was Sara who looked at David now and saw that he was looking a little uncomfortable, and frowning at the client, and she smiled and made a note.

"Then the flats were finished and we started to sell them and pay off our debts. Eventually we had accumulated a little 'nest egg' which we could invest after we sold the flat to Johns. God how I wish we hadn't now!"

David looked towards Sara. She was now staring at Hugh, clearly feeling some sympathy for her uncle.

Hugh did not seem to notice as he continued, "I've already told you how Johns and I became friends. He used to tell very amusing stories. We shared an interest in military history. He told me of his time in the RAF."

Hugh laughed, "I remember one of his stories was about the 'precision bombing' of the day. He and another pilot were told to bomb some Argentinian positions near the capital of the island, Port Stanley. They saw these black shapes in a field where they were told to bomb and assumed they were Argentinian soldiers. They dropped the bombs and returned to their carrier, only to find they had bombed a field of black sheep! There was apparently hell to pay and after the Argentinians surrendered, the Ministry of Defence had to pay the owner a fortune to hush the matter up!"

Hugh hesitated before continuing, "Of course though, you never knew with Johns if he was telling the truth or just spinning a good yarn!"

David decided it was now time to intervene.

"We know you became friends with Johns until that time you discharged the firearm into his pillow. What we need to know is, is your wife right, did you deliberately fire into the pillow or did you deliberately fire at Johns and just miss him?"

Hugh looked surprised at the question and paused before answering, "I was standing less than 10 feet away. If I wanted to hit him, even if I was heavily intoxicated, I wouldn't have missed him.

Certainly not twice!"

CHAPTER 17

COSTA SMERALDA

"So what's she really like?" asked Wendy.

David raised his eyebrows slightly as he sipped from his Sardinian beer. They had chosen to have a two week break on the Costa Smeralda, on the north east coast of Sardinia. Wendy's diary had not allowed for a summer holiday so David was happy when she agreed to a late September break. They had flown here on the 26th September and enjoyed a few days lazing about. The weather had been perfect, around 24 degrees Celsius in the daytime, so he had spent plenty of time relaxing around the pool of the villa they had rented.

Wendy chose this location as she had heard so much about it and had found a villa to stay in the village of Pantogia. It was a beautiful setting but outrageously expensive. David had mused silently, that the amount they spent could have funded a three-week all-inclusive holiday in the Caribbean. Still, it had been relaxing although he was becoming irritated by Wendy's frequent references to his junior, Sara, and their forthcoming three weeks together in Newcastle conducting the Hugh Petford-Williams trial.

He put his beer down and looked longingly at the glimmering pool before answering her, "As I've told you several time already, she's a perfectly pleasant individual. She's hardworking and mature for her age and quickly grasps legal issues. I am sure she will make an excellent junior."

He picked up his beer again and took a further sip as if to punctuate the end of that conversation. He slid further down into his pool lounger, shielding his eyes from the blazing Sun and hoping Wendy would take the hint.

Wendy shrugged but would not let this topic go.

"I think it's wrong for a second six month's pupil to act as junior counsel in a murder case. What if you are taken ill? She cannot very well be expected to conduct the case on her own can she? You should have refused to take the case with her as a junior."

David took another sip of his beer, noticing with some regret that the bottle was now empty. He turned to look at Wendy who was dressed in a lightweight flowing white dress worn over her colourful, figure hugging, swim suit. She had bought it in Harrods especially for the holiday. Momentarily he looked down at his frayed swimming trunks which he had owned for years, then he replied, "I suspect you took on quite a few cases when you were a solicitor advocate that were, perhaps, slightly beyond your then ability?"

He watched as a frown appeared on her face and he quickly added, "In any event, the client insisted that his niece be instructed. I can't do anything about that, it's nothing to do with me."

He put the beer down again, it was definitely time for a few lengths in the pool. He raised himself from the lounger with a grunt and got ready for a quick get-away before she started on again about Sara, but he was stopped by an icy stare as Wendy replied, "I didn't have a choice when I was a solicitor advocate, I was employed by a firm that wanted to maximise its profits. That does not apply to you. You are a self-employed barrister, as is your pupil, and our standards should be better!"

It never ceased to amaze David how the barristers who were most biased against solicitor-advocates tended to be ex-solicitors!

He nodded diplomatically and said, "You're undoubtedly right," as he jumped into the deep end of their pool and submerged himself into the water. After a few seconds he emerged to hear Wendy ask, "Did you ever see that Tatiana girl again?"

With a big gasp of air and a groan he disappeared under the surface again.

Two hours later they were walking around the town of Porto Cervo, hand-in-hand, enjoying the sights of the luxurious yachts. David offered to buy Wendy a present in one of the local shops but was surprised to find they all seemed to cater exclusively for billionaires. He had noted with shock how designer cashmere sweaters were retailing at 2,000 Euros. Fortunately, Wendy had not seen anything that she thought worth the price. He was very grateful for that. Although he had been paid some money recently, the cost of this holiday had meant his primary credit card had reached its limit again.

After a cappuccino in a local café they drove off in their hire car to explore the beautiful coastline, travelling south, towards the small island of Tavolara. It was times like these that David realised just how much he enjoyed his life at the Bar, allowing as it did, frequent opportunities to enjoy fantastic breaks, far away from chambers and all the concerns and worries about his practice.

He had made his decision before coming on holiday and tonight was the night.

They returned along the coast road and at 7pm they stopped at a restaurant called Isobella, opposite the coastal resort of Capriccioli. They were soon seated at a balcony table overlooking the sea, sipping a couple of Prosecco Sbagliatos.

The waiter, Antonio, was very attentive and soon suggested they try the local specialities. The zuppa quatto, a bread and cheese soup interested them both, although David was careful to ask what cheese it was made out of. He had heard that Sardinia had some unusual cheeses like Casa Marzu, a strong creamy cheese full of live maggots. He had decided against indulging in that delight. They both turned down the offer of Bistechhe di Cavallo when Wendy translated it as Donkey steak. They also turned down the choice of live lobsters that were brought to their table, as they looked distinctly small and unhappy. In the end, both chose the Cinghiale alla Sulcitana, a wild boar stew washed down with a bottle of Turriga, which their waiter recommended as an excellent accompaniment.

Soon they were enjoying the Turriga and understanding why Sardinia had received the name, 'insula vini', the 'wine island'.

David looked out at the lights of the port which reflected in the waters of the bay and then turned to Wendy, uttering one word, "Stunning."

She followed his gaze and looked out at the view and replied, "It really is breath-taking isn't it?

"I was referring to you," said David smiling sheepishly.

Wendy grinned back at him, "That's as cheesy as the soup!"

"True, but I mean it," he said reaching for her left hand.

"Wendy, we've been together quite a long time now. We love each other. I cannot imagine being without you. Will you marry me?"

Wendy withdrew her hand slowly and hesitated before replying. David suddenly felt a deep knot tighten in his throat. She then took his hand in hers and asked, "Didn't you think it might be better to wait and ask me once I'd drunk a lot more wine?"

David eyes widened in disappointment. Wendy's smile broadened, "I'm only kidding you fool, of course I'll marry you, but only on one condition."

He breathed a big sigh of relief and smiled lovingly at her, "And what is that?"

"We buy the engagement ring in London. If you buy it here, you won't have any money left to take me on a really expensive honeymoon and I insist on that!"

CHAPTER 18

BACK TO REALITY

David walked into chambers on Monday morning, 12th October, at 10am, in an excellent mood. Wendy and he had arrived back on Saturday, both thoroughly relaxed and happy. David had a tan and was feeling quite fit, despite carrying a few extra holiday pounds around his waist.

They had both agreed to visit Hatton Gardens in London the following Saturday to buy an engagement ring. They had also agreed that they would not tell anyone in chambers until Wendy had the ring on her finger.

It was now back to business. There was just one week to go before the Hugh Petford-Williams trial began. He needed to start his final preparation.

As he approached the clerks' room he bumped into Sara.

"Hello David, hope you enjoyed your holiday, sorry - got to rush, I'm on in the Bailey at 10:30! Incidentally, there has been some more evidence in Hugh's case. You should have a copy in your pigeon hole, perhaps we can talk later. Bye."

With that she rushed out of the building with her robes and wig under her arm and a folder under the other. David momentarily thought how the youngsters of today always seemed to leave things to the last minute, but then dismissed the thought. After all, he had done his fair share of rushing around all over the place during his career!

He exchanged pleasantries with the clerks, discussed his holiday briefly, accepted compliments for his tan and then made his way to his room with a cup of hot filter coffee in his right hand.

Once he was seated and had had a preliminary look at all the correspondence that had arrived for him, most of which was consigned to the waste bin, he opened the brown paper envelope from Mark, Wright and Rogers.

It contained a Notice of Further Evidence containing three witness statements from witnesses called Timothy Granger, Walter Doyle and Rachel Harris, a Forensic Scientist.

Rachel Harris's statement referred to analysing swabs taken from Hugh's hands when they were swabbed at the police station. She used a scanning electron microscope equipped with an energy-dispersive X-ray spectroscopy detector to determine that he had trace elements of firearms residue on his hands. This suggested to her that Hugh had either fired a weapon within a few hours of the swab being taken or had been in close proximity to the firing or had touched something that was in the presence of the gun when it fired. As Hugh admitted firing the gun that night, the statement did not take the case any further whatsoever and David was surprised that the prosecution had gone to the expense of carrying out the tests.

Timothy Granger and Walter Doyle were actually friends of Hugh's and were members of his club. They both gave similar evidence that Hugh regularly visited the club most weekdays and occasionally on a Saturday.

It was clear to both of them how much he loved his wife as he frequently spoke about her, although occasionally he could make a caustic comment about her 'demands' but he never went into detail about this.

Hugh also discussed his neighbour, William Johns, with them both. Their distinct impression was that he could not stand Johns and both were surprised that Johns was such a frequent visitor to Hugh's home. On one occasion, a few months earlier in around February, Granger remembered Hugh saying, 'I'd like to shoot that bastard and I would too, if it wasn't for the fact Rosemary likes him so much!" Granger had not asked any more questions because Hugh was clearly drunk at that time and was getting maudlin. Doyle remembered this comment in similar terms, adding that he had thought little of it at the time.

They had both been at the club on the day Johns died. Hugh had arrived around 9:15pm. They had both noticed that he had been drinking. He bought them both a drink at the bar and then suggested they toast the Duke of Wellington's victory at Waterloo. Doyle remembered him making some comment about 'nothing to do with mud', but he had no idea what he was talking about.

They both said that Hugh appeared a little more tense than usual and seemed to be in a great hurry to get back to his flat. Walter Doyle had asked him what the hurry was and both claimed Hugh said in a 'jokey sort of way', 'I have to get back, you never know what those two might get up to in my absence and I might need to put a stop to it!'

Both of them said they thought nothing of the comment at the time. After one more drink, Hugh left at about 9:45pm.

Nick Mark had managed to take Hugh's comments on the statements already. Hugh had confirmed the contents were basically true. He accepted he made the comment about wanting to shoot Johns, but said he had not meant anything by it. He had made the comment earlier in the year and he knew at the time he made it, that Johns and Rosemary would be having sex whilst he was in the club.

In relation to the night of the shooting, he did not think he had been tense although he might have appeared that way because of the drink he had consumed and the fact he was tired. He had not wanted to stay long in any event and the comment he made was a joke. He had not expected them to get up to anything that night because he had not placed a red silk ribbon on the door, as per their agreed ritual. He claimed it was a personal joke because he knew that normally they would get up to something, but no one else did.

Just after midday, Sara returned from Court and came into David's room. He had finished reading the latest witness statements and was now preparing notes on cross examination of the prosecution's witnesses.

He looked up as she entered the door, "Hello Sara, how was the Bailey?"

She groaned, "Horrible! I was in front of some judge called Tanner. He was just mean. I was dealing with someone else's mention hearing, a barrister in another chambers who had been taken ill. I was trying to find out what had happened when the Judge insisted on me coming into court and explaining everything. I told him I had only just been instructed and needed time to get the details, and he just tore into me. He accused me of unprofessionalism, appearing in front of him without being properly prepared!"

David grinned, "I wouldn't worry about it. Tanner has quite a reputation. He's an unpleasant tribunal at the best of times. I should know, he was my Pupil Master when I started at the Bar. What you now call a Pupil Supervisor."

"You don't think he will report me do you?"

"What for? It wasn't your fault someone else was taken ill, you were trying to help out. In any event, he makes a lot of noise but doesn't usually do anything about it. Just don't ask him for a reference!"

He smiled at his own joke remembering his own first years at the Bar when he had unknowingly received a number of bad references from Tanner. Sara just looked puzzled, wondering why David would think she would ask this judge for a reference!

David moved on to Hugh's case. "Anyway, Sara, we need to start thinking about Hugh's case. Have you seen the latest witness statements?"

Sara smiled and took the seat in the seat in front of David's desk. "Yes I managed to read them all and make some notes on them. I don't think they alter anything at all. The firearms residue evidence adds nothing and Hugh's friends' evidence really does not take it any further save for the unfortunate comment about wanting to shoot Johns."

David nodded in agreement, "Yes, that was not the most helpful comment he could have made, but it was made months before the actual shooting.

I am slightly more concerned about the evidence of him being tense and in a rush to get home that night. The prosecution will claim that is clear evidence he thought something might happen and he needed to get back home to stop it, and that's exactly what he did.

Permanently!"

CHAPTER 19

THE TRIAL COMMENCES

A week later on Monday 19th October, David and Sara were in Newcastle Crown Court. He had arrived on Sunday and stayed in his usual hotel. Wendy and he had spent Saturday going round the jewellery shops of Hatton Garden, accepting numerous glasses of champagne in various shops until Wendy had chosen the ring she liked. There was little change out of fifteen thousand pounds and David had been forced to use his reserve credit card. He reflected that fine wines would have to be off the agenda for some months to come!

At 09:30am, he entered the robing room. A few faces looked at him again but soon turned away again when they did not recognise him as a local advocate.

At 9:35am, Jeremy Asquith QC entered the robing room, carrying his bags. He was a local Newcastle silk and a well-known face in that court. He was greeted by a few of the barristers and solicitor advocates present. One older barrister shouted out, "What you up today, Jeremy, another of your weird sex cases?"

Jeremy laughed in response. He had recently been prosecuting and defending in a series of cases involving serious sexual offences, "No, thank God, I've got something normal today, a straight forward murder!"

He looked towards David who was putting his silk robes on.

"And, if I'm not mistaken, this is my opponent."

David was struggling to put on a severely starched wing collar over his shirt and did not welcome all eyes falling on him just then. However, he adopted a friendly expression and looked towards Jeremy. "That's right, David Brant, nice to meet you."

Jeremy acknowledged him and once they were robed they agreed to go for a coffee to discuss any remaining issues in the case.

Seated in the advocates' canteen, sipping hot coffees, they discussed David's objections to the jury seeing certain evidence at this stage. Jeremy handed him a copy of a jury bundle that he was proposing to give to the jury when he opened the prosecution case. David quickly looked at the index:

Page 1. Indictment

Page 2. Plan of Flat 1, the Elms, Manor House Road, Jesmond

Page 3. Photo of all the flats in Manor House Road, Jesmond.

Page 4. Front door of Flat 1

Page 5. Photo inside Flat 1, showing base of stairs and the lavatory directly opposite

Page 6. Photo of lavatory

Page 7. Photo of stairs with rifle resting against side and cartridge resting on stairs

Page 8. Photo of the spare room showing the bed and pillows

Page 9. Photo of the kitchen with table and bin

Page 10. Computer generated image of Mr Johns' head showing the area of the wound

Pages 11-14. Photos of firearms expert in different firing positions on the stairs

David flicked through the bundle stopping at pages 11-14 showing the firearms officer demonstrating where a person would have to stand on the stairs to have fired the shot that killed William Johns.

"Surely you have no intention of relying on these. They are a bit one-sided. I'm not sure the jury will be able to put these images out of their minds and concentrate on what actually happened."

He paused at a particularly graphic one taken with the barrel pointing directly at the camera.

"These are extremely prejudicial and I notice that you don't have one from the position of where my client says he was standing!"

Jeremy looked through them again. "I can make it plain to the jury that you do not agree these photographs and they are for illustrative purposes only."

"If they were for illustrative purposes, surely you would have one showing where my client says he was situated when he accidentally fired the shot?"

Jeremy looked at David with an innocent expression. "Well, we do have such photographs of course, but this is the prosecution bundle. I have no objection to you putting such photographs in a defence bundle, should you produce one, but I want to keep this purely as the prosecution bundle, illustrating what we say occurred."

They continued to disagree and eventually David told him he would argue the point in front of the judge when they went into court.

David and Sara then made their way down to the cells to see Hugh. Hugh had little to say. He confirmed that he was as ready as he ever would be for the trial and only asked who the jury would be.

David answered, "We know nothing about them. We are provided with no material about them, not even their names until they are called into court. All we can assume is that they will have been selected from the Newcastle area.

Hugh nodded, "I suppose most of them are unemployed and on benefits! The only people unable to avoid jury service." He laughed as he added, "I read a good comment about that somewhere, "Never in the field of social existence has so much been given to so many undeserving, by so few taxpayers!"

David looked surprised as he replied, "I hope you don't express that view in court, Hugh, otherwise it won't take very long for the jury to find you guilty of murder!"

A few minutes later David and Sara went upstairs to Court 8 and sat in the advocates' row of benches, nearest the jury box. Sara was seated to David's right slightly further away from the jury. Jeremy Asquith QC was seated to her right, furthest away from the Jury.

Jeremy was prosecuting the case on his own, with no junior. The Crown Prosecution Service had refused to allow the expense of instructing a junior to assist him and the only assistance he had was from Janice, a secretary from the

Crown Prosecution Service, who was there simply to take a note but who played no further part in the proceedings.

At 10:30am, Mr Justice Bright QC entered the courtroom. He acknowledged the barristers as he entered and gave a questioning stare towards Janice. He was aware that in these austere times fewer advocates were being instructed to conduct cases but he still considered that the prosecution should have a junior in a murder case, and preferably a barrister!

He had been at the Bar for twenty-five years before he took up his appointment as a High Court judge. His father and grandfather had both been barristers and he had not got used to the idea of solicitors conducting cases as advocates.

He sat down wondering whether to say something on the subject in open court, but decided not to. It would not change anything and may earn a rebuke from the Lord Chancellor's Office, so there was no point.

Seated in front of him was Jane Duffy, his clerk. She had come to Newcastle with him from London and had sorted out accommodation in the Judges' lodgings in the countryside and arranged for his transport every day to the court. She was a blessing in such a place so far away from home. He smiled as he thought to himself, that it also helped that she was a reasonable conversationalist over dinner and the fact she was quite attractive was definitely a bonus!

Jeremy Asquith QC waited until Hugh had been brought into court and identified before he rose to address the Judge. He had noted the Judge's expression and had no idea why he was smiling, it was a murder trial after all.

Jeremy introduced the parties, making the point that he appeared in the case alone and that Janice was solely there to take notes. He expected the judge to say something and was surprised when he merely nodded without saying a word.

"My Lord, before we swear a jury there is just one matter that we seek Your Lordship's ruling on. The prosecution has served upon my Learned Friends, a draft jury bundle containing the usual types of documents, an indictment, a plan of the area, a plan of the flat where the shooting took place, photographs of the scene and then the item that is objected to, photographs of a firearms officer recreating what the prosecution say happened in this case. My Learned Friends, Mr Brant and Ms Petford-Williams, object to those photographs being put before the jury."

The judge looked up, "Ms Petford-Williams, is she related to the defendant?"

151

Jeremy looked back at Sara and smiled, "Ms Petford-Williams is the defendant's niece, My Lord."

The Judge looked surprised at this news and frowned. He made a note in his red notebook and turned to David, "Is that correct, Mr Brant?"

David stood and addressed him, "Yes, My Lord, that is correct. I should say there is no possible conflict. Ms Petford-Williams has checked the position with the Bar Council and there is no conceivable objection to her representing her uncle, particularly as he insists upon it."

The Judge wondered whether to say anything more but decided against it. It was a sign of the times he supposed, solicitor advocates defending defendants and now their nieces defending them as well!

"Very well, Mr Brant. What is your objection to this evidence? I would have thought it will assist the jury."

David adopted a slightly stern expression, it was becoming an increasing trait in cases that he was conducting, that judges made such comments before listening to any objections. He would have liked to say, 'Would you do me the courtesy of listening to my objection before ruling upon it.' But he knew it would not help. It would only antagonise the judge and he needed him to be on his side, for as long as possible.

"My Lord, one can see at first sight why Your Lordship might think that. However, when one looks at the photographs, it is noticeable that they all show the position from which the prosecution 'thinks' the shooting might have happened. What they do not show, is the position from which Mr Petford-Williams says it actually happened!

Visual images can be a useful tool for a jury. They can amount to very powerful evidence but they can also bring with them the potential for real prejudice. The photographs are unnecessary in this case because the firearms expert can describe the bullet hole and the trajectory and produce diagrams which are already in the jury bundle and which we do not object to. However, these photographs provide powerful images of the officer aiming the rifle at the lavatory door. These are images that the jury may have difficulty dispelling from their minds when deliberating."

Mr Justice Bright looked at him as if he could not understand what the problem was, as if everything David just said made no sense whatsoever.

David observing the expression decided to try a different approach. "It would not be so bad if there was some balance. If the prosecution had supplied a number of photographs of the expert in the position Mr Petford-Williams said he

153

adopted, as he stumbled on the stairs and fired the fatal shot, but sadly the prosecution are only providing one side of the story."

The Judge looked up at this, he saw an easy solution. Turning to Jeremy he asked, "Are such photographs available Mr Asquith?"

Jeremy stood to answer. "They are available, a large number of photographs were taken by the firearms expert but we did not want to clutter the jury bundle with them. As I have told My Learned Friend, if he wants to produce a defence bundle, I would have no problem with his including such photographs in it."

The judge frowned, "I do not see any need to over-complicate this case for the jury by giving them several bundles of evidence in what, on the face of it, is a straightforward case. If you have such photographs is there any problem placing them in the prosecution's jury bundle?"

Jeremy hesitated before replying, "I suppose we could place one or two in the bundle demonstrating what the defendant claims happened."

The Judge smiled and turned to David, "Would that satisfy your objection Mr Brant?"

David returned the smile, "It would My Lord, provided my junior and I might be allowed to choose the appropriate photographs."

The judge nodded, happy to solve the first issue of the trial without needing to deliver a judgment. "I see nothing wrong with that, do you Mr Asquith?"

Jeremy hid a dissatisfied scowl, "Not at all, My Lord."

CHAPTER 20

THE PROSECUTION OPENING

One hour later, Jeremy stood to deliver his opening speech. He had taken the precaution of having extra photographs available and after David and Sara had selected the one they thought most appropriate, the jury bundle was re-jigged and page 15 added, headed 'Photo of firearms expert showing the position adopted if the shot was accidental.'

Jury selection had not taken long. There were no objections to any of them from David. As he had explained to Hugh in the cells, he could only object to potential jurors for 'cause' and as the court deliberately told him nothing about the jurors, he had no reason to challenge anybody.

Jeremy asked for the jury bundles to be distributed to the jury and then he began outlining the prosecution case.

"Ladies and gentlemen, I appear to prosecute this case. I will be assisted by the lady behind me, Janice Saunders from the Crown Prosecution Service, who has kindly agreed to provide me with a note of the proceedings. You will see that she is not wearing robes like myself or my Learned Friends. That is because she is not an advocate and therefore you will not hear from her during the trial.

The defendant, Hugh Petford-Williams, is represented by my Learned Friend, David Brant of Queen's Counsel, who sits nearest you and also by my Learned Friend, Sarah Petford-Williams, who sits next to him."

It seemed to David that Jeremy emphasised Sara's surname so the jury would realise she must be related to Hugh. There was nothing he could do about that so he just ignored it and continued listening.

"His Lordship has already briefly addressed you. Let me just make this point. His Lordship is the judge of law in this court and you will take the law from him, not from my Learned Friends or from myself, but from him and only him.

May I ask you now to turn in your jury bundles to page one, just after the index. There you will see a document headed 'the Indictment.' That is just another word for the charge sheet setting out the allegations against the defendant.

You will see that the defendant faces one charge on this Indictment, the most serious charge of murder.

As I have just stated, you should take the law from His Lordship, but as I am the first person to address you, it is only appropriate that I inform you of a basic proposition of law. The prosecution has charged Mr Petford-Williams with murder and it is only right that the prosecution assumes the burden of proving it. The burden is a high one. You cannot convict Mr Petford-Williams unless you are satisfied, so that you are sure of his guilt.

That is an important part of the criminal trial process and therefore it is important and appropriate that I deal with it first."

There were nods from a few members of the jury. David always loathed this approach from prosecutors. Assuming an air of fairness when all they were doing was dealing with the most basic proposition of criminal law.

"This is a strange case and one where you may feel some sympathy for the defendant because of the personal position he found himself in. You may also feel some understandable sympathy for the victim in this case, William Johns, whose life was taken from him. Again, it is only appropriate that I say at the outset that sympathy should play no part on your deliberations or your verdicts. You should look coldly and clinically at the evidence in this case and determine your verdicts entirely on that evidence and not on any feelings of sympathy.

In a short time, I will be calling the evidence before you but, before I do, let me tell you the facts of this case so that you can see the importance of that evidence and how it falls into the picture as whole.

The Defendant is a married man. He met his wife, Rosemary, at University and they married a few years later and went to live with the Defendant's parents in an eight bedroomed home, known as The Elms, Manor House Road, Jesmond. The Defendant's father ran a clothing business and both the Defendant and his wife worked with his father.

Eventually, the Defendant's father retired and later died. Unfortunately, although the Defendant tried to keep the business afloat, it went into liquidation. He tried his hand at other businesses but was not successful and when his mother died he could not pay the inheritance tax due on her estate and he could not afford to keep the family home.

He and his wife decided that in order to pay the bills, they would turn the family home into four flats and sell three of them and live in the fourth. They managed to do this and this enabled them to pay the inheritance tax and have an amount of capital that they could use to invest and provide some income.

Two of the three flats were sold to two couples who you will hear give evidence later, Dr Jeffries and his wife Janet, and Gerald Payne and his wife Clare.

The third flat was sold to William Johns, the victim in this case.

In interview, the Defendant explained to the police that he met Mr Johns in a public house and discovered that they had similar interests. Both were interested in military matters and indeed Mr Johns had been a harrier pilot during the Falklands war over thirty years ago.

They became friends and Mr Johns was a frequent visitor to the defendant's home where they would often drink wine into the small hours and discuss military matters.

The defendant's wife, Rosemary, was also present during these visits and, as you will hear, she became particular fond of Mr Johns as well.

Let me move on to deal with an important aspect of this case. Unfortunately, over the years the defendant began to suffer from type 2 Diabetes. This affected him in a number of ways, but perhaps the most important was that he found that he could not obtain an erection or, if he did, he could not maintain it.

You will hear that he tried various remedies including Viagra, but nothing worked and his sex life with his wife deteriorated until it became just a distant memory. On the other hand, her sex drive did not diminish and, as he put it in interview to the police, she still had her needs.

Matters first came to a head on 24th October 2014. The defendant's niece was offered the position as a trainee barrister in a London chambers, a pupillage as it is known."

David looked at the jury to see how they would react to this information. Jeremy had made it clear with a glance over his shoulder that Sara was the niece he was referring to. A few looked in her direction but most kept staring at Jeremy with blank expressions.

"The defendant and his wife decided to celebrate her good fortune with a few drinks. They invited Mr Johns to join them, which he did, and they consumed probably six litre bottles of wine between the three of them during the evening.

The defendant is a member of a local club in Jesmond and frequently visits the club for a drink and to socialise with his friends. That Friday, 24th October, he again visited his club to have a few drinks with his friends.

Regrettably, on his return he discovered that his wife's 'needs' had got the better of her and she and Mr Johns were in the spare bedroom. If you look at page two of the jury bundle you will see a plan of the property. The spare bedroom is positioned downstairs, the second door on the left when you enter the property. The first door on the left is a lavatory and opposite that you will see the stairway that leads to the first floor and the master bedroom and bathroom.

Mr Johns and Rosemary were together in that room engaging in sexual intercourse.

As I said, the defendant is a military enthusiast. Some years before he had purchased an old rifle, a .22 Winchester rimfire rifle. It was not in working order but he restored it, obtained ammunition for it and used it for firing at targets in a target range he had set up in his garden.

On 24th October 2014, however, he found another use for that rifle. He went upstairs to his bedroom where he kept it, loaded it, came back down and threatened Mr Johns with it. Mr Johns treated it as a joke and made an unpleasant comment to the effect, 'Excellent Hugh, you've finally found something you can get up.'

The defendant was angered by the comment and he fired the rifle twice, both shots hitting the pillow Mr Johns was lying on, just inches from his head. Whether he was deliberately aiming at the pillow or Mr Johns' head may be an issue in this case, but in any event, Mr Johns was not hurt, but he was clearly shocked.

When the smoke settled and the defendant calmed down, the three of them all went to the kitchen where they consumed more wine and discussed what had happened.

Again you will hear that the defendant told the police he came to an 'arrangement' with Mr

Johns and his wife. It was, you may think, an unusual arrangement which almost inevitably led to Mr John's death. The defendant agreed that his wife and Mr Johns could have sexual intercourse, but only when he gave his permission.

It was agreed that he would signal that permission by tying a silk red ribbon to the door handle of the spare bedroom when he went out. If there was no red ribbon, they were not permitted to have sex. If there was, then they could.

This strange triangle of sexual tension and pent up emotion continued until the night of 18th June 2015, the night when Mr Johns was killed.

The 18th June 2015 was the two hundredth anniversary of the battle of Waterloo and Mr Johns and the defendant, with their keen knowledge of military matters, discussed the battle. They argued with each other as to why Napoleon lost and Wellington won.

At just after 9pm, the defendant decided to visit his club for a few drinks. He did not intend to be long and so he did not tie a silk ribbon around the door handle of the spare bedroom. The message, or perhaps I should say, the lack of a message was clear. There was to be no sexual intercourse for his wife and Mr Johns that night.

Unfortunately, their passion and lust took over and they went into the spare bedroom and had sexual intercourse.

The defendant arrived at the club around 9:15pm. There, he met two friends, Mr Timothy Granger and Mr Walter Doyle, who will give evidence about his demeanour and what he said to them. They both say he appeared tense and in a hurry to get back. Their impression was that he did not like Johns and he made an interesting comment to them, 'I have to get back. You never know what those two might get up to in my absence and I might need to put a stop to it!'

The defendant left the club at around 9:45pm and returned home at around 10pm. It is clear that he came across Mr Johns and his wife having sexual intercourse in the bedroom.

He had not given permission and was clearly angry. He went upstairs to get his rifle."

Jeremy picked up the rifle to show the jury.

"He either loaded it there or it was already loaded and therefore obviously in a dangerous condition. This is a pump action rifle and as you will see, pumping the rifle like this ..."

He pulled the bottom of the rifle back and the jury heard an audible click.

"... a cartridge is loaded into the breach of the gun, the trigger goes forward into the firing position and the hammer goes back, ready for firing.

It is clear that Mr Johns left the spare bedroom and went to the ground floor lavatory. The defendant then came downstairs and stopped, probably on the landing facing the lavatory.

What happened next is an issue between the prosecution and the defence. According to the defendant he stumbled on the stairs and accidentally pulled the trigger. The rifle was discharged and the bullet went through the lavatory door and hit Mr Johns in the neck. Despite considerable efforts by paramedics and hospital staff, they were not able to save him and he effectively bled to death.

The prosecution's case is that this was no accident. It was murder. The defendant deliberately aimed this rifle at the lavatory door towards the seat area, knowing Johns was behind that door.

At 10:08pm, the defendant telephoned the emergency services. It may have been that he felt some remorse, it may have been his wife who insisted, we shall probably never know, but he did make the call. You will hear that call played to you. You may think that the defendant sounded impatient. He admitted firing the rifle, but claimed it was an accident.

The prosecution say it was no such thing and the defendant was merely trying to protect himself when he realised the enormity of what he had done.

At 10:15pm, the paramedics arrived and began working on Mr Johns. He was found lying on the lavatory floor, bleeding to death. Two minutes later, police officers arrived. They saw that the defendant still had the rifle in his hands and it appeared to them he was pointing it at the paramedics. Fearing that he might use it, one of the officers, Police Constable Ray Savage, rushed over to him and applied a Taser, an electronic gun, directly to the defendant incapacitating him. He was then forced to the floor, arrested and handcuffed.

There was a loud grunt of dissatisfaction heard from the back of the court from Hugh as he listened to this. The Judge stared at him and David turned round and shook his head from side to side. Hugh quietened down as Jeremy smiled smugly at the Jury. He was already planning his cross examination of Hugh, it would probably not be too difficult to make him angry and show the jury his aggressive side. He paused for a few seconds and then continued.

"Ladies and gentlemen, you will hear that the defendant was interviewed the following day by Detective Sergeant Bull of the Newcastle CID. He chose not to have a solicitor and answered all

166

the questions that were put to him. He relayed a lot of what I have told you. He admitted the shooting but continued to claim it was an accident.

It will be for you to consider this evidence and the defendant's claim. The prosecution say you can be sure this was murder. His Lordship will direct you on the law in due course, but, in short, murder is the unlawful killing of a person with the intention of killing that person or at the very least intending to cause him really serious injury.

The prosecution say that there are five factors that clearly point to this being murder:

Firstly, there had been the previous warning, if that is what it was, firing the bullets into the pillow on which Mr Johns lay.

Secondly, although you might consider it to be bizarre, he had given Mr Johns permission to have sexual intercourse with his wife on occasion, but on the night in question, he had not given his permission.

Thirdly, he had clearly suspected that they might breach their agreement with him from the fact he was tense when he was in his club and wanted to leave quickly because he did not know what his wife and Johns might be getting up to.

Fourthly, you will hear from the neighbours in this case. Dr Richard Jeffries and his wife, Janet, heard him say, clearly, 'I'm going to kill you, you bastard', followed by the sound of a rifle shot.

Fifthly, you will hear from a witness in this case who is an expert on firearms. Dr Henry Roper will explain the workings of this rifle to you, the amount of pressure needed to pull the trigger and the bullet's trajectory. He will tell you that although the bullet hit Mr Johns in the neck, it was deflected upwards and to the left by the door. Once the trajectory is followed back from the door to the stairway it is clear that this was a well-aimed shot aiming at the position Mr Johns' heart would have been if he was seated on the toilet.

This was a cold calculated act by a man who felt he had been betrayed in his own home, by his wife and his best friend. At the time he pulled the trigger, he had one clear intention.

He wanted to kill Mr Johns."

CHAPTER 21

THE NEIGHBOURS

Jeremy called his first witness to give evidence, the neighbour, Clare Payne. It was some distance between the witness room and the court room and so it took a few minutes before she arrived. Everyone waited quietly and patiently, the court clerk sat speaking in hushed tones on the telephone in front of him, his well-practised whisper meaning it was almost impossible to hear his words.

As the witness entered the court, everyone turned to look at her. She was wearing her best dark blue business suit with a matching handbag and scarf tied loosely round her neck despite the fact it was a warm October day. Her hair was perfectly arranged in a neat twist at the back of her head. She had clearly visited the hairdressers before court today. She took the oath and gave her name and Jeremy then took her through a few background questions.

"Do you prefer Ms or Mrs Payne?"

"Mrs Payne."

"Mrs Payne, you are a married lady, married to Gerry Payne, who is also a witness in this case?"

She replied quietly, "That's right."

Mr Justice Bright intervened, "Now, Mrs Payne you will have to do better than that, everybody in court has to hear your evidence so please would you kindly speak up."

She went slightly red, "Sorry, Your Honour?"

He smiled at her politely as Jeremy continued with his questioning. "Mrs Payne, I understand that you work in the Financial Services Industry in Newcastle?"

"Yes, that's right."

"What exactly is your role?"

"I work in risk analysis in the Finance Investments' Section of my company."

"Thank you."

Jeremy was quite content that he had effectively established her good character and that she was therefore less likely to lie. After all, it was unlikely that she would have criminal convictions if she was working in finance.

David was amused that Jeremy had raised the issue of finance, after all, most juries were not fond these days of anyone who worked in finance!

Jeremy moved on, asking, "Do you know Hugh Petford-Williams, the defendant in this case?"

She looked towards the dock at Hugh and replied, "Yes I do."

"In fact, you and your husband purchased your current property from him, didn't you?"

"Yes, we did."

"That was sometime in late 2012, wasn't it?"

"Yes, in December 2012."

"Did you have many dealings with the defendant or his wife?"

"Not after we bought the flat from them."

It was clear from her expression that this had been intentional on her part.

"I want to ask you about an incident that occurred last year, in October. Do you recall anything of potential relevance to this case, happening around then?"

"Yes, I do."

"Can you tell us what it was?"

"My husband Gerry and I were at home, sitting downstairs in the living room watching television. I can't remember what was on now, probably the News, but it was around 10pm when I heard two loud bangs in short succession."

"Did you know what they were?"

"No, but they sounded like gunshots."

"What did you do?"

"I told my husband that I heard gunshots." She looked triumphant, "At the time, he just dismissed me, telling me not to be silly, but we know differently now!"

Jeremy grinned at her answer, "Did you know your next door neighbours, Dr Jeffries and his wife Janet?"

"Only to say hello to."

"What about the late William Johns?"

"Again, I just knew him to say hello to." She could not help adding, "He seemed a perfectly nice man."

Jeremy nodded so that the jury would hopefully make a mental note of his gesture, before he went on to ask, "Let me move on to June of this year. In particular, the evening of 18th June. Do you recall that day now?"

Clare looked at him with an expression that clearly said, 'how could I forget that day.'

"Yes, I do recall it."

"Where were you in the evening of 18th June?"

"I returned home about 6pm. Gerry was home already, he goes into work earlier than me and therefore leaves earlier."

"Can you recall anything happening in the evening when you were both together."

"Yes, it was around 10pm again. We were both downstairs in the front room, watching television again." She looked sheepish as she said this, almost ashamed to admit it. She hastily continued, "I heard a single bang. It certainly sounded like a gunshot to me. I mentioned it to Gerry and he again told me not to be silly. He said it was probably a car backfiring as he didn't think anyone around here would be firing a gun at this time of night. Again, he was a little dismissive of the idea of a shooting."

"Did you do anything?"

"Yes, I decided to look out of our front room window. I opened the curtain and at first, I couldn't see anything. Then I'm sure I saw Mr Petford-Williams approaching his front door."

"Could you tell whether he had just left his flat or not?"

"He appeared to be returning to it."

"Was the door of his flat open?"

"I couldn't see that from where I was."

"Was he carrying anything at all?"

"I didn't notice anything, but he might have been."

Jeremy smiled, thanked her and asked her to remain there in case David had any questions.

David got up from his bench and faced her. He had very little to ask her in truth, but she was the first witness and it helped the jury to see the defence ask something vaguely relevant and demonstrate that there were some issues in the case!

"Mrs Payne, you have told us that you and your husband purchased your flat from Mr and Mrs Petford-Williams?"

"Yes."

"Effectively, those were the only dealings you had with them?"

"Yes."

"In fact, most of those dealings were with Mr Petford-Williams, weren't they?"

"Yes, I suppose so."

"You had no problems with Mr Petford-Williams during those negotiations did you?"

"No."

"He was perfectly honest with you?"

"Yes, as far as I was aware."

"He never misled you in any way?"

"No."

"He didn't try to raise the price just before you completed on the property or anything like that?"

"No."

"You are aware that your flat was one of four converted from a former large eight bedroomed house?"

"Yes."

"Have you been in the other flats?"

"No, never."

"Please turn in the jury bundle to page two where we have a plan of Mr Petford-Williams' flat."

Everyone in court with access to a jury bundle followed his direction.

"You will see here a plan of Mr Petford-Williams' flat. You will see that it is different to the layout of yours, isn't it?"

She looked at the plan for a few seconds before replying, "Yes."

"We don't actually have a plan of your flat, but am I right in thinking that if you face towards your front door from outside, your flat is on your far left, situated at the corner of the building?"

"Yes, that's right."

"Your living room is to the front of your flat on the far left of the building?"

"Yes."

"In between yours and the Petford-Williams' flats, is the one owned by Dr Jeffries and his wife. You are probably unaware that their flat is a mirror image of yours, so the living room is on the right as you face their front door?"

"I've never been inside, but I can easily see into their front room when I leave my property."

"Of course. Now, in relation to the incident in October, you heard two bangs in short succession?"

"Yes."

"Presumably only a second or so apart?"

"Yes, something like that."

"It sounded like someone had fired one shot and then deliberately fired another?"

"Yes, it did."

"However, on 18th June, you only heard one shot?"

"Yes."

"It was not followed by the deliberate firing of another shot?"

"No."

"Having heard that single shot, you then spoke to your husband and looked out through the curtains?"

"Yes."

"Do you know how long it was between hearing the bang and looking out of the window?"

She hesitated before saying, "Probably seconds."

"Might it have been a little longer, say minutes not seconds?"

"I don't think so."

"In any event, you saw Mr Petford-Williams outside his house?"

"Yes."

"Shortly afterwards, did you see an ambulance arrive, followed by police officers?"

"It was about fifteen or twenty minutes later. I wasn't looking out of the curtains then, but I heard the sirens and saw the flashing lights through our curtains."

"You cannot say for certain, but Mr Petford-Williams might have only left his residence a few seconds before you saw him and could have been returning when you saw him?"

"I suppose so."

"When you saw him was he looking around as if he was looking for something ..." He paused, "...like an ambulance?"

"I don't remember what he was doing, I only saw him for a second or so."

"So you cannot say one way or the other?"

"No."

David thanked her. He had achieved little but had tried to convey the impression that Hugh was honest. More importantly, the firing of two shots in October was a deliberate action whereas the one fired in June might be an accident. He had also tried to create the impression in the jurors' minds that soon after the shot was fired, Hugh must have phoned the ambulance service and was probably waiting outside for an ambulance when Clare saw him. Hopefully all of this would not be lost on them

CHAPTER 22

MORE NEIGHBOURS

After an adjournment for lunch, Gerry Payne gave evidence of what he had seen and heard. His evidence did not take long and David had very few questions to ask him. He confirmed his wife's account, although he stated that he had not heard any bangs the previous October and had dismissed his wife's comments that she had heard gunshots as fantasy on her part. He attributed any such sound to the fact that Hugh owned an old car which quite frequently backfired. When asked about why he dismissed his wife's account, he said he thought she watched too much television.

Some members of the jury laughed when he said he had been forced to give her a grovelling apology when he found out she had been right!

At 2:45pm, Janet Jeffries walked into court to give evidence. She was well-dressed and looked a good few years younger than her 55 years of age.

Jeremy did not bother to ask whether she preferred Ms to Mrs and called her Mrs throughout his questioning. He started with some background information about when they purchased the property, its location and he asked her to confirm that her flat was a mirror image of the Payne's flat.

"On 18th June, 2015, you heard the firing of a shot from the defendant's home?"

"Yes, that's right."

"I want to take you back to October of the previous year. Did you hear anything similar in that month?"

She looked a little puzzled but then said, "Well, frequently we have heard shots being fired from his garden. I have looked out of the window and seen a firing range that he has created in his garden. It was a little annoying as he did it at any time of the day!"

"In October 2014, did you hear any sounds of shots coming from inside his flat?"

David wondered for a moment whether to object to this obviously leading question but decided against it. Janet Jeffries witness statement did not refer to hearing such shots, but, as Hugh admitted firing two shots into Hugh's pillow on that occasion, it did not really matter whether she heard them or not.

Janet looked at Jeremy and paused as she searched her memory. Finally, she said, "No I don't think so. When was this? We went on a holiday in late October 2015 to New York."

David smiled, it would be quite clear to the jury that Jeremy was unaware of this fact and it just might suggest he did not have detailed knowledge of his own case.

Jeremy clearly had the same thought as he tried to recover, "Yes, thank you, I thought that might be the case. Very well let us move on. What were the Petford-Williams' like? Were they quiet or noisy neighbours?"

She grimaced, "At times they were very noisy. There was the shooting in the back garden but also we could frequently hear raised voices in the house."

"Do you know who was making these loud noises?"

"Yes, I often heard Mr Petford-Williams arguing with Mr Johns. The arguments always got very aggressive and on many occasions it sounded like they were about to hit each other!"

Jeremy paused so the jury would note that answer, and then asked, "Let's now move on to the evening of 18th June 2015. Can you tell us in your own words what happened?"

Janet nodded and answered, "Yes, certainly. It was around 9pm that my husband made a comment that he had seen Mr Petford-Williams leaving his address. I was reading a novel at the time and did not take much notice."

181

Jeremy smiled and tried to introduce a little levity, "Can you remember what the novel was?"

Janet reddened slightly when she looked over at the jury. "I can't remember now, it was probably a classic, maybe Jane Austen or something like that."

Jeremy quickly glanced at her witness statement and the reference to 'The Thrusting Rapier and the Royal Maid', but decided not to say anything. Instead, he simply asked, "Do you recall what your husband's comment was?"

She reddened even more as she answered, "I think it might have been something about Mrs Petford-Williams and Mr Johns doing something."

"Can you recall what?"

"He made some comment about them having sexual intercourse!"

"Do you know why he made that comment?"

"Probably because we had heard them having sexual intercourse in the past on many occasions."

"How frequently did this occur?"

She glanced over at Hugh in the dock and gave him a sympathetic look as she answered, "It

182

seemed to be whenever Mr Petford-Williams left the flat!"

Jeremy saw the gesture and quickly asked a question in case the jurors saw it and also started to feel some sympathy for Hugh. "I appreciate that this might be a little embarrassing for you, but can you tell us how you realised they were having sexual intercourse?"

She was bright red now as she answered, "Because we heard Mrs Petford-Williams moaning a lot. She does make a great deal of noise on such occasions, and unfortunately our walls are paper-thin."

"Did you hear such noises on the night of 18th June?"

"No, not really, but we were upstairs in bed with the television on."

Before Jeremy could ask her, she said, "I think Richard was watching some science programme. We had noticed in the past that they would always have sex in their spare bedroom, which is downstairs, right next to our living room. That's why we heard so much noise. Fortunately, we were upstairs this time."

"Did anything else happen that night?"

"Yes, about an hour later, just before 10:00pm, we both heard loud voices coming from next door. That wasn't unusual. However, on this occasion, I heard a high-pitched voice shout, 'I'm going to kill you, you bastard.' I actually thought it was a woman's voice."

Jeremy quickly intervened in case the jury got confused, "Yes, it is sometimes difficult to tell the difference in a heated situation."

It was a totally inadmissible comment but David did not object as Hugh admitted that he probably said something like this.

Jeremy continued, "What happened next?"

"Almost immediately afterwards, we both heard a loud bang. Richard said it sounded like a gunshot and made some comment about someone getting shot. I didn't think it was a gunshot. It was just a loud bang and could have been anything. It didn't sound like the gunshots you hear on the television."

"Did anything else happen around this time?"

"I didn't hear anything more until the ambulance arrived, about 20 minutes later."

"Did you hear any similar bangs or noises after the first one?"

"No, I did not, but I do recall Richard saying he thought he heard another bang. He had just started watching another documentary and I was reading my novel when he mentioned this,

184

but I didn't hear anything and I thought he was imagining it."

Jeremy thanked her for her evidence and asked her to wait there. Again David had very little to ask her as Hugh accepted most of what she said. Nevertheless, there were one or two matters she might be able to help with.

"Mrs Richards, did you know Hugh Petford-Williams or his wife very well?"

She thought for a few seconds before answering, "No, not really, we had very few dealings with them after we bought the flat."

"Did you know Mr Johns very well?"

"No, I don't think I ever said more than 'hello' to him and that was only once or twice."

"So, in reality, you did not know any of them personally?"

"No, I didn't."

"You mention frequently hearing loud voices coming from Mr Petford-Williams' flat. Did you ever hear what they were arguing about?"

"Often it sounded like they were discussing battles or wars, something like that."

"To you, these voices sounded loud and possibly aggressive?"

"Yes, very much so."

"Would you accept that some people can be having perfectly reasonable discussions but can be very emphatic and often loud at times?"

She hesitated before answering, "I suppose so."

"As you have told us, you did not know these men. In reality, you cannot say whether they were being aggressive or just having a heated discussion about a mutual interest, such as military history."

"Well, it sounded aggressive to me."

"Yes, but there were loud discussions like this frequently weren't there. You did not witness the police being called to any previous incident; you never saw either of them with bruises or injuries suggesting they had hit each other and, despite what you heard, these men still met up frequently to have these discussions?"

"I suppose so."

"As you recall it, on 18th June you heard a voice shouting, 'I'm going to kill you, you bastard' and this was followed shortly afterwards by the sound of a gunshot?"

"Yes, that's right."

"You actually thought it was a woman's voice?"

"I did."

There was a noise from the dock as Hugh cleared his throat and made a disapproving grunt. David ignored him and continued, "The only other matter I wish to ask you about is whether there may have been a period of up to a minute between you hearing the comment and then hearing the shot?"

"No, I'm certain the shot was within a few seconds of the voice."

"These situations can be very confusing. Are you sure it was within such a short space of time?"

"Yes, I'm sure."

David could see he was not going to get any further and he thanked her and sat down.

The final witness of the day was Dr Richard Jeffries. He came into court with an air of arrogance and annoyance about him. He glanced towards Hugh with a calculated look of distaste. It was clear to everyone he was annoyed that he had been brought here. In his mind, he had far better things to do than wait around all day before giving evidence in something that had nothing to do with him.

Jeremy asked him the usual introductory questions. Where he could, Richard answered with monosyllabic replies.

Jeremy then moved on to 18th June. "Dr Jeffries, can you tell us where you were late in the evening of 18th June?"

Richard looked at him as if he was an idiot. "I was at home as I explained to the police in my statement."

Jeremy smiled, "Thank you but the jury do not have your statement and have to hear all of your evidence from you."

Richard looked at him and adopted a piercing scowl.

Jeremy ignored the look and continued, "What was the first thing of importance that you can remember happening that night?"

"What, do you mean the gunshot?"

"If that is the first thing of importance you remember, then yes."

Richard's scowl intensified. He had never liked courtrooms and he did not like barristers. He remembered back to when he had defended himself in a Magistrates Court when he was charged with careless driving. He had crashed into the rear of some silly woman who had suddenly braked. The prosecutor had been a smarmy barrister who had led the magistrates to convict him through his impertinent questioning. That had led to a six-month driving ban. This barrister reminded him of the prosecutor in that case.

"The first thing of importance I recall is being in bed watching a particularly interesting programme on Artificial Intelligence. I remember that it was coming to an end at about 10pm when I heard a voice from the Petford-Williams flat, shout, 'I'm going to kill you, you bastard.' This was followed a few seconds later by what was clearly a gunshot coming from next door. I had heard gunshots from their garden before, as Mr Petford-Williams had a home-made firing range there. This was different though and was clearly from inside his flat."

Jeremy was silent for a second, surprised that Richard had answered in such detail instead of trying to get away with a 'yes' or 'no'!

"What did you do?"

"I made some comment to my wife, who was reading some trashy novel."

He adopted a contemptuous look on his face as he added unnecessarily, "She has recently taken to reading cheap romantic thrillers."

Jeremy could not resist, "I presume you are not talking about Jane Austen then?"

Richard looked at him as if he were mad and exclaimed, "Pardon?"

189

Jeremy looked at the jurors, hoping they would enjoy this private joke with him, "Never mind, Dr Richards, just tell us what happened next."

"I thought Mr Petford-Williams had shot somebody. That was no surprise to me considering what went on in that household!"

"What do you mean?"

"Well, we have seen Mr Petford-Williams leave the flat on several occasions and, almost immediately after, we would hear the sounds of Mrs Petford-Williams making loud groaning noises whilst she and Mr Johns fornicated!"

"What happened after you heard the shot?"

"I remember my wife saying that the voice shouting, "I'm going to kill you, you bastard", belonged to Mrs Petford-Williams who may have shot her husband. We then decided we must be mistaken as it all sounded so ridiculous. My wife went back to reading her novel and I started watching another documentary."

"Did you hear anything else from next door?"

"Yes, a few minutes later I was sure I had heard another gunshot. However, this was more muffled and sounded like it came from the garden."

"Did your wife hear this noise?"

"No, she didn't, she thought I had heard a door banging or something like that. I probably had. I just thought it was a gunshot at the time."

"What did you do after that?"

"I carried on watching my documentary until I heard the sound of an ambulance about ten minutes later. I looked out of our window and saw it was going to the Petford-Williams' flat. I saw Mr Petford-Williams outside his address waving the ambulance technicians in.

I then decided to go outside to see what was happening. A few minutes later, a couple of police cars arrived and police officers went rushing into the flat. Minutes later I saw Mr Petford-Williams being led away in handcuffs."

Despite his best efforts, Dr Jeffries could not help smirking slightly. Jeremy thanked him and asked him to wait there.

Again, David had no real challenges to this evidence, but he stood and asked, "Dr Jeffries, did you like Mr Petford-Williams?"

Richard paused and thought before answering neutrally, "I neither liked nor disliked him."

"It's just I noticed you smiled when you mentioned him being led away in handcuffs, why was that?"

"I didn't mean to, it's probably nerves," he added unconvincingly.

"No because it's not an amusing matter is it. Someone died."

Richard blushed slightly, "I realise that." He wanted to add 'and it was your client who killed him' but thought better of it.

Having achieved what he wanted, to shake the witnesses' confidence before asking him more important questions, David continued, "Your wife told us that you went to New York on holiday in late October 2014. When you returned, did you notice any difference in the Petford-Williams' household?"

Richard looked confused, "What do you mean?"

"Did you notice that, from about that time, Mr Petford-Williams would leave his flat on some evenings and his wife and Mr Johns would start, as you put it, fornicating?"

"I think it was some weeks after we returned from New York that we first noticed Mrs Petford-Williams' incessant groaning."

"How frequently would this occur?"

"At least weekly, sometimes more often."

"On every occasion that you heard this, Mr Petford-Williams would be out of the flat?"

"Yes."

"He would return though?"

"Yes."

"You never heard any arguments on any other occasions after he returned to the flat?"

"Well they would argue, but usually that was before he went out."

"So on previous occasions, when Mr Petford-Williams returned, after his wife had apparently had sexual intercourse with Mr Johns, you never heard him arguing with Mr Johns about having sex with his wife?"

"Not that I can recall, no."

"On 18th June, you heard someone shout, 'I'm going to kill you, you bastard', followed by a gunshot a short time later?"

"As I've already said."

"Please bear with me. Can you now recall the distance in time between those words being said and the gunshot?"

"Seconds."

"Could it have been longer, perhaps a minute or so?"

"Definitely not."

"Obviously you were not timing it?"

"No, but I'm sure it was seconds."

"It was a few minutes later that you heard what sounded to you like another shot but which you now think was possibly a door slamming?"

"Yes."

"The next matter you recall is the ambulance arriving, followed shortly afterwards by the police?"

"Yes."

"You saw Mr Petford-Williams at his door when the paramedics arrived?"

"Yes, he was outside."

"Presumably it looked to you like he was waiting for them?"

"I suppose so."

"Did you have a clear view of him?"

"Yes."

"He wasn't carrying anything was he?"

"Not that I recall."

"You would recall it if he came to his front door with a rifle in his hands?"

"Of course."

"I would like to put this into some sort of timescale if we can. Firstly, you heard the shout followed by the shot at just before 10pm?"

"Yes."

"Your second documentary started presumably at around 10pm?"

"Yes."

"Then, a few minutes later, you heard another noise, sounding like another shot but probably a door slamming or something like that?"

"Yes." Dr Richards was clearly getting impatient.

"Then about ten minutes later you saw an ambulance arrive followed a few minutes later by the police?"

"Yes, I've already said this."

David smiled, "Now you will not be aware of this but we have an exact record of when the ambulance and the police arrived. The paramedics arrived at 10:15pm and the police two minutes later at 10:17pm."

Dr Jeffries just shrugged dismissively at this information.

David continued, "We also have the time of the 999 call which was made at 10:08pm." David turned towards the jury, "We know that call was made by Mr Petford-Williams." A few nodded.

David turned back to the witness, "So it appears the 999 call was made at around the time you heard the second bang?"

Dr Jeffries decided to say something, "I've no idea."

David ignored the comment, "The call was clearly made by Mr Petford-Williams a few minutes after the shot was fired and the ambulance and police arrived shortly after that?"

"I suppose so."

"So it appears there was a shot, as we will hear, the toilet door had to be broken down and then towels pressed onto Mr John's wound and then within minutes at most, Mr Petford-Williams made the 999 call for assistance?"

Richard looked completely confused and answered, "I've no idea."

Jeremy rose to his feet to object to the questioning, which it was clear Dr Jeffries was not in a position to answer and amounted more to comment than questioning.

David ignored him, looked at Dr Richards and said, "Thank you, you've been very helpful in establishing what happened here."

He then sat down before Jeremy said anything. He hoped he had made his point. Hugh had phoned the ambulance within minutes of shooting Johns. He had even waited outside for them and directed them to where Johns was bleeding to death. Surely, that was more consistent with an accidental shooting than a deliberate attempt to kill?

CHAPTER 23

SEVERAL SHADES OF RED

Dr Jeffries had been the last witness of the day and David now trundled back to his hotel by the River Tyne, carrying his wig and gown and some papers he wanted to look at overnight. Monday night's menu in the restaurant was the same as every night, with just five main courses to choose from, of which only three interested him. The choice for him was steak, sea bass or curried lamb. He would have to venture out of the hotel for dinner at some stage in the next few days. He could not face such a restricted menu night after night. He was thankful he was only likely to be in Newcastle for a maximum of two weeks.

He arrived at court early on Tuesday morning, just after 9am. The lifts had still not been repaired and it was another trek upstairs carrying his cases.

He met Sara in the robing room and they walked down to the cells to see Hugh before the case started.

After exchanging pleasantries with the security staff and temporarily forfeiting their mobile phones, they were led to an interview room. After a few minutes Hugh was brought in to see them. They exchanged the usual greetings and then David adopted a reassuring tone as he addressed his client,

"Well Hugh, we've had the first few witnesses now. There was nothing that took us by surprise in their evidence, however, we decided to come and see you just in case you had anything to say about the evidence you've heard to date."

Hugh studied them both for a few seconds before answering, "No, I agree, there was nothing surprising. Even that silly Jeffries' woman saying I sounded like a female did not surprise me. You warned me that she'd said that in her statement. I always thought she was a bit doo-lally!"

David moved on, "Today we have a couple of your friends giving evidence from the club. They will be followed by the paramedics and, finally, the police officers will give evidence. Again, there should be nothing surprising in any of their evidence.

Is there anything you have thought of since you last looked at their statements?"

"Only one thing, ask Tim Granger about William Johns. He met him once at my house and told me he did not trust him. I told him Johns was all right when you got to know him. That was just a few weeks before this tragic accident."

David looked at him closely, Hugh had never mentioned this before, which was surprising considering Timothy Granger's statement said that he thought Hugh disliked Johns.

He looked at Hugh with a steely glint in his eyes, "Have you had any communication with Granger recently?"

Hugh could not hide the sly smile when he answered, "No, certainly not!"

The denial was just a little too emphatic for David's liking, but he said nothing and he and Sara left the cells a few minutes later.

At 10:20am they made their way upstairs to the court. It did not take long before the judge and jury filed in and Jeremy called his first witness of the day.

Timothy Granger was a large man just under six feet tall and about sixty years of age, balding and ruddy faced. He entered the courtroom dressed in an ill-fitting tweed suit. It was clear from his features that he enjoyed his food and drink enormously and the suit had probably fitted him well once, it certainly looked like it was tailor made.

As he walked towards the witness box he looked straight at Hugh in the dock and nodded. Few, if any, in court missed the gesture to the great annoyance of David. It did not help Hugh for prosecution witnesses to be too friendly towards him, the jury might doubt any favourable evidence they gave.

Jeremy did not miss the gesture and once Timothy had taken the oath to tell the truth and given his name, Jeremy asked, "We just saw when you came into court that you nodded at the defendant. There is nothing surprising in that, you are close friends aren't you?"

Timothy was clearly embarrassed that his innocent gesture was being referred to in this way. His normal ruddy complexion reddened further as he replied, "Yes, we've known each other for a good thirty years."

Jeremy nodded gratefully at the witness, "You presumably have spent a good deal of time together over that period. Have you met him weekly or even daily perhaps?"

"Probably most week days, except when one of us is away on holidays."

He quickly added, "We are members of the same club in Jesmond, and we regularly meet there."

"Have you discussed your personnel affairs with him?"

"Yes."

Timothy was now looking suspiciously at Jeremy. Jeremy just beamed at him and said, "Don't worry, I won't ask you about them."

A couple of the jurors on the front row smiled at this. Timothy simply turned even redder.

Jeremy continued, "I presume the defendant has shared a few secrets with you?"

Timothy looked concerned by the comment, replying, "I don't know what you mean."

Jeremy looked towards the jurors to see how they were reacting to this witness. It was beginning to look to him that Timothy knew more than he had told the police, but as he was a prosecution witness there was very little that Jeremy could actually do. He could not cross-examine him as the rules did not permit him to do so unless the witness was openly hostile. He would have to be a little subtler than that.

"Mr Granger, don't worry, I'm not asking you to break any confidences."

Timothy managed to somehow look both suspicious and grateful at the same time. Jeremy continued, "It is no secret that you are a close friend of the defendant in this case and met him frequently. I want to ask you about one of those meetings that took place on 18th June this year. Do you recall that evening now?"

Timothy nodded and replied at the same time, "I do."

"Tell us in your own words what you recall happening."

"Well it was an ordinary evening. I'd gone to the club early, at around 7pm. It was quiet at first but, within half an hour, a friend of mine, Walter Doyle, arrived. We chatted and bought each other a few drinks. Then, sometime after 9pm, Hugh arrived at the club."

Jeremy quickly interjected, "Do you recall the exact time the defendant arrived?"

Timothy hesitated before replying, "I think it was around 9:10pm to 9:15pm. I can't be more precise, I wasn't consciously looking at the time."

"Did the defendant join you both?"

"Yes, he bought us both a drink."

"You had been drinking for over two hours by then, could you tell whether the defendant had been drinking at all?"

Timothy smiled at the question, "Hugh likes a drink but you can never really tell that he's been drinking because it never seems to affect him. However, he did tell me he had been drinking with his wife and Mr Johns."

"Had he ever discussed his wife or Mr Johns with you?"

"What, previously?"

"Yes."

Timothy looked down and then immediately glanced in Hugh's direction before answering. "He often told me how much he loved his wife, Rosemary. He used to say she was his only love and he would do anything for her."

"Did he say anything else about her?"

"Well like any marriage it had its ups and downs. He used to say she had certain demands which he could not fulfil, but he never said what they were. Generally, though I got the impression that they had a close loving relationship."

"What about Mr Johns, did the defendant ever say anything to you about him?"

Timothy nodded at the question, "He did say a few things about him. Generally, they seemed to get on together. I once saw them together at Hugh's flat…"

Jeremy looked up from the witness statement wondering where this was coming from. Timothy just continued, "I can't say I took to Mr Johns. He seemed a little pushy to me. I remember telling Hugh this but he said that Johns was alright, once you got to know him."

Jeremy's eyes widened at this statement. He was clearly not expecting this answer. He paused before asking, "You visited the defendant's address and met Mr Johns. When was this?"

"Oh, a few weeks before the accident."

"Accident?"

"Yes, when Hugh accidentally shot Mr Johns."

Sara smiled at the answer, David avoided smiling, this evidence was probably not going to help Hugh in the end.

Jeremy slammed his papers on the bench in front of him. "Mr Granger you were not there, kindly tell us what you witnessed, not what your close friend has claimed happened!"

Timothy reddened further and looked a little chastened, "I'm sorry."

Jeremy picked up his papers again. "Did the defendant ever express an opposite view to you about Mr Johns?"

Timothy hesitated, "Not that I recall."

Jeremy looked at him with an icy stare for a couple of seconds before asking, "Did you make a witness statement to the police in this case shortly after the incident?"

Timothy looked surprised, "Yes."

"Do you think that your memory might have been significantly better at the time you made that statement than it is today?"

"I suppose so."

"Unless there is any objection, I will show you a copy of that statement."

Jeremy looked in David's direction. David said nothing, knowing there was no possible objection he could raise as referring to the statement was admissible under section 139 of the Criminal Justice Act 2003. Jeremy produced Timothy's witness statement and showed it to him. "Could you turn to page two please, where it says, 'I got the distinct impression that Hugh could not stand Johns.' Do you recall saying that now?"

Timothy blushed as he read the line and looked at Hugh before answering quietly, "Yes."

Jeremy was not inclined to show any mercy, "Please speak up Mr Granger, you accept that this statement records what you said, was it true?"

"Yes, it was true, but it was only an impression."

"I see, what was the impression based on?"

"I can't recall now."

Jeremy smiled, "Let me see if I can assist you. Could you look at your witness statement again? Page two again please. Do you see the line, 'In February Hugh came into the club and was really upset? He had clearly been drinking. He started complaining about Johns and said, 'I'd like to shoot that bastard and I would too, if it wasn't for the fact Rosemary likes him so much!'

Does that help you recall why you had this impression that he did not like Mr Johns?"

Timothy went bright red, this was clearly not going the way he had thought it would. He was quiet for a few seconds so Jeremy prompted him further, "Do you recall that conversation now?"

"Yes, I do."

"Was that why you thought the defendant could not stand Mr Johns?"

"I suppose so, but that was months ago. I know he told me just a few weeks before the acci...,"

He immediately corrected himself, "... the incident that he thought Johns was alright once you got to know him."

"Is this a recent memory?"

Timothy looked surprised at the question, "I'm sorry, I don't understand the question."

Jeremy pulled his sagging gown tightly over his shoulders and looked away from the witness. He faced the jury as he asked, "This reference to the defendant saying Mr Johns was alright once you got to know him, does not appear anywhere in your witness statement, I was wondering why you were referring to it now?"

David rose quickly to his feet, "My Learned Friend is now attempting to cross-examine his own witness which of course he is not permitted to do. I wonder if he could restrict himself to legitimate and admissible questions."

Jeremy quickly responded, "I was simply seeking clarification from the witness."

Mr Justice Bright immediately intervened to avoid what he saw as an unnecessary squabble between counsel, "Mr Asquith, you were venturing into a cross-examination of your own witness, I am sure the jury have got your point, could you move on!"

Jeremy's smile widened as he answered, "Of course My Lord." He turned back to Timothy, "Let us move on to what happened after the defendant came to the club on 18th June of this year. Do you recall what he said?"

Timothy visibly relaxed and the deep red in his face lightened to a less conspicuous pink, "I recall that after he bought us a drink he suggested we toast the Duke of Wellington's victory at Waterloo. Hugh was a great one for history and there was nothing unusual in this although I had no idea it was the anniversary of the battle."

"Do you recall if he said anything else at that stage?"

"No, that was it really."

"How did the defendant appear at this stage?"

"He seemed a little tense. He looked at his watch a few times and seemed to want to get back home."

"Did he say why?"

"He made some comment, 'I have to get back you never know what those two might get up to when I'm away.' He said it in a jokey way so I didn't take any notice of it."

Jeremy looked at Timothy's witness statement before asking, "Did he say anything else?"

The colour in Timothy's face deepened as nerves set in again, "Not that I can recall."

Jeremy raised his eyes to the ceiling of the court in a gesture the jury could clearly see. He then asked, "Could you please look at page three of your witness statement, where it says that the defendant said to you, 'I have to get back, you never know what those two might get up to in my absence and I might need to put a stop to it!' Was that what he said?"

Timothy looked down before answering. "Yes, but it was said in a jokey sort of way. He clearly didn't mean anything by it."

Jeremy ignored the last comment and asked, "Did he leave the club a short time after saying that?"

"Yes."

"What time was that?"

"I recall buying him another drink and he left shortly after that, sometime around 9:45pm."

Jeremy looked at Mr Justice Bright and said, "I have no further questions." Pointedly he did not thank Timothy for giving his evidence in chief.

David immediately tried to put Timothy at his ease, "Mr Granger, I represent Mr Petford-Williams and need to ask you a few questions on his behalf."

Timothy nodded as David continued, "You have already told us that you have known Mr Petford-Williams for thirty or so years and seen him quite frequently during that period. Have you been able to form an opinion of his character in that period?"

Timothy did not hesitate this time and immediately answered, "Yes I have. He is one of the most honest, kind, generous, decent people I have ever met. He would help out any friend in need."

"Is he a violent man by nature?"

"Good God, no!"

"Is he the type of person who easily gets angry?"

"No, he can be very emphatic when he argues but I wouldn't say angry."

"From your knowledge of him, is he the type of person to deliberately shoot someone?"

"Certainly not. I doubt he would even shoot a rat, never mind a man."

David quickly looked towards the jury to see how they were taking this evidence. He saw that two were taking notes. Satisfied, he turned back towards Timothy. "You have told us about a conversation you had with Mr Petford-Williams, some months ago where he said words to the effect, 'I'd like to shoot that bastard and I would too, if it wasn't for the fact Rosemary likes him so much!'

You had known Mr Petford-Williams for thirty years, did you think he meant this?"

"Certainly not! He was obviously distressed about something but, knowing Hugh, I took this to be frustration, not that he meant it."

"In any event, as you have told us, you visited Mr Petford-William's address just a few weeks before this incident and you met Mr Johns there?"

"Yes."

"We do not need to go into any detail but you formed an unfavourable opinion of Mr Johns didn't you?"

"Yes I did. I don't like to talk ill of the dead, but I thought he was arrogant and very dismissive of others."

"You told Mr Petford-Williams this was your opinion and he was in fact supportive of Mr Johns wasn't he?"

"Yes, he said Johns was alright once you got to know him."

"And that was just a few weeks before this incident?"

"Yes."

"Moving on to the 18th June, you say that when you saw him in the club, Mr Petford-Williams seemed tense and wanted to leave quickly?"

"Yes."

"However, he stayed for a couple of drinks and chatted to you and your friend Mr Doyle?"

"Yes he did."

"Isn't it right he didn't normally stay that long when he visited the club. Usually he would stay between half an hour and an hour and a half unless there was a special event?"

"Yes, I believe that's right."

"The night of 18th June was no different from any other night in this regard?"

"No it wasn't."

"You have told us he made this jokey comment, 'I have to get back, you never know what those two might get up to in my absence and I might need to put a stop to it!'

You will recall, you were reminded of that part of your statement. What you weren't reminded of was the next line where you said, 'I thought nothing of the comment at the time.' Was this because it was the typical type of comment made by Mr Petford-Williams, with nothing significant in it whatsoever?"

"Yes that's right."

David made a point of thanking him for his evidence. Timothy had been a very useful witness for Hugh, hopefully the next one would prove to be as well.

CHAPTER 24

THE FRIEND

Jeremy did not re-examine Timothy but immediately called his next witness Walter Doyle.

Walter was a very different person to Timothy. He was in his early fifties, stood at about 5 feet 6 inches tall, wore a full head of hair, and was pale and skinny. He entered the courtroom and went straight to the witness box without looking at Hugh or even in the direction of the dock.

Jeremy waited until he had been sworn by the usher, and then asked him to confirm his name and a few background details. With the formalities out of the way, Jeremy aimed for the target, "Mr Doyle, you are well-acquainted with both the defendant in this case, Hugh Petford-Williams, and his friend Mr Timothy Granger?"

"Yes I am."

"How long have you known them both?"

Walter paused as if to calculate the time then answered, "I've known them both for about the same period of time. About four years ago I moved to Jesmond from London. I joined the local club and there I met Tim first and became friendly with him. A few nights later, I met Hugh. Both were regular members of the club. Tim would spend most of his time there, almost always being there when I arrived. Hugh would usually arrive later, but he would visit almost every night."

"Would you call yourself a friend of either of them?"

"I suppose so. We would meet in the club and have a drink together. I've never been to their homes though and they've never been to mine. I wouldn't say we were close friends."

Jeremy nodded and then asked, "Would you say the defendant and Mr Granger were close friends?"

"Oh yes, they've known each other for years."

Jeremy smiled as he looked towards the jury, then he turned back and faced Walter and asked, "Did the defendant ever discuss his wife with you?"

Walter now looked towards the dock before answering, "He did occasionally. He made it plain that he was infatuated with her when he met her and he still is. He frequently said he would do anything for her."

David noted how Walter emphasised the word 'anything.'

"Did he ever discuss his neighbour, Mr Johns, with you?"

"On a few occasions he did. I got the impression that he did not like Mr Johns. Something about him being too attentive towards Rosemary."

He paused and then quickly added, "Hugh's wife."

"Can you recall when this conversation or these conversations first took place?"

"Not exactly. He was always talking about Rosemary, probably from the first time I met him. He started talking about Johns sometime before last Christmas."

"What did the defendant say?"

"He said he thought Johns was a little too familiar with his wife and was generally an obnoxious man. I remember earlier this year he even said he would like to shoot him!"

"Do you recall when this conversation took place?"

"Not precisely, probably February or March this year."

"How did he appear when he said this?"

Walter glanced at Hugh's neutral expression as he listened to this from the dock, and replied, "Like he meant it!"

David made a note of the words whilst thinking to himself, 'so much for friendship'.

Jeremy waited ostensibly for the judge to make a note, but actually using the time so that the answer would be absorbed by the jury. He noted that a couple of jurors made a note and then he moved on. "I want to take you back to 18th June of this year. Do you recall going to the club and meeting the defendant?"

"I recall going to the club and meeting Tim first. We were there for about a couple of hours before Hugh arrived."

"What time did the defendant arrive?"

"It was sometime after 9pm, probably about 9:15pm. I remember thinking at the time that it was perfect timing because Tim and I were just finishing our drinks when Hugh came in and bought a round."

"Did he say anything to you?"

"Yes, he suggested we toast the Duke of Wellington's victory at Waterloo two hundred years before, so we did."

"Did he say anything else?"

"He said something like, 'It had nothing to do with mud'. I had no idea what he was talking about and I didn't ask him as I had no interest in battles."

"What was his demeanour like that night?"

Walter paused before answering, "He seemed a little preoccupied with something, a little tense."

"Did he say what was concerning him?"

"He did make a comment just before he left that I thought was a bit strange at the time. He said he'd better get back as he didn't know what those two might be getting up to in his absence."

"Did you know who he was referring to?"

"Yes, it was clearly his wife and Mr Johns."

Jeremy sat down satisfied that at least this witness had followed his witness statement and not provided any surprises, indeed his evidence was better than he thought it would be.

David felt the opposite, expecting that a friend of Hugh's would not have given such unhelpful evidence against him. He did not waste any time on background matters, "Mr Petford-Williams was more of an acquaintance rather than a friend wasn't he?"

"I thought of him as a friend. We did meet quite regularly at the club."

"Yes, but you never visited each other's homes or shared anything else in common other than buying each other drinks in a club?"

Walter hesitated before answering, "I suppose not."

"Did you even like him?"

Walter looked down at his shoes but then immediately looked up and replied, "Yes, he could be good company."

"Then why is your evidence so against him?"

"I'm not sure what you mean."

"Well, let's look at it. You told us you did not think he liked Mr Johns, didn't you?"

"Well, he did make the comment about shooting him."

"He made the comment but it was obviously a joke wasn't it?"

"I don't know."

"According to your witness statement, he said, 'I'd shoot that bastard if it wasn't for the fact that Rosemary likes him so much!"

"Yes, that's how I recall it."

"In giving your evidence to this jury, you never mentioned the words, 'if it wasn't for the fact that Rosemary likes him so much.' Why was that?"

"I don't know, I must have forgotten."

"You did not think he was being serious, did you? He didn't seem to mean it, did he?"

"I did think he was being serious."

"In your witness statement, which was taken from you much nearer the time of the incident, you said, "I thought little of the comment at the time."

"I don't recall saying that."

"I can show you your statement if you wish? In any event, I would be corrected by prosecution counsel, if I put to you something that did not appear in your statement."

"No it's alright, I don't need to see the statement, I'm sure it's there."

"I presume you call yourself a good citizen?"

The witness looked at David suspiciously, "Yes, I do."

"If you had thought he was serious about shooting someone, you, as a good citizen would have reported it to the police, but you didn't report it, did you."

"No."

"And you would have done if you thought he was serious wouldn't you?"

"I suppose so."

"So when you were asked by my learned friend, 'How did he appear when he said this?' and you answered, 'Like he meant it', you weren't saying what you thought at the time but presumably what you thought with the benefit of hindsight?"

Walter looked distinctly uncomfortable, "I don't know now."

David did not want to give him time to recover as he had made some inroads, so he moved on quickly and asked, "On the 18th June, Mr Petford-Williams visited the club and bought you a round. It was like any ordinary evening wasn't it?"

"Well, he doesn't usually buy the first round, he always seems to appear when it's my round and I have to buy one for him!"

David stared at him. "Mr Doyle, we are not dealing with who buys the first round here. This is a much more serious matter, this is a murder trial!"

Walter looked down at his feet again before apologising.

"It was an ordinary evening and Mr Petford-Williams only stayed for half an hour or so. Usually, he only stayed for half an hour to an hour and a half didn't he?"

"Something like that."

"He was not unusually tense or in a hurry to get home was he?"

"It seemed to me that he was in a hurry."

"Again, I suggest that you are using the benefit of hindsight? You are presuming that is what he must have felt?"

"No, that's the way it seemed to me at the time."

"Have you used the benefit of hindsight in any of your other answers?"

"I don't think so."

David looked at Walter's witness statement. "Let's deal with the comment Mr Petford-Williams made just before leaving the club that night and returning home. In your witness statement you refer to him making the comment, 'I'd better get back home now, you never know what those two might get up to when I'm away and I might need to put a stop to it!' Do you recall that now?"

"Yes, I couldn't remember the exact words earlier."

"Don't worry, I'm not dealing with your exact words. The truth is, you never thought anything of the comment at the time did you?"

"I thought it was a bit strange."

"Please look at page three of your witness statement, where it states, 'I never thought anything about it at the time.' That statement was made on 20th June, just two days after you met him in the club. It deals with an incident that took place four months ago now.

That was the truth wasn't it. You never thought anything about it at the time? It's only now with the benefit of hindsight that you think it was strange?"

Walter looked perplexed, "I was sure I thought it strange at the time, but I do remember what is in my statement, I'm a little confused now."

David sat down with the words, "Yes, that's what usually happens when a person relies on hindsight!"

CHAPTER 25

THE EMERGENCY SERVICES

At the conclusion of Walter's evidence, Mr Justice Bright adjourned the case for lunch. As only one lift was working, and there was a long queue for it, David and Sara walked down the stairs to the second floor to have a sandwich in the advocate's canteen.

Once they had bought lunch, they took a seat in the corner of the room and Sara asked David a question that had been puzzling her, "Do you still get surprised when witnesses change their accounts in court like that?"

David put his tuna and salad sandwich down and after swallowing a small, surprisingly tasteless bite, he replied, "No, not at all. Experience teaches you that what appears in witnesses' statements and the evidence given in court months later are frequently two different accounts. You have to remember that the police take the statements and have their own agenda. Consciously or subconsciously they can influence the statements given by the witness. Similarly, a witness may have his or her own agenda. Either they want to protect someone, like Timothy Granger in this case, who has obviously bent over backwards to help Hugh,

225

and probably perjured himself in the process, or a witness might be seeking a minor revenge for hurt feelings, which is possibly the case of Walter Doyle. I thought Doyle came across as someone who was enjoying the opportunity to put obstacles in Hugh's way, for reasons best known to himself."

Sara nodded, "I was a little surprised at Mr Doyle. I thought he might give helpful evidence and be a character reference for Hugh. I can't think why he didn't! I was wondering at the time why you didn't seek a character reference from him but I guess you were concerned about what answer you might get."

David nodded, "Originally, when I read his statement, and Hugh said he was a friend, I had decided to ask him about Hugh's character. However, having listened to his answers to the prosecutor I decided against it. You never know what he might have said!"

He smiled at Sara, "It's what makes the job so interesting. Despite having their witness statements in advance, you never know what a witness is actually going to say until they've said it!"

Sara took a sip of what just about passed for coffee. After grimacing at the taste she asked, "Do you think it's worth asking the solicitor to look into Mr Doyle to see if there's any reason we can discover for his being unhelpful?"

David beamed at her, "You can ask if you like but legal aid won't cover such an investigation and I doubt the solicitor has the time or resources to carry one out himself."

At 2:05pm, they returned to court and, once everyone was assembled, Jeremy announced that he was going to play the CD recording of the emergency 999 phone call made by Hugh on 18th June. Normally, David objected to 999 calls being played as being too emotional for a jury. Usually the call was made by the victim or someone one discovering a loved one's body and would be full of emotive language, but this call was from Hugh and it would be the first time the jury would hear him speak. It was also his first account of what happened, claiming that what had occurred was an accident. David was happy for the jury to hear every word of the call, even though Hugh came across a little annoyed and impatient with the operator.

Within minutes, the equipment had been set up and Detective Sergeant Charles Bull was playing the CD to the court.

David watched the faces of the jurors as they heard the call. It was always surprising to David that these calls sounded much more dramatic when played in open court as opposed to when he listened to them through earphones. He still thought Hugh sounded genuinely concerned for Johns' life. He took particular interest in their faces when they heard Hugh say, 'Yes, I shot him ... It was an accident. My rifle went off and shot him through a lavatory door. I didn't mean to shoot him. Now I am worried that he might die and it will be my fault.'

There was the usual mixture of expressions on their faces although most were showing no emotions. A couple looked like they had no idea what was going on, but a few seemed to be taking it in, nodding with interest as they listened to the call.

As David acknowledged, he could never tell what a juror was thinking, but he thought he had made the right decision in asking for the call to be played.

Once the CD ended, Jeremy rose to his feet and addressed the Judge in front of the jury, "My Lord, my next two witnesses are members of the ambulance crew who called at the defendant's address on 18th June. I had hoped to be in a position to call the police officers who also attended shortly after them, but unfortunately neither officer is available to give evidence today. Both are available tomorrow though. It will probably mean we will run out of evidence early this afternoon. I apologise if that causes any inconvenience but I should add that we are making good progress in this case."

Mr Justice Bright turned to face the jury before stating, "I suspect none of us will be too disappointed if we have an early afternoon for once."

A few members of the jury dutifully smiled, some frowned, appearing to prefer court than returning home early!

A few minutes later, Paul Holland, a paramedic walked into court. Once he was sworn, Jeremy asked him his age and occupation and what qualifications he had before moving on to the important aspects of his evidence.

"Mr Holland, we know that the 999 call was made at 10:08pm because that is the time recorded on the CD we have just played to the court. The emergency operator then contacted the ambulance service and the police. When did you receive the call to attend Flat 1, the Elms, Manor House Road, Jesmond?"

Paul Holland had given evidence in court before. He was not a novice. It was a sad fact of his occupation that he was no stranger to violent crime on the streets of Newcastle. He turned away from Jeremy and looked directly at the jury as he answered the question.

"It was almost immediately, my colleague, James Marshall and I were on standby and we received the call from dispatch and I logged it at 10:09pm. We then immediately set off for the address in Jesmond."

"What is your normal response time?"

"We aim to make it to the patient's address in eight minutes. Of course, we cannot always make it in that time because of traffic, but that is our aim."

"In this case, you made it by 10:15pm according to your records so congratulations are due. You beat your normal time and made it within seven minutes of the 999 call!"

Paul nodded, he rarely received congratulations or thanks. By the nature of his work, he spent a lot of time dealing with injured alcoholics who would rather take a swing at him than give him any praise.

Jeremy continued, "What did you do when you arrived?"

"I was the driver that night so I parked just outside the address and waited."

"Why did you wait?"

"It's the protocol when you are dealing with a potentially violent scene. The person who caused the injury may still be armed, dangerous and violent and we are told to wait until the police arrive so they can enter the property first and ensure that it is safe for us to enter."

"Is that what you did in this case?"

"We intended to, but within seconds of arriving we both noticed a large, portly man with silvery hair outside the address. He was pointing to us and shouting."

"Do you recall what he shouted now?"

"Yes, it's in my notes."

Mr Justice Bright intervened and addressed David, "Is there any objection to Mr Holland referring to his notes?"

David rose and said, "None whatsoever, I am happy for Mr Holland to refer to them, indeed I was going to ask him a few questions based upon them."

The judge turned to Paul, "There you are then Mr Holland, please feel free to refresh your memory from your notes if you need to."

Paul opened a notebook and turned to the notes he had taken on the day. He then answered Jeremy's question, "The man was waving at us and shouting, 'Come on in here. There's a man dying.' I looked at James and we both shrugged our shoulders. I had parked a little bit too close to the property. I should have parked to the side of the building but I'd been unable to do so as once I pulled up the driveway I noticed that there was a barn straight ahead, a few feet away from the side of the house and there was no room to park the ambulance there.

James and I realised that the man could easily have harmed us already if he wanted to, so we felt it was safe to go straight into the property and not wait for the police."

David made a point of audibly underlining something in his notes so that the jury could see that this was important for the Defence.

Jeremy ignored him and asked, "What did you do then?"

"We both picked up our equipment and ran into the flat behind the man."

"What did you see?"

"We ran through the front door. I recall there was a stairway on my right as I came in and opposite the stairs was a lavatory. The door was open and a man was on the floor, his body lying half in and half outside of the room. A woman was applying a blood-soaked towel to his neck. Her clothing was covered in blood and there was a great deal of blood pooling on the floor around his neck, increasing every second."

"Could you tell what state the woman was in?"

"She seemed heavily intoxicated to me. Once I came in, I asked her to move out of the way. Her eyes were glazed and she did not seem to understand what I was saying. I eventually got through to her and James had to gently push her out of the way so we could get to the man on the floor. She got up from the floor but stumbled and almost fell over. Strangely, I noticed her arms seemed to be wet through with water which I thought was unusual, as though she had tried to wash the blood off and then returned to help the man. She did try to talk to me but she was slurring her words and I couldn't make out exactly what she was saying."

"Do you have any note of what she said?"

"It was something like, 'He's dead!' then something inaudible, followed by, 'It's my fault.' She may have said something else but I couldn't make it out."

"What did you do?"

"I assembled an intravenous drip to put some fluid in his veins to prevent them from collapsing from blood loss. James meanwhile applied pressure to the wound. We both knew that we were losing him and we would have to work fast if there was any chance of saving him."

"You mentioned that a man directed you to the address telling you that someone was dying in the house. There is no dispute that was the defendant in this case, Hugh Petford-Williams. Do you recall him saying anything when you were trying to help the man?"

"For the most part he was mumbling something. I couldn't make it out. I thought he said 'mud' at one stage but I might be wrong about that."

"Do you recall now what he was doing if anything?"

"He was just standing watching us as we did our job."

"Do you recall if he had anything in his hands?"

"I can't recall now."

"Did you manage to stabilise the injured man?"

"As well as we could in the circumstances. We knew there was only so much we could do and we had to get him to hospital as soon as possible."

"We will hear that the police arrived shortly after you. Do you recall them coming now?"

"Yes. I had my back to the front door so I didn't see them enter. I just heard the noise of a scuffle. I tried to carry on with what I was doing as every second was clearly going to count, so I didn't see exactly what happened."

"That's understandable, Mr Holland, the police officers will give their own evidence relating to that. You took Mr Johns to the hospital didn't you?"

"Yes, I was the driver, so James stayed in the back with Mr Johns."

"Did you have any further dealings with him once he arrived at the hospital?"

"No, none."

Jeremy thanked him and sat down.

David rose to cross-examine. He could see that the calm way in which the paramedic had given his evidence had impressed some members of the jury. He knew they would be sympathetic to him owing to his job, so there was no point in cross-examining him harshly.

He began by making the point that he wanted assistance, not confrontation, "Mr Holland, I want to say at the outset that there is no criticism whatsoever of you. Quite the opposite. It is clear that you did everything you could in the circumstances to save Mr Johns' life."

Paul smiled to himself, he had been cross-examined like this before and then immediately ripped into by the barrister. He had no reason to doubt that the same would happen here, but he would pretend that the question had disarmed him. "Thank you sir, we do our best in what are often difficult circumstances."

David nodded, "Mr Holland, there were only two of you in the ambulance that night. Usually wouldn't the contingent be higher?"

Here it comes, thought Paul as he replied, "Yes, we would normally have three or four crew members, but we were short-staffed that night."

"As you have told us, you made notes of this incident?"

"Yes that's right."

"Presumably, they were not made at the time as you were too busy?"

"That's right, I made them after we had taken Mr Johns to the Accident and Emergency centre at the Royal Victoria Hospital in Newcastle."

"You also made a witness statement in this case, a few days later?"

"That's right."

"Obviously your witness statement to the police was more detailed than your original notes."

"Yes, the police asked me a number of specific questions and I used my memory to answer them as accurately as I could."

"As you have told us, when you first arrived at the address, you were going to follow protocol and wait outside for the police to arrive?"

"Yes."

"But you saw Mr Petford-Williams outside the address and realised he was no threat?"

"Yes, we both thought if there was any risk of danger, it had passed. If he was going to shoot us, he could have done it when I parked right outside his front door!"

"You were asked by my Learned Friend whether Mr Petford-Williams had anything in his hands and you said you cannot recall now?"

"That's right, it is a number of months ago and I have no notes about it."

"I can see you don't refer in your notes to him carrying anything nor indeed is there such a reference in your witness statement."

"That's right."

"However, you had assessed it was safe to enter the house. If Mr Petford-Williams was carrying a rifle, you would surely not have assessed it as safe to leave the vehicle and enter the house?"

"Certainly not."

"So it follows that you did not see him with a rifle in his hands?"

"No, I think I would have remembered that!"

"Do you recall seeing a rifle anywhere in the house?"

"I don't recall seeing one but then I only went into the hallway and the toilet area and as I was concentrating on saving the man's life I wasn't really looking at anything else."

David nodded, "Perfectly understandable Mr Holland. Could you just look at page 7 in the jury bundle? It's a photograph taken later on 18th June showing the rifle resting against the side of the stairs. Does that help you recall where the rifle was when you entered the flat?"

Paul looked at the photograph but shook his head, "I'm afraid it doesn't, I don't recall seeing a rifle."

"Very well, let me move on to one final matter. You were obviously occupied when the police arrived, but you do recall them arriving?"

"They were behind us. I heard them come in and shout something and then I heard a crackling noise and a scuffle behind me. I was worried that they were going to knock over the intravenous drip I had just set up, fortunately they didn't."

"Do you remember if the police swore at Mr Petford-Williams, using words like, 'Police, get on the fucking floor now!', or something like that?"

"I don't recall what they said. They might have used words like that but I was not really concentrating on what they were saying."

"Mr Petford-Williams did not say anything in response, did he?"

"I think he may have said something but, again, I can't really recall."

"I suggest he never had any time to say or do anything?"

"I can't really recall now."

"As far as you can recall, he did not make any sudden move?"

"Not that I'm aware of, but I did have my back to him."

"Did you see the police put a Taser to his back and use it on him?"

"No, I didn't, but I did hear a strange crackling noise which I later assumed was the Taser."

David thanked him and as there were no further questions from Jeremy or the Judge, the witness left the court thinking that had been one of the easiest experiences he had had in a court room.

Jeremy then called his last witness of the day, John Marshall, the second paramedic.

After John was sworn, Jeremy asked a few questions establishing his qualifications and experience before moving on to the night of 18th June.

"Mr Marshall, we have heard that night you were part of an ambulance crew of two, driven in an ambulance by your colleague, Paul Holland?"

"That's right. Paul was the designated 'blue light' driver that night?"

"It's probably obvious, but what is a 'blue light driver'?"

"It means he has had special training and is allowed to drive using blue lights and can ignore certain traffic restrictions when it is safe to do so."

"Thank you. Now I would like to move on to when you arrived at the defendant's address. Do you recall what you saw?"

"Yes, Paul should have parked slightly away from the address but he parked right in front. I think he intended to go past it but then found that he couldn't hence he pulled up outside with the nearside of the vehicle opposite to the front door."

"The nearside would be the side you were on?"

"Yes."

"So your view would have been of the front door of the defendant's property. Did you see anything when you parked?"

"Yes, I saw Mr Petford-Williams at the door of his address. He was shouting to us to come in saying that a man was dying in there."

"Did you see whether he was carrying anything?"

"I don't recall seeing anything."

"What did you do?"

"We decided not to wait for the police. We both looked at each other and decided that if he wanted to hurt us, he could have done so when we arrived, because Paul had parked so close to the house!"

"Did you follow him into the address?"

"We did, Paul collected the equipment and went in first. I followed."

"What did you see?"

"There was a woman, she was covered in blood but I ascertained that it wasn't hers but was Mr Johns' blood, so I gently moved her aside and started applying a pressure bandage to Mr Johns' neck."

"Did you see what happened to the woman?"

"She got up and stumbled. She was saying something but I couldn't make out what, she was clearly drunk and slurring her words."

"Do you recall if the defendant said or did anything?"

"No, he did mutter something but I couldn't make it out. To be fair, I was concentrating on trying to save the man's life and not really listening."

"We have heard that the police arrived shortly after you. Do you recall them arriving?"

"I do, they made an almighty racket."

"Did you see them or were you still concentrating on Mr Johns?"

"I was concentrating on Mr Johns, but I was positioned to his right side so I did see them enter the house and arrest Mr Petford-Williams."

"You took Mr Johns to the Royal Victoria hospital and we have heard you were in the back of the ambulance with him."

"That's right. I was trying to keep him stable but I knew there was no real chance."

"Why was that?"

"He'd lost too much blood. I was surprised he lasted as long as he did."

Jeremy thanked him and sat down.

David took James to the plan of the flat at page two of the jury bundle and asked, "Mr Marshall, can you show us where you were when you were applying pressure to Mr Johns' neck?"

James pointed to the toilet area demonstrating he would have been almost facing the front door.

"So you would have had a good view as the police came into the flat?"

"Yes, although I was concentrating on Mr Johns."

"Of course, I think we all understand that. Do you recall where Mr Petford-Williams was standing when the police came into the flat?"

"He was to my left near to where the stairs are."

"Can you recall what he was doing?"

"Just standing there."

"We know he had phoned 999 and called for an ambulance, we also know that he called you into the house and explained that there was a man dying in there. Did he appear keen that you save the man's life?"

"I don't know if I can answer that. He certainly encouraged us to come into the house to try and help Mr Johns."

"He did not hinder you in any way?"

"No."

"He was not a threat to you in any way while you were there attending to him?"

"No, I didn't think so."

"He was taking an interest in what you were doing?"

"Yes."

"Before arriving at the property, you had been told some of the details of this incident?"

"A few, yes."

"You knew a rifle was involved?"

"Yes."

"Did you see the rifle?"

"Yes, I think it was propped up against the stairs when we came in."

David smiled, "Please look at page seven of the jury bundle."

James opened the bundle that had been left in the witness box and looked at the photograph.

"That is a photograph taken later on 18th June after you had left the flat. Was that where the rifle was when you went in to the flat and saw it?"

"Yes, I believe so."

"You never saw it in Mr Petford-Williams hands at any stage?"

"No."

"When the police arrived, do you recall that one of them had a Taser in his hand and was pointing it at Mr Petford-Williams?"

"I do. I was concerned because I was so close to him. I thought I might get hit if he fired it."

"Do you recall the police shouting at Mr Petford-Williams?"

"I do."

"Do you recall what they said?"

"Not exactly."

"Let me see if I can jog your memory, I suggest they burst into the flat, one was carrying a Taser which was already unholstered and he said, 'Police, get on the fucking floor now!' Do you recall an officer saying that?"

"It was something like that. I do remember the police officer swearing at the man."

David could not resist letting a slight grin appear on his face as he added, "Mr Petford-Williams did not do or say anything did he?"

"Not that I can recall."

"The police officers then jumped on him?"

"Yes."

"One of them applied a Taser to him?"

"I saw that and heard a loud noise as it was used."

"Others pinned his arms behind his back and attached handcuffs to him?"

"That's what I saw."

"As they jumped on him, they almost knocked the intravenous drip that Mr Holland had struggled to place in Mr Johns' right arm?"

"Yes, I was surprised at the time because Mr Petford-Williams wasn't doing anything, except looking at us as we tried to save Mr Johns."

"So you saw no reason for them to jump on him and force him to the ground?"

"None whatsoever."

CHAPTER 26

THE TASER

At 10:35am on Wednesday 21st October, Police Constable Ray Savage entered the court room. He was 6 feet 2 inches tall and weighed 17 stone. He was an imposing sight as he walked slowly and purposefully towards the witness box. As he did so, he took one quick look at the barristers, then a slightly longer one looking at the Judge before his eyes finally rested on the jurors. He knew he would probably be in for a tough time today. After all, it went with the territory. He was licenced to use a Taser and, by virtue of his duties, he came across violent individuals who then complained in court if he had used force against them!

Still he felt fine. He had arrested a murderer and it was the only time he had done that in his career and already he had shared the story with a number of colleagues over a drink or two! He could not help having a slight smirk as he stood there. As far as he was concerned, there was nothing the defence barrister could do to take away the sense of satisfaction that he felt from taking down a violent, armed criminal.

Jeremy noticed the smirk, but ignored it. He waited until the officer had taken the oath to tell the truth and then, after requesting his name, he asked, "Officer, I understand that as part of your duties you are licenced to carry, and in the right circumstances, use, a Taser. For the benefit of those of us with limited knowledge of Tasers, can you tell us a little about them?"

Ray smiled at Jeremy, happy to discuss his particular expertise, "Certainly, sir. Perhaps I should first discuss what a Taser actually is. Basically it's classified under the Firearms Acts as a firearm but it's less lethal than say a handgun ..." he paused before adding, "... or a rifle! Its purpose is not to kill but to incapacitate a person who is a threat to police officers or to ordinary citizens. The Taser has a slightly different shape to a handgun and has yellow markings so it can be easily distinguished.

It can be used in one of two ways. Either by using a cartridge and firing out two dart-like electrodes that hit the offender but remain connected to the Taser by conductive wires. An electric current is then applied through the darts which causes the muscles of the offender to spasm and incapacitates him.

It can also be used directly against a person not by firing the darts but by simply applying the electric charge. This is referred to as the 'drive-stun' mode and is the mode I used here. This can also incapacitate the offender and is a safer use of the Taser than firing the darts, particularly when there are other innocent people in the immediate vicinity and you are in a small enclosed space."

Jeremy nodded, "Can you help us with details of the training you received in the use of the Taser?"

"Yes, sir. Officers who are assigned to use Tasers have to attend an intensive three-day course. Not everyone passes it, I believe 20% fail. I passed the course in the top half of my class," he added proudly.

"Before you can attend the course, you have to be up to date with Officer Safety Training, and Emergency Life Support, you also have to pass a fitness test, have a valid eyesight test, and be recommended by your unit Inspector. Also your professional and disciplinary record is considered."

"What were you taught on the course?"

"We were taught not just how to use the Taser but also about decision making in its use, when the use of force is justified and the medical implications of using a Taser."

David noisily underlined his note when he heard the words, 'medical implications.'

The officer looked over at him suspiciously but carried on with his evidence, "We were taught to use the Taser on a range and then in certain scenarios. We were also taught when to use the Taser in the 'drive-stun' mode."

"Is that all the training you do, a three-day course?"

"No, sir. Thereafter, we attend a one-day annual refresher course to keep us up to date."

Jeremy smiled, he felt he had covered every aspect of Taser training and the officer could deal with any of David's criticisms. He decided to deal with the officer's actual use of the Taser in this case.

"Officer, I want to deal with the 18th June of this year and your involvement in this incident. Firstly, on that date, did you receive a call to attend the defendant's address?"

"Yes, sir, we did."

"Can you tell us what information you received?"

"Yes, sir, I was with Police Constable Rimmer when we received a call telling us that a man had been shot by someone with a rifle and that the shooter was still present at the scene and was presumed to be still armed and dangerous. We were also told that an ambulance team had been dispatched to the address and that we should attend the property first in order to ensure their safety."

"And is that what you did?"

250

"Yes, sir. Police Constable Rimmer and I drove to the address. I was the designated driver on this occasion. We attended the property first and, just after we arrived, another vehicle containing two other officers arrived."

"Who were they?"

"Police Constable Hervey and Police Constable Walker."

"What did you do when you arrived?"

"I saw that an ambulance was parked outside the property. The ambulance was empty so I assumed the occupants had already entered the property in breach of the set protocol that states they should wait outside until police officers arrive."

"Did you have any concerns about this?"

"Yes, sir, I thought there was a possibility that they had been taken into the house under force by the gunman."

"What action did you take?"

"Expecting there to be a man in the house with a loaded rifle, I drew my Taser from its holster and activated it. I disengaged the cartridge as I could not envisage a situation where I might need to fire it in a closed space and thereby potentially injure others than the gunman."

"What happened next?"

"I ran into the house. I was the first to enter with the other officers directly behind me."

"What did you see?"

"I saw the staircase on my right and opposite that was a small downstairs lavatory. I saw the body of a man on the floor half in the lavatory and half in the hallway. He was bleeding profusely. There was a paramedic on either side of him. One was holding an intravenous drip and the other was trying to staunch the flow of blood from his neck. I could see a woman to my left who was crying and was covered in blood. I then saw the defendant. He was standing over the paramedics and was pointing a rifle at them.

I was immediately worried for their safety, as well as the woman's, and my fellow officers and of course, myself. I was also worried that the defendant may use the rifle to shoot himself."

"What did you do?"

"I acted as quickly as I could. The training took over. I ascertained the dangers to everyone and shouted to the defendant, 'Police, get on the floor!"

"Did you swear?"

"Certainly not, sir! The situation was difficult enough without my antagonising it by swearing."

"What did the defendant do, if anything?"

"He said nothing but he started to move and I saw the barrel of the rifle turning quickly towards me. Worried for my own safety and that of others, I ran over to the defendant who was now side on to me and applied the Taser in drive-stun mode to the right hand side of his torso. I felt him collapse from the pain and I then brought him to the ground and took the rifle out of his hands. I stacked it against the staircase and then helped other officers to apply handcuffs to him."

"Officer would you look at page 7 of the jury bundle?"

The witness opened the jury bundle and looked at the well-thumbed photograph.

"Is that the rifle you took from the defendant?"

"Yes, sir."

"And how did it get in the position we see in the photograph?"

"I placed it there."

"Did you take any other steps?"

"I took the defendant to the police car with Police Constable Rimmer. As the arresting officer, I got into the back of the car with the prisoner and

Police Constable Rimmer drove us back to the police station."

"Did the defendant say anything on the journey back?"

"I think he muttered a few words but I couldn't make anything out. I also told him it was in his interests to remain quiet until he was at the station."

Jeremy smiled at the officer, happy that he had covered everything and thanked him as he sat down.

David rose from his seat to question the officer, but there was no smile on his face.

"Officer, I presume you are aware that the rifle was examined and it was found that it did not contain any cartridges?"

"I understand that now, sir. Of course, at the time, I did not know that. Your client had a rifle pointing at the paramedics, and, as he had by his own admission shot someone, I thought there was a real risk he might shoot someone else!"

David did smile now. The officer could have answered that question with just his first sentence but he was clearly keen to add a line or two to make matters worse for Hugh. He wondered whether the jury would notice this.

"Of course officer, he could not shoot anyone if the rifle was not loaded at this stage?"

Ray grinned, this was going to be easy. "As I've stated sir, at the time I was unaware that the rifle was not loaded."

"Where was the rifle when you first came into the flat?"

"It was in the defendant's hands, pointing at the paramedics."

David picked up the jury bundle and asked, "Officer, can you look at the photograph at page seven again?"

Ray looked again.

"Officer, I suggest that is where the rifle was when you first came into the property?"

"No, sir, that's where I placed it."

"That's not true is it officer, you've made this up to cover yourself for your unjustified and unnecessary use of the Taser?"

"No, sir, I haven't made anything up. Your client had a rifle in his hands and, because of that fact, I believed lives were in danger. I used the Taser as I thought it necessary to do so."

"Very well, let's look at your account shall we. You received a call that a man had shot someone with a rifle?"

"Yes, sir," replied the officer with a patronising tone.

"Were you informed that the man had made a 999 call asking for an ambulance and for police to attend, saying the shooting was an accident?"

"No, sir, the information I received was that a man had shot someone with a rifle and that he was still armed and dangerous."

"When you arrived you noted that the ambulance was empty. Clearly the paramedics had entered the property by the time you arrived?"

"Yes, sir."

"Did you think they would have entered the property if a man was waving a rifle about?"

"I didn't know what had happened to them, he could have taken them hostage for all I knew!"

David looked at the officer's statement and asked, "You were the first officer to enter the property?"

"Yes, sir."

"So your view was not obscured by other officers?"

"No, sir."

"Did you have a clear view when you entered the flat?"

"Yes, sir."

"You could clearly see the rifle in Mr Petford-Williams' hands?"

"Yes, sir, I had a clear view."

"No room for mistake?"

"None sir."

"You shouted out, 'Police get on the fucking floor' didn't you?"

"I didn't swear sir, I shouted out 'Police, get on the floor'."

"This was clearly in the hearing of the paramedics?"

Ray hesitated for a moment before answering, wondering for a split second what the paramedics might have said before resuming his air of calmness and control and answering, "I don't know what they heard, you will have to ask them."

David looked at the jurors and smiled, replying, "I already have."

Ray started to sweat a little, but tried to keep calm as David asked, "Did you swear because you were angry or because you wanted to look aggressive?"

"I never swore."

"Officer, I doubt anyone will criticise you for swearing. Lying about it on oath is a different matter however!"

"I am not lying. I did not swear"

David ignored the answer and continued, "Having shouted, 'Police, get on the fucking floor!', you immediately pounced on Mr Petford-Williams before he had time to say or do anything."

Ray shook his head from side to side, "I considered he was a serious threat to myself and others and I acted to prevent him from harming anyone else."

"I suggest he was unarmed and was not a threat to anybody?"

"No, sir, he still had hold of the rifle and I considered he was a credible threat."

"How did you get the rifle out of his grip after you applied the Taser?"

"I pulled it away from him."

"Surely whilst you applied the Taser his muscles would spasm making it more difficult to pull it away?"

Ray thought for few seconds, "I had no trouble, sir."

"Are you right or left handed?"

"Right handed, sir."

"Which hand did you use to take the rifle away from him?"

"I used both, sir."

David put a puzzled expression on his face. "How could you use both hands, officer, the Taser must have been in your right hand?"

Ray paused again before replying, "I must have put the Taser back in my holster by then."

"Are you making this up as you go along."

"No, sir."

"You applied the Taser to Mr Petford-Williams in the drive-stun mode didn't you?"

"Yes, sir."

"Just help us with that, will you."

David picked up a small file of papers that Sara had prepared relating to Taser use and held them out in front of him, "Officer are you aware there is a considerable amount of literature available about the drive-stun mode of a Taser?"

Ray looked at the file in David's hands. "No, sir, I wasn't, but I'll take your word for it."

"As you told us, you had a three-day intensive course on Taser use, followed by annual refresher courses. Were you taught how to use the Taser in the drive-stun mode on any of those courses?"

"Not as such, sir. We were told that it could be used in that fashion but weren't given any demonstrations."

"No, that's because the drive-stun mode has been open to heavy criticism hasn't it?"

"I'm not aware of any."

"Oh come, officer, at the very least you would have been told this on your annual refresher course?"

Ray remained silent so David pressed him, "Officer, in your last annual refresher course, were you told that in the United States, as long ago as 2011, guidelines were issued recommending that the use of drive-stun, as a pain compliance technique, be avoided. The guidelines were issued by a joint committee of the Police Executive Research Forum and the U.S. Department of Justice Office of Community Oriented Policing Services. The guidelines stated, 'Using the ECW to achieve pain compliance may have limited effectiveness and, when used repeatedly, may even exacerbate the situation by inducing rage in the subject.' Were you aware of that?"

Ray wiped some sweat off his brow and replied, "No."

"Surely you must be aware of guidance in this country then. Are you aware of the Independent Police Complaints Commission's report, the 'IPCC' report of July 2014 headed 'the IPCC review of Taser Complaints and Incidents.'

Ray looked uncomfortable as he answered, "I think I've heard about it."

"The report indicates that most of the complaints against Taser use in this country, are made because of the use of drive-stun. You must be aware of that?"

"No."

"Well, surely you have heard the opinion expressed in that report that, 'Officers are no longer trained to use Tasers in 'cartridge off drive-stun' mode, although they are still shown that it can be used in this way. This seems counter-intuitive if they are not supposed to be doing so.' Do you recall that comment?"

"No."

"Officer, you know all about Taser use. In order to use it to its best effect, as an incapitator, the darts have to be a few inches apart when they hit the target. However, when used in drive-stun mode the two ends of the Taser that contact the body are only 1.6 inches apart. Consequently, the drive-stun mode does not incapacitate a person, it just causes immense pain. You presumably knew that when you used it in this mode on Mr Petford-Williams?"

Ray was silent and started to fidget in the witness box, David was not going to let it rest, "Will you answer my question, officer?"

Ray was silent for a moment, "It's not unlawful to use the drive-stun mode and I judged it to be the best way to use the device so as not to hurt anyone else in the flat."

"No, officer, you were 'Taser happy' that day. No doubt your adrenalin levels were raised. You knew there was no need to use the device because Mr Petford-Williams was not a threat but you went ahead and used it anyway."

"That's not true."

"You used it in a way you knew would not incapacitate Mr Petford-Williams but in a way that would cause him the most suffering."

"That's not true."

"How old are you officer?"

Ray looked slightly confused but answered, "Thirty-two."

"How tall are you?"

"Six feet two inches,"

"How much do you weigh?"

"Seventeen stone."

"Not satisfied with inflicting unnecessary pain with your Taser on this five feet six inches tall, sixty-four-year-old, diabetic, man, you and other officers, of a similar size to you, then found it necessary to jump on him and flatten him, didn't you?"

Ray was now gripping the edges of the witness box, "No, we saw that he was a threat and we acted to contain that threat."

"Really officer, I suggest you were 'Taser-happy'. You had your Taser out and you were determined to use it."

"No, sir."

"Just how many times have you drawn and used your Taser since you were first issued with one, ten, twenty, a hundred times…" David paused before adding, "…or even more?"

Jeremy quickly rose from his bench, "I cannot possibly see the relevance of that question."

Mr Justice Bright looked at David who looked pensively back at him and then turned to the jury announcing, "Very well, if my Learned Friend doesn't want the officer to answer that question, I don't need to pursue it."

He sat down quickly before Jeremy could reply. Jeremy looked at him with an open mouth, but said nothing. David had no idea how many other times the officer had used the Taser, if any, or in what circumstances. He had therefore decided he preferred the lack of an answer to an actual one. The jury would no doubt be drawing their own, probably wrong, conclusions, courtesy of Jeremy's intervention!

CHAPTER 27

THE NOTEBOOK

Police Constable Timothy Rimmer was different to his partner, Ray Savage. Not only was he physically unlike Ray, being shorter and thinner, his whole demeanour was dissimilar as he entered the witness box and looked at the usher as he took the oath.

Jeremy took him through the usual background questions before moving onto the events of 18th June.

"Officer, we have already heard from your colleague, Police Constable Savage, that you received a call to attend the Defendant's home in Jesmond. We have also heard that Police Constable Savage was the driver. Can you help the court by telling us what happened when you arrived?"

Rimmer turned to the Judge, "Can I rely on my statement your honour?"

Jeremy asked him a number of questions about whether the statement was made within a short period of the events depicted and whether matters were more fresh in his mind than they were today. Once the officer confirmed they were, Jeremy asked if the officer could have permission to refer to his statement. Mr Justice Bright turned towards David and in a bored tone asked, "Is there any objection, Mr Brant?"

David rose slowly to his feet, "Yes, my lord, there is. The officer made notes in a pocket notebook before making the statement, based presumably on those notes. Surely it would be better if he refreshed his memory from the most contemporaneous document?"

The Judge looked at Jeremy, "That seems to be a fair point Mr Asquith?"

Jeremy had the statement in front of him and had not seen the officer's notebook, but not wanting to admit that, he replied, "I know the statement is more detailed but I'm content for the officer to rely on his notebook unless he needs to remind himself of any more detail later on."

David nodded a respectful thanks towards Jeremy and sat down looking quickly at Sara. Sara had scoured the unused material and come across a copy of the officer's notebook. She had then notified David of the contents.

Jeremy continued by asking Police Constable Rimmer, "Officer, I was asking you what happened when you arrived at the Defendant's address?"

Rimmer looked down at his notebook, "Yes, sir, Police Constable Savage was the first to enter the property followed by me. Two other officers were behind me, Police Constables Hervey and Walker. As we entered the flat, I saw the defendant with his back to me. He looked like he was watching the paramedics who were busy working on a person who was prone on the floor. I later learnt this was Mr Johns. Police Constable Savage shouted out to the defendant, "Police, get on the floor.""

David observed that two jurors were noting this answer. Jeremy noticed this as well and interrupted the officer, "Are you sure those are the words used?"

"Yes, sir, positive."

"Did Police Constable Savage swear at all?"

"Certainly not."

"Very well, what happened next?"

"There was a sudden move by the defendant and Police Constable Savage applied his Taser to the defendant in order to temporarily incapacitate him."

"Did you see why this was necessary?"

"Yes sir, the defendant had a rifle in his hands and was pointing it at the paramedics. There was clearly a threat to them."

"What happened next?"

"Police Constable Savage applied the Taser and whilst the defendant was incapacitated I moved in to help apply handcuffs to him."

"Was anything said whilst this was happening?"

"Not that I can recall, sir."

"What did you do then?"

"We got the defendant up from the floor and then took him out to the car. Police Constable Savage got into the back of the vehicle with him and I drove back to the station."

Jeremy thanked him and sat down as David rose holding a photocopy of the officer's notebook in his hand. "How well do you know Police Constable Savage?"

Police Constable Rimmer looked surprised at the question, "I don't understand sir."

It was David's turn to feign puzzlement, "I'm sorry officer, it's not a difficult question. How well do you know your partner, colleague and no doubt, friend, Police Constable Savage?"

The officer continued to have a puzzled expression. So David tried again, "Come now officer, let me try a different approach then, is Police Constable Savage a close friend?"

268

"He's a friend, sir. I have known him five years and we have been partners for the last three."

"Finally officer, thank you! I presume you socialise together?"

"Occasionally sir." He smiled and tried to inject some humour, "Not that we have much spare time to socialise in the police force!"

David looked at him with a stern expression. "Officer, you have known Police Constable Savage for five years, been partners for three of them and as a consequence, I suggest you have a very close friendship?"

"We are friends, sir."

"And friends help each other out, don't they?"

The puzzled expression returned to Police Constable Rimmer's face. "I'm sorry, sir, I don't understand what you mean."

"Simply this, officer, you would lie to protect your friend."

"No sir."

"Indeed, you have lied, haven't you?"

The officer assumed a hurt expression as he answered, "No, sir."

"You have lied to cover up for his misuse of the Taser on this occasion. There was no justifiable reason for using the Taser and therefore you have got together with your partner, your friend and lied. You claim Mr Petford-Williams had a rifle in his hands when in fact the rifle was propped up against the stairs?"

Rimmer turned slightly red. "That's not true, sir."

"Officer, you made a statement a day after this incident didn't you?"

"Yes, sir."

"Why?"

"It was important to have an accurate record of what happened."

"But you had an accurate record. You had written notes in your notebook as soon as you got back to the police station."

"They weren't as detailed, sir."

"No, but I suggest they were more accurate."

Police Constable Rimmer gave his puzzled expression again as David continued, "Were you with Police Constable Savage when you made your statement?"

"I think so."

"Did you confer at all when you wrote that statement?"

"We might have asked each other about names and addresses but the statements were our own."

"Really? I note that you both use the same expressions in your statements. For example, Police Constable Savage stated in his witness statement, 'I entered the property and immediately saw the Mr Petford-Williams with his back to me, holding a rifle pointing at the paramedics. I was immediately concerned for their safety. I shouted, 'Police, get on the floor'. Mr Petford-Williams began to turn round and I saw the barrel moving quickly towards me so I rushed and applied the Taser to his side in order to incapacitate him'. Have you seen that statement officer?"

"No sir."

"But you have obviously seen your own?"

"Of course, sir."

David picked up Rimmer's statement and said, "Your statement is in almost exactly the same words. 'I entered the property and immediately saw the Mr Petford-Williams with his back to me holding a rifle pointing at the paramedics. I was immediately concerned for their safety. Police Constable Savage shouted, 'Police, get on the floor'. Mr Petford-Williams began to turn round and I saw the barrel moving quickly towards Police Constable Savage who rushed over to the

Mr Petford-Williams and applied the Taser to his side in order to incapacitate him.' Do you recall writing that?"

"Yes, sir."

"Was it the truth?"

"Yes, sir."

"Then let's look at what is in your notebook. Did you make your notes alone as soon as you got to the police station?"

"Yes."

"Where was Police Constable Savage?"

"He was in the Custody Suite dealing with the defendant."

"Your notes state this, "We arrived at the address and noticed that an ambulance was parked outside but was empty. We assumed that the paramedics had entered the property and we quickly went into the address to ensure that they were safe. Police Constable Savage was the first in the property and I was directly behind him, followed by two other officers. Police Constable Savage shouted, "Police, get on the ..." David stopped abruptly and stared at the notes, "There is then something written next, it looks like the letters 'f' and 'u' which are then crossed out. Is that because you were writing what Police

Constable Savage said, namely, "Police, get on the fucking floor!'?'

"No, sir, he never swore, I must have made a mistake."

"Come now officer, you are clearly writing 'fu' in your notes, what else could it stand for except 'fucking'?"

The officer paused, desperately trying to think of something, "I wasn't writing that, sir, I don't know now what I was writing, I probably misspelt the word, 'floor'."

David just looked at him without bothering to respond for a few seconds, then he added, "Very well, officer, let us see what else you wrote in your notes. 'Police Constable Savage then launched himself at Mr Petford-Williams and applied the Taser in order to incapacitate him.' Do you notice what is missing officer?"

Police Constable Rimmer looked at his notes and stared before replying, "No sir."

"There is no reference to Mr Petford-Williams having a rifle in his hands?"

The officer looked again at his notes and turned over a page as if looking for a reference he knew should be there, but could not find. Finally, he replied with resignation, "No, sir."

"That's because the rifle was not in his hands but propped up against the stairs?"

"No sir, it was definitely in his hands," he replied with a final attempt to sound convincing,

"If it was in his hands, you would have made a note of it at the soonest opportunity. You only later made a note of it in your statement, a day later, to help your friend Police Constable Savage, who you knew had acted inappropriately in using his Taser."

"That's not true, sir."

David sat down and looked at Sara mouthing the words, 'Thank you.' He was happy to make some headway with the jury, some of whom had been nodding enthusiastically whilst he cross-examined the officer.

Of course, David realised that, in reality, the point had nothing to do with the central issue in the case, did Hugh deliberately or accidentally shoot William Johns? Still, he had enjoyed himself at the officers' expense and that always made the job seem worthwhile!

CHAPTER 28

THE SEARCH

After lunch Jeremy announced to the court that he was calling Police Constable Andrew Hervey to give evidence about the search of Hugh's flat. A few minutes later, the officer was standing in the witness box and giving his name to the court. David noted that this officer appeared more intelligent than the last two and he might need to take a different approach with him.

Jeremy treaded more carefully with his questions. He had not been impressed with the answers given by his last two witnesses and had no doubt the jurors would have a few concerns. He did not want to lose this case on the issue of whether there was a justifiable use of a Taser or not. He decided to ask the officer about the search and nothing else. "Officer, we have heard that you attended the defendant's flat in the company of other officers. Police Constables Savage and Rimmer went in first and you followed with your colleague, Police Constable Walker. We have heard about the arrest of Mr Petford-Williams and I am sure you can answer any questions my learned friend asks about that matter. I want to take you to a point after the arrest, when I understand you searched the property?"

"Yes, sir."

"When did the search begin?"

"As soon as the defendant had been arrested, and removed from the premises, I commenced my search of the property, assisted by Police Constable Walker."

"What was the purpose of the search?"

"We wanted to secure the rifle and any ammunition for it and check for any other illegal weapons or potentially relevant evidence."

"Tell the jury what you found."

"Could I refresh my memory from the Search Log, which I wrote at the time?"

There was no objection from David.

Jeremy turned to his own copy of the Search Log, "Officer, I only want to ask you about a few specific items. Starting with the rifle. Where was that found?"

The officer looked through the log and announced, "It was resting against the side of the stairs."

"Did you see how it got there?"

"I believe it was placed there by Police Constable Savage."

Jeremy smiled as he asked hopefully, "Did you observe that yourself, officer?"

"No, sir, it was what I was told by Police Constable Savage."

"Very well, officer, just tell the jury what you saw and heard at the time."

Hervey clearly felt a little rebuked by the tone of Jeremy's instruction. After all, as far as he was concerned, he was only answering the barrister's question! "Yes, sir," he replied in a slightly surly way.

Jeremy ignored the tone and continued, "Did you find anything else of interest near the rifle?"

"Yes, sir, there was a small table with a bowl on it next to the bottom of the stairs. In the bowl were 8 live .22 cartridges."

"Did you search the area around the stairs?"

"Yes, sir, I did and I found a spent .22 cartridge case just on the level opposite the lavatory door."

Jeremy picked up the jury bundle, "Yes, I think we can see the cartridge in the photograph on page 7 of the jury bundle."

Everyone with a jury bundle turned to page 7.

"Did you find anything else of interest in the house?"

"Downstairs in the kitchen there was a bin near to the back door containing three empty one litre bottles of red wine. On a table nearby, was a half-finished bottle of red wine and three glasses. Two were half full the other was empty."

Jeremy nodded, "Yes, I think we can see that in the photograph at page 9 of the jury bundle." Again everyone followed his lead and looked at the photograph.

"Are those the bottles and wine glasses you are referring to officer?"

The officer looked closely at the photograph as if he needed to verify this was not a picture of some wholly different house. After a few seconds he announced, "Yes, sir."

"I believe you searched the rest of the house?"

"I did, sir."

"I'm not going to ask you about anything else found in the house as it does not seem to me to be relevant. However, I understand you also searched the garden. What did you find there?"

"There was an area near the house which was surrounded by thick bales of hay shaped in a rectangular shape. Furthest from the house there was a row of bales with targets pinned to them. I should say they were stacked double thick, I assume for safety. Directly opposite them, placed around 25 metres from the targets, was a leather mat and on that I found one discharged cartridge."

Jeremy turned to the jury, "I believe there is no dispute, the defendant stated in interview that he had a target range at the bottom of his garden which he used for firing the rifle."

He turned back to the officer, "That's all I wish to ask you. Will you remain there, there may be questions from the defence."

David was already asking his first question before Jeremy had sat down. "Officer, you were in a separate police car to Police Constables Savage and Rimmer?"

"Yes, sir."

"Nevertheless, I understand you are all from the same police station and no doubt know each other well?"

"Yes, sir."

"Are you all friends? Do you socialise together?"

"We occasionally meet after work but not often. We have a large number of officers at our station, I wouldn't say I was friends with either of them. I would describe them as work colleagues, not friends."

"When you entered Mr Petford-William's address, what did you see?"

"I saw Police Constables Savage and Walker trying to restrain the Defendant."

"What do you mean, 'trying to restrain'? They were either restraining him or they weren't?"

Hervey gave David an annoyed look, "When I came in I saw them pulling his arms behind his back in order to apply handcuffs. I saw him resisting. At that stage they were 'trying to restrain' him. After a few seconds they succeeded."

"So you weren't immediately behind them when you entered the property?"

"They entered the property a few seconds before me."

"You never saw Police Constable Savage use his Taser on Mr Petford-Williams?"

"No, sir."

"Your first view was both those officers trying to apply handcuffs?"

"Yes, sir."

"Did Constable Savage still have the Taser in his hand?"

"I believe so."

"Did he have anything in his other hand or was he trying to force Mr Petford-Williams' hands behind his back."

"I never saw anything in his other hand."

"So you never saw the rifle in the hands of Mr Petford-Williams or Police Constable Savage? Indeed, the first time you saw it was when it was resting against the stairway, next to a table that had a bowl containing live cartridges?"

"Yes, sir."

"It no doubt looked to you like someone had emptied the cartridges from the rifle, making it safe and then placed the rifle against the stairs?"

Jeremy was quickly on his feet, "I don't see how the officer can answer that, it is calling for speculation."

David smiled, "I won't seek an answer to that question. Thank you, that's all officer."

He sat down whilst looking at the faces of the jury, quite content that his point had been made.

The rest of the afternoon was spent listening to Jeremy reading out witness statements in open court. These statements had been made by witnesses who had not been required to attend court to give live evidence or be questioned by either side. At just after four pm, the court adjourned for the day and David took Sara for a quick drink to a public house that was near the court. Sara had a gin and tonic and David tried the local draft beer. After they were served and had seated themselves near a window, it became obvious to David that Sara was worried about something. He looked at her kindly, "Are you ok, is your uncle's case getting you down?"

Sara looked up, "No, it's not that. I was just wondering about the spent cartridge that was found."

David looked puzzled, "I don't understand, we've always known there was a spare cartridge on the stairs. Its presence is consistent with both the prosecution and defence versions of what happened."

"No, I wasn't thinking about that one. I was wondering about the one found outside at the target range."

David looked surprised, "I don't see what the problem is with the police finding a spent cartridge at a rifle range!"

Sara nodded slightly, "There wouldn't be normally, my only concern was why was there only one cartridge. If he regularly used the range, as he says, why weren't there more of them? If he regularly cleaned up the cartridges, why was this one left?"

David nodded and tried his best not to appear condescending as he stated, "You often find in cases there are missing pieces where there's no obvious explanation. In this case, Hugh might have simply missed the cartridge case or been distracted and not picked it up. In any event, I don't think it's really going to help us discover whether this was an accident or a deliberate murder."

Sara nodded and sipped at her gin and tonic. She realised she had a lot to learn about trials but she still had a nagging doubt about this one.

CHAPTER 29

THE PATHOLOGIST

Dr Henry Roper made his way into the witness box carrying a large file of documents. It was 10:45am on Thursday. There had been a slight delay in starting, as the High Court Judge was held up in traffic on his journey from his lodgings outside Newcastle.

David watched as the noticeably confident Dr Roper set out his papers in front of him. He had never met him before, probably because David had not practised in or around Newcastle, where Dr Roper was based.

To David, he was typical of the new breed of pathologist that he now met. Younger than him, probably by twenty years, highly intelligent and not as dogmatic as the pathologists David first came across when he started as a barrister, thirty odd years ago.

Jeremy was relishing the opportunity of going through the pathology evidence. In his opinion, it was an important part of the prosecution case in a murder trial even when there was no issue as to the cause of death. It gave the prosecution the opportunity to remind the jury that a person had died and to go into minute detail about the circumstances and to emphasise that the cause of that death was the defendant.

He took Dr Roper through his impressive qualifications and then continued, "Dr Roper, your post-mortem was carried out on Saturday 20th June, the day after Mr Johns was pronounced dead."

Dr Roper looked down at his notes, "Yes, that's right. My notes state he was pronounced dead at 3am on 19th June."

"Please take us through your pathology report, starting with your findings in relation to Mr Johns' general health."

Dr Roper looked at his notes, "Mr Johns was a 59-year-old male, 1.85 metres tall, so six feet one inch, weighing 101 kilos, or 15 stone 12 lbs. Generally, he had a healthy appearance and his organs were normal, save for his liver which showed some signs of disease, suggesting he had over-indulged in alcohol throughout his life.

I have a note here of his blood reading taken on admission to hospital to match his type. It read 245 mg per 100 ml of blood, which is three times the drink driving limit in England and Wales. It could have been and probably was higher than that earlier in the night as clearly some time passed between his being shot and his arrival in hospital. His alcohol reading would have been decreasing as time passed during that period."

Jeremy quickly intervened, "Is there any suggestion that his death might have been as a result of his liver or any other part of his body being diseased or otherwise unhealthy?"

"None whatsoever. He was generally a fit man apart from the condition of his liver. His death was solely due to the bullet wound."

Jeremy nodded, "Could you please turn to page 10 of the jury bundle."

He waited whilst everyone turned to the appropriate page.

"This is a computer representation of the injury caused to the neck. I understand that it was created from photographs taken at the time of the post mortem?"

"That's right."

"Please describe the injury to us."

"After the autopsy, I was given a ballistic report which suggested that the bullet that struck the deceased, had been deflected by the lavatory door. This was in accordance with my findings. Normally a bullet fired from a short range will hit the body and cause a small entry wound and a larger exit wound as it tumbles within the body and hits its structures. There was a wound here to the neck which was in a 'teardrop' shape. This was undoubtedly because the bullet had hit the lavatory door and was deflected by that structure, causing the bullet to tumble or hit his neck at an angle.

The bullet then sliced through his jugular vein and missed the spinal cord before exiting through the back of his neck, causing a larger exit wound. There are a large series of blood vessels in this area and a great deal of damage was caused. The paramedics did a wonderful job keeping him alive as long as they did, as did the hospital staff, but, in my experience, a wound of this type was almost inevitably going to be fatal."

"So the cause of death was?"

Dr Roper looked at Jeremy as if he was stupid before he answered, "The cause of death was as a result of a single gunshot wound to the right side of the neck which cut through the jugular vein and other structures, causing severe haemorrhaging from which Mr Johns bled to death."

Jeremy had noticed the look, "Sorry Doctor, it was no doubt an obvious answer, but I did have to cover it with you."

He smiled at the witness, hiding his own irritation, "Can you tell us whether there was anything unusual about the wound?"

"Not really. There was an element of compression around the entrance wound but this is normal. When a bullet hits the skin it tends to cause compression and indentation. Once perforated, its elasticity causes the skin to recoil. In a perpendicular entry, the skin can recoil such that the entry wound is smaller than the calibre of the bullet."

He looked directly at the jury, "Contrary to what television programmes tend to suggest!"

He looked down at his notes again, "There was a greasy rim around the entrance wound, often called a 'bullet wipe', which frequently occurs with lead alloy or even dirty bullets. I suppose the only unusual feature was the presence of some minute wood splinters around the area of the entry wound which I assume came from the lavatory door."

"Can you tell us anything in particular about the exit wound, were there, for example, any wood splinters?"

"No, nor would I expect any. The minute wood splinters did not penetrate very far."

Jeremy thanked him and sat down. David just had one matter to deal with.

"Dr Roper, you were able to examine the deceased's body in detail?"

"Yes, as I've already said."

"You have described the entry and exit wounds and the cause of death with a significant degree of certainty?"

"Yes, I think so."

"Yet for all that, you cannot answer one simple question, can you? Namely, was this a deliberate or an accidental shot?"

Dr Roper looked straight at the members of the jury, "No I can't, from a pathological point of view both scenarios are equally consistent from my examination. You will have to look for other factors to answer that question."

CHAPTER 30

THE FIREARMS EXPERT

A few minutes later, Dr Christopher Brown, the prosecution's firearms expert, walked into court. He took the oath, gave his name, and then went through his extensive firearms experience with Jeremy. Having established that he was an expert, Jeremey moved onto the facts of the case.

"Dr Brown, you had an opportunity to visit the defendant's home and to examine the firearm that was seized from there, as well as to take photographs and measurements?"

"Yes, I did."

"We have produced a selection of the photographs you took. Could you open the jury bundle please at page 7? You will see that is a photograph taken inside the defendant's flat, showing the staircase and a rifle placed against it by ..."

He looked towards David and added, "... by someone. Is that the rifle that you examined?"

"Yes, it is."

"Can you tell us a little about the rifle?"

"Yes certainly, I have it here."

He produced the rifle from a large bag that had been given to him by Jeremy outside court and held it up for the jury to see. He then continued, "This is a Winchester Model 62A, 1890 rimfire rifle. As the name suggests, the first model was produced in 1890. There were subsequent adaptations, particularly in 1906, which then became the 1906 model, although effectively the rifle remained much the same.

It is a rimfire rifle, in other words, the firing pin, instead of striking the centre of the cartridge strikes the rim, causing it to ignite the propellant and forcing the bullet to fire from the barrel.

It was a popular model at Fairgrounds in both the USA and in this country at the turn of the century. It was easy to load and maintain and quite accurate. It was advertised in the USA at the time as a rifle that could also be used to kill vermin or to shoot small animals to put meat on the table."

"Thank you. Was there anything different about this rifle to a normal 1890 model?"

Dr Brown nodded, "I noticed that certain adaptations had been made to the rifle. The firing mechanism was not the original and probably dated to later than 1890 as did other parts of the rifle. As a result, I noticed that the trigger required more pressure to fire a round than would have been the case with the original model."

"Can you demonstrate that to us in court? I assume the rifle is not loaded!"

Dr Brown smiled, "No, it has been made safe but I can demonstrate how it is loaded and fired."

He took the rifle and pumped it and then pulled on the trigger and the hammer snapped into place with a loud click. It was noticeable that it required some pressure to pull the trigger.

Satisfied with the demonstration, Jeremy asked, "We will hear that, in due course, the defendant in this case was interviewed and stated this was an 'antique' firearm and therefore he considered that its possession or use was covered by the firearms legislation in this country. As an expert, are you able to assist on this point?"

Dr Brown nodded. "Yes, I believe so. The firearms legislation in this country is quite complex, I believe there are currently some 34 different Acts of Parliament dealing with it. The law is intentionally strict with severe penalties for its breach. Possession of a firearm without a firearms certificate is a serious offence. There are, however, exceptions for certain firearms such as war trophies and those that are classed as 'antiques'. These can be possessed without having a firearms certificate. 'Antique' is not defined within the legislation but is covered by a Home Office guide which refers generally to pre-1939 firearms. This, of course, is a pre-1939 firearm, but the guidance states that it does not apply to .22 rimfire rifles and it does not apply to firearms that have been extensively modified or adapted after 1939, which appears to be the case here. In any event, the exemption only applies to 'antiques' possessed as 'curiosities' or 'ornaments'. I understand that this rifle was used to fire ammunition at targets set up in the defendant's garden. In accordance with the guidance, that means it was not possessed simply as a 'curiosity or ornament'.

"Thank you doctor. So, in the circumstances, this was not an 'antique' and therefore not exempt from the firearms legislation?"

"Correct."

"Now, as you told us, you visited the defendant's home to take measurements and photographs. Why was that?"

Dr Roper nodded at the question, "It is important to go to the scene of an incident in order to better judge what occurred. It allows the expert to have a better view than by just looking at photographs and allows accurate measurements to be taken of the distances from which a firearm might have been fired and it also allows for a more accurate estimation of the trajectory of the bullet."

"In this case what did you find?"

"I started from the area of the toilet and worked backwards. I knew the height of Mr Johns, I knew he was sitting on the toilet when he was shot and I was able to estimate where his neck would have been relative to his body. I then noted that the door was quite thick and there was a bullet track. Applying a long steel rod through the hole and lining it up with the area of where the site of the wound was likely to be at the time, I was able to estimate, with a good degree of accuracy, where the bullet had originated from. My assistant then took a series of photographs of me in the position the defendant was likely to be in when the shot was fired."

"What degree of accuracy?"

"About 95%."

"And what is that figure based on?"

"There is always an element of uncertainty and we act within limits. There may be deviations in the potential tracks due to the wood or the exact position of the victim, hence my estimate is 95% accurate rather than 100%."

Jeremy nodded, "Thank you, could you now turn to pages 11-15 in the jury bundle?"

Dr Roper picked up the bundle and described each photograph in turn, "You will see that page

11 is a photograph of me in a position where the defendant would be if he had aimed a shot at the centre of the door. Pages 12 and 13 are similar positions assuming that the shot was aimed and accounting for the degree of deviation either side that I have referred to. As you will see, each position is within a few centimetres of the other."

He turned to page 14, "This photograph shows the position the defendant would have to be in if the rifle was fired from the hip. You will see that he would have to have been a step higher to make up for the distance between the hip and the shoulder which is where the rifle would have been if this was an aimed shot. It is not a practical way to fire a rifle but was included here to show the range of potential positions."

He turned to photograph 15 and raised his eyebrows slightly, no one had informed him that this photograph was going to be included in the bundle. "This is a photograph of me in a position the defendant would have to have been in if the shot was accidental. You will see it is similar to page 14, in that the position in which he would have had to be, is approximately the same."

"From your examination, are you able to assist the court with which is the most likely position he would have been in when the shot was fired?"

"No, they are all equally possible. You would have to take into account factors other than just the ballistics to determine that."

David took a full note of the answer with a noisy double underlining to emphasise the point.

Jeremy ignored David and looked down at Dr Brown's report. "Dr Brown, can I ask you to look at your conclusions at paragraph 37 of your report?"

Dr Brown looked at his report and turned to the appropriate page and read it. He then nodded, "Yes, I see that, I did conclude it was more likely to be a deliberate, aimed, shot."

Jeremy gave him a practiced patient stare, "Is there any reason then why you say today that they are equally possible?"

"I consider there are a number of possible factors in this scenario. It is true it appeared like an aimed shot because of its location and the fact that the trigger requires quite a lot of force, which is not necessarily consistent with an accident. However, I must point out that I cannot rule out that it was an accident."

David again used his pen to underline something in his notes in a most noisy and obvious way. Jeremy in turn just stared at Dr Brown in disbelief for a few seconds before remembering he was on his feet, he quickly continued, "Can you tell us what happened once the bullet was fired?"

"Yes, it hit the door, roughly at the level and position where Mr Johns' heart would have been located behind the door. The bullet was then deflected by the door."

"How can you tell that?"

"As I have said, the door was made of thick wood, English Oak I believe. We can see the track through the wood and where the bullet exited the door. It made a much larger exit hole surrounded by splinters. This was because the bullet tumbled after hitting the door meaning it left at an angle. I estimated that the door deflected the bullet upwards by about 15 cm and by 10 cm to the left hitting Mr Johns on the right hand side of his neck."

Jeremy looked down at his notes before asking, "Dr Brown, in this case we will hear that the defendant admits that he had firearms residue on his hands and clothes. Can you tell us what the significance of that is?"

"Certainly. When a firearm is discharged, the propellant fires the bullet but also gases and fine particles are discharged which we call 'firearms residue' or 'firearms discharge particles (FDRs) or 'cartridge discharge residues' (CDRs). All the terms are interchangeable.

These particles consist of both organic and inorganic material. The organic material consists of unburnt or partially burnt propellant. The inorganic material is produced by the effect of the hot gases on the bullet. When the firearm is discharged, these particles will settle on nearby objects or people. They will therefore have traces of lead, antimony or barium on their person. The person firing the gun will have such residue on their hands and arms and clothing. Persons near to the person firing will also have such residue on them, including the victim, if he is near to the weapon when it is discharged. The significance of finding firearms residue on a defendant means that he either discharged the firearm or was near to it when it was discharged.

In this case, I understand there is no issue that the defendant fired the weapon, so the presence of firearm residue has less significance. It just confirms what he admits, that he fired the rifle."

CHAPTER 31

CHALLENGING THE FIREARMS EXPERT

Jeremy thanked Dr Brown and asked him to remain where he was. David rose from the advocates bench and immediately asked, "Dr Brown, you were asked to give your expertise on whether, in your opinion, this rifle was an antique?"

"Yes, and I am firmly of the belief that it is not."

"Do assist me on this, you are not a practising lawyer are you?"

"No."

"Do you hold any legal qualifications?

"No."

"Parliament used the word 'antique' in the Firearms Act 1968 and you were giving an opinion based upon a legal interpretation of that word."

Dr Brown looked slightly uncomfortable as he replied, "It is true that I am not a lawyer but I am an expert on firearms and feel qualified to give an opinion on firearms in general."

"I don't question your expertise as a firearms expert but I think it fair to say the law on antique firearms is not clear even to a firearms expert, is it?"

Dr Brown looked questioningly at David, "I agree that it is not a straight-forward area."

"No, and, indeed, as you have dealt with the subject, you will be aware that the courts have held that it is a question of fact and not law as to whether a gun is an antique or not?"

"I believe so."

"You are presumably aware that the burden rests entirely on the prosecution to prove that a firearm is not an antique?"

"I believe so."

"And, you are no doubt aware that it is always a question for the jury to determine that fact."

"I believe so."

"Further, the Home Office guidance you referred to is just that, guidance only. It has no force of law."

"It is important guidance."

"But guidance nevertheless?"

"Yes."

David picked up a list that Sara had prepared and studied it for a few seconds, "Being an expert, you will be aware that in the Crown Courts in this country, juries have held that far more powerful weapons than this rifle were antiques, for example, in Norwich Crown Court in 2008, a 9mm Parabellum calibre Lancaster sub-machine gun made in 1940 was held to be an antique firearm. In Oxford Crown Court in 2007 ..."

Jeremy quickly intervened, "With respect to my Learned Friend, I cannot see the relevance of this line of questioning. I have been asked in due course to admit that Mr Petford-Williams pleaded guilty to possession of the rifle without possessing a firearms certificate, so there is no issue that this rifle was not an antique!"

Mr Justice Bright QC looked up from his notes and looked at David with a slight frown on his face, "Surely that must be right Mr Brant?"

David turned to the Judge and adopted his most disarming smile, "Actually, it's not! It is right Mr Petford-Williams has pleaded guilty to the possession charge because he is guilty of that offence. However, that does not mean that the rifle was not an 'antique'. As Your Lordship is aware, the antique exception only applies in law if the 'antique' was held as a curiosity or ornament, as Mr Petford-Williams was in the habit of using the rifle to fire at inanimate

301

targets in his garden, it is accepted that he did not have the antique rifle merely as a curiosity or ornament and that he had adapted it. The purpose of my cross-examination was to demonstrate that the area is complex even for lawyers and firearms experts, never mind laymen like Mr Petford-Williams. He believed the rifle was an antique and therefore did not obtain a firearms certificate. As Your Lordship knows, ignorance of the law is no defence, and he has pleaded guilty to that offence but it was important to put this matter in its proper and fair context. It was not a deliberate attempt to flout the law by Mr Petford-Williams, but done simply through a lack of knowledge. However, in the circumstances, I won't cross-examine further on this point and will move on."

David turned towards the witness watching the red-faced and clearly very annoyed prosecutor sit down. By objecting to his question, Jeremy had allowed David to make a speech and put across the reason for Hugh's plea of guilty, something he would have been unable to do at this stage if he had simply been allowed to finish his cross-examination of the witness.

Sara hid a grin as she made a note in the margin of her notebook, 'Don't object to a question unless you really are on firm ground and don't allow your opponent to make speeches during cross-examination!'

David turned back to the witness, "Dr Brown, let's move on. I note that you used steel rods and tape measures in order to carry out your investigations?"

Feeling a little more confident, Dr Brown replied, "Yes, that's right."

"As I understand it, for some years now, Firearms experts have been using more modern tools. Most experts use 3D laser scanning to recreate 3D images of the scene and to work out the zone from which a bullet was fired. Why didn't you use such methods?"

Dr Brown looked a little annoyed, "It is right that such techniques are regularly used in complex cases. However, such techniques are very expensive and time-consuming. In this case, there were financial constraints put on me by the Crown Prosecution Service. Also the firing distance was not great and I was told there was no issue that the defendant had fired the fatal shot. In those circumstances I considered that a cheaper, tried and tested method could be used."

David looked at him for a few seconds before asking, "Dr Brown, Mr Petford-Williams has been charged with murder. He admits he fired the shot but it is his case that it was a tragic accident. Using a potentially more time-consuming and potentially more expensive method could have answered that question in his favour!"

Dr Brown, reddened slightly, "I don't believe so. I don't think it would have made any difference to my conclusions."

"But it could have done?"

Dr Brown was clearly uncomfortable, "I suppose it's possible but I don't believe it to be likely."

David looked down at his notes and asked, "Earlier, in answer to my Learned Friend's question, 'From your examination, are you able to assist the court with which is the most likely position he would have been in when the shot was fired?' You answered, 'No, they are all equally possible. You would have to take into account factors other than just the ballistics to determine that.'

Do you stand by that answer now?"

Dr Brown knew he had no choice but to stand by it, he had given it under oath. "Yes, I do. There are a number of different factors here that will have played a part in addition to an examination of the scene."

"As you have told us then, any one of these photographs in the jury bundle could show the position Mr Petford-Williams was in when the shot was fired?"

"Yes."

"They are all equally likely, from what you say?"

"Yes."

"Please look at page 15 of the jury bundle."

David waited a few seconds whilst everyone opened the bundle. "Your evidence means that photograph, which would be the position he was in if he had stumbled and fired the shot, is as equally likely to have been the position he was in as any of the others we see in the jury bundle?"

"Yes."

CHAPTER 32

FURTHER EVIDENCE

The rest of Thursday was taken up by Jeremy reading out further witness statements from prosecution witnesses who had not been required to attend court. The prosecution and defence had also agreed that some admitted facts should be read out, in order to reduce the issues in the case before trial. These had included the fact that Mr Petford-Williams had firearms residue on his hands and clothing when he was arrested and also that he had pleaded guilty to the offence of possessing the rifle without having a firearms' certificate.

It was now Friday morning and a short day was expected. Mr Justice Bright QC had announced the day before that he would not be sitting after 1pm, as he had to catch an early flight back to London for an urgent meeting. No one said anything to object. No one was going to complain about finishing the week early on a Friday afternoon. It was also fortuitous for David as he had received a text message from Tatiana asking if they could meet Friday evening at about 7pm to discuss her brother's case. He wondered whether there might be a brief there for him after all.

Once the court was assembled, Jeremy announced that he was calling his last witness, Detective Sergeant Charles Bull.

Charles Bull walked slowly towards the witness box. It had been a long night with his squad celebrating the fact that one of their colleagues was taking early retirement and far too many drinks had been consumed. Still despite the fact he had a hangover, Charles Bull was an experienced policeman and he did not expect to run into any problems today.

As soon as he was sworn, and had given his name to the court, Jeremy asked him to explain what the duties of an officer in the case were. He told the jury he was in overall charge of the investigation, and of the papers and was responsible for submitting them to the Crown Prosecution Service who would decide on the appropriate charges.

Jeremy then asked him about his dealings with Hugh and he explained he interviewed him. Copies of an edited transcript of the interview were then handed out to the jury. The interview had been edited by agreement to take out repetitious questions and answers. Jeremy and Charles Bull then read out the transcript of the interview, Charles Bull taking his own part and Jeremy taking the part of Hugh.

Sara had asked David before this if he would prefer the DVD of the interview to be played as it showed how Hugh responded to the questions. David pointed out that it was not customary to show such videos or play tapes in the court. In any event, he had watched the DVD and had not liked the fact that Hugh smiled and even appeared to joke with the officer at times. It did not fit well with the picture of a man who, just a few hours earlier, had accidentally shot and killed one of his best friends.

Once the interview had been read out to the jury, Jeremy looked down at his papers and then looked at the officer. He paused as if wondering what to do, but then said, "That's all I have to ask at the moment, officer, will you wait there."

David noted the pause and wondered for a moment if Jeremy had wanted to ask something else but had thought better of it. He dismissed the thought as he turned to the witness, noticing how Charles Bull was gulping down water regularly supplied by the usher. He was fully aware what that meant.

"Officer, are you feeling all-right? I only have a few questions but I don't want you to be uncomfortable."

Charles reddened slightly as he said, "I'm fine, thank you, sir."

He put the empty glass of water down and waved away the usher who was about to refill it.

David nodded, "Good, then let me ask you one or two questions. Firstly, as you know, from the moment Hugh Petford-Williams phoned the emergency services, he has always admitted shooting Mr Johns."

"Yes, sir."

"As he made it clear in that call, it has always been his case that this was an accident."

"Yes, sir."

"He made that clear to you when you interviewed him."

"Yes, sir."

"The issue in this case therefore has always been, and remains, whether this was an accident or not?"

"I agree, sir."

"As an officer in charge it was your duty to investigate the case, both matters that further the prosecution case, but equally any matters that assist the defence?"

"That's right, sir and I believe I have."

"One of the matters you did arrange was for a firearms expert to visit the scene, examine the rifle and to prepare a report?"

"That's right, sir."

"However, instead of getting an expert who used the most modern equipment, you instructed someone who used rods and tape measures. We were told by him this was for cost reasons. Is that correct?"

"Yes, sir. He did offer to obtain the latest equipment but told us that the whole operation would be very costly because once the scans were taken he would then have technicians spend some time creating a 3D model which would then be used in court and require the use of further computer equipment to display it. We were advised by the Crown Prosecution Service that it was not needed in this case as the only issue was whether this was an accident or not."

"But using the most up to date equipment may have answered that question in favour of Mr Petford-Williams?"

"It might, but we were led to believe by Dr Brown that it would not make a difference."

"Very well, did you carry out any other investigations into Mr Petford-Williams' version of events?"

"I'm not sure what you mean, sir."

"Well, his diabetes comes to mind. Did you ever request medical records or a medical examination of Mr Petford-Williams to discover, firstly, whether he did suffer from diabetes and secondly, whether he is prone to being unsteady on his feet as a result of that condition?"

"No, I didn't."

"You are aware that the defence commissioned such a report which was served on the prosecution in advance of the trial?"

"I am, sir, I have been shown a copy by the Crown Prosecution Service."

"So you are aware that Mr Petford-Williams has suffered from diabetes for a number of years and one of the side effects has been…"

David picked up a medical report and quoted from it, '…to weaken the sensation in his legs and make him unsteady on his feet'."

"I am aware of that now."

"Very well, you can also confirm that Mr Petford-Williams pleaded guilty to possession of the rifle without having a firearms certificate, before this trial commenced?"

"Yes, sir."

"Apart from that, it is correct that he has no criminal convictions, cautions or reprimands recorded against him."

"That's right, sir."

David thanked him and sat down. Jeremy immediately rose to his feet and turned to the judge, "My Lord, I have no questions in re-examination for the officer and it was intended that he would be my last witness. However, before I close my case there is a matter of law I would ask you to deal with."

David looked at him quizzically wondering what possible matter of law could have resulted from his questioning. Mr Justice Bright QC looked similarly confused but asked the jury to retire. Once they had left the courtroom he asked Jeremy, "Well, Mr Asquith, what matter of law has arisen at this very late stage of the case?"

"I appreciate it is late and the prosecution case is about to close. Nevertheless, there is one important matter that does arise at this stage. My Learned Friend's questioning of the officer elicited that his client has no previous criminal convictions save for the possession of the firearm without a certificate. He has also sought to refer to the basis of that plea in court, namely that the defendant was ignorant of the law."

Mr Justice Bright QC nodded, "Yes, and unless you are able to persuade me otherwise, I shall give a modified good character direction to the jury in due course telling them to treat him as a man of good character save for the firearms offence."

312

"That is the point My Lord. Now that the defence have raised this issue in this way, I seek to rely on a witness statement that has hitherto been in the 'unused' statements. It is a statement of Rosemary Petford-Williams and deals with the earlier incident that took place in October 2014. She makes it quite clear that she believed the defendant deliberately shot at Mr Johns on that occasion, but missed. As the defence are raising good character as an issue in this case, I submit that statement should be read to the jury as a hearsay statement under the provisions of the Criminal Justice Act 2003, on the basis that, 'it is in the interests of justice that it be adduced to put in context, the modified good character direction you are likely to give.'"

The judge turned to David, "I presume that you object Mr Brant?"

David rose to acknowledge him, "I do My Lord on a number of grounds. Firstly, this is too late. The prosecution have known about this statement for months and no attempt has been made to issue either a bad character notice or a hearsay notice to adduce it. Secondly, it is made by Mr Petford-Williams' wife. In law she is not a compellable witness against him because she is his wife and she cannot be forced to give evidence in this court. Therefore, the prosecution could not force her to give this evidence and should not seek to go behind a centuries old common law protection by seeking to read her statement. That is particularly so in such a serious matter as a murder case. I ought to add that Rosemary Petford-Williams has refused to give evidence for either the prosecution or the defence so I will not be in any position to ask her questions about this statement. In all those circumstances I suggest it will not be in the 'interests of justice' to admit this evidence at this very late stage."

The Judge turned to Jeremy, "What do you say to that, Mr Asquith?"

Jeremy put on his most serious expression to deal with the enquiry, "Of course, my Learned Friend is quite correct, I could not force Mrs Petford-Williams to give evidence against her husband, nor would I wish to do so, which is why I make an application to read her statement under the hearsay provisions of the Criminal Justice Act 2003. The defence have chosen to emphasise the defendant's lack of previous convictions. I only seek to put that in context by pointing out that on one previous occasion a witness who was closer to him than anyone could be, saw him use the rifle with what appeared to be murderous intent. It is true that the defence is denied the opportunity to cross-examine the witness, but that can easily be remedied if the defendant chooses to give evidence about this matter and tells the jury what his intent actually was. It should also be noted that the prosecution is denied the opportunity of calling this evidence live, and therefore the forceful impact that would have. I submit that in the interests of justice the prosecution should be allowed to adduce this evidence, albeit at this late stage."

Mr Justice Bright QC thought for a few minutes before stating, "I agree, in view of timing constraints I will give my detailed ruling on Monday, but Mr Asquith I rule that you can read the statement to the jury. I suggest you do that on Monday, there seems little point in having them back into court just to hear one statement read to them. Unless anyone objects, I shall tell the usher to release them until Monday at 10:30am."

David looked straight at his grinning opponent. He was annoyed because it was obvious to him that Jeremy had deliberately waited until the last moment in the prosecution case to make this application. At the same time, and slightly ironically, he had a renewed respect for him and made a mental note to watch closely when Jeremy cross-examined Hugh.

By successfully making this application at the end of the prosecution case he had taken away an important option from Hugh. Hugh now had no real choice in the matter. He would have to give evidence in his own defence and be cross-examined by a very competent prosecutor!

CHAPTER 33

A NEW CASE?

As usual, Sara decided to spend the weekend with her parents who lived nearby, whilst David made his way to Newcastle train station for the four-hour journey back to London.

It felt good to finish early but he was slightly apprehensive at the thought of meeting Tatiana again and the inevitable resulting comments from Wendy. Just to avoid any misunderstandings and prying eyes, he had arranged to meet Tatiana in the wine bar 'Vino Veritas' rather than 'Briefs' as it was further away from chambers.

At 6:55pm, he walked into the crowded wine bar and saw Tatiana seated alone at a table by the window. She had a quarter full flute of champagne in front of her. She saw him and waved and then downed the contents of her glass, David walked across to join her.

"Hello, David!" she said, greeting him with a particularly attractive smile.

David returned the greeting and sat down. Almost immediately, a young waitress appeared and asked them if they wanted anything. David ordered a glass of the house claret, whilst

Tatiana stared at the drinks menu and ordered a glass of the most expensive champagne. David immediately knew it was going to be an expensive night again!

As they sat waiting for their drinks to arrive, Tatiana spoke to him in her most seductive voice, "David, I am so grateful that you agreed to meet me tonight. I do not know what I would do without you as a friend."

He smiled, waiting for the inevitable punchline.

"I wanted to see you about my brother David. I am afraid he has fled the country. We have no idea where he has gone. We all believe that he has returned to Russia and is staying with friends."

David nodded, it made sense to him as he recalled that Russia would not extradite its own citizens to face trial in a foreign country. His personal thought was, 'Oh well, there goes that brief!', but obviously he chose to say something sympathetic, "I'm sorry to hear that Tatiana, it must be a great strain for you and your family."

She thrust her right hand out across the table and grabbed his right hand, "It is David, it has been an intolerable strain for all of us, particularly me!"

He felt the need to ask, "Why particularly you?"

"The police came to see me to talk about him. They seized my laptop computer 'to interrogate it' they said."

David looked puzzled, "Why did they seize your laptop, you have nothing to do with your brother's involvement in all this?"

The drinks arrived and Tatiana took a large sip of champagne before replying. "That's what I'm worried about David and why I wanted to see you. I'm worried about getting into trouble!"

"But why?"

"My brother used to visit me in my flat and used my laptop computer on a few occasions when he was there. He used to say I got a far better and faster internet signal than he did in his flat."

David watched her carefully as he asked, "Did you tell the police about this?"

"No, I was too scared. I didn't want to be arrested."

"Tatiana, you are undoubtedly aware that computer hard drives and the internet leave a trail each time they are used. If you have nothing to do with this, it's in your interests to tell the police sooner, rather than later, that your brother used your laptop."

She took another long sip of the champagne almost finishing the glass. David watched her and immediately wondered about his credit card allowances. He no longer had a reserve card! Perhaps he should try and extend his allowance on his remaining card before the bill arrived?

"David, I am worried about this and my involvement in my brother's companies."

David took a sip of his own wine before replying slowly, "What involvement?"

He noticed as Tatiana turned ashen before replying, "Anton asked me to sign some papers for him once and to become a Company Secretary for one of his companies. He told me it was a speculative venture and he wanted to keep it in the family rather than ask some stranger to become involved."

"What was the name of the company?"

"I believe it was called, SEAL, Speculative Emergency Acquisitions Limited."

David nodded, he recalled the company name from when he had a consultation with Anton. He did not recall Anton making any mention of Tatiana being involved. He had a thought and asked her, "Did you sign in your own name?"

She was looking into her empty glass now so David called over the waitress and ordered a bottle of the champagne. He decided his credit cards, battered as they were from holidays expenses, an engagement ring and spending a week in Newcastle, could extend to an expensive bottle of champagne. After all, he felt from the way this conversation was going, there was a potential big fraud brief coming his way!

Tatiana did not wait for the bottle to arrive before answering his question. "I did sign in my own name but ..."

David looked at her closely as she carried on.

"... I signed in my married name, Tatiana Luckov because that is the name on my passport. Do you think I will get into trouble?"

David put his hand across the table to hold hers. He had a mixture of emotions. He felt sorry for her but relished the idea of receiving a good fraud brief. He gave her a reassuring look as he replied, "Not if I can help it."

CHAPTER 34

THE DEFENCE CASE

It was Monday, and a sunny October morning in Newcastle. David smiled to himself as he walked into the court building. 'Sunny', 'October' and 'Newcastle' were not words he had ever expected to put together in the same sentence.

He had spent the rest of the previous Friday night and Saturday with Wendy and after a ropey start had a good weekend. His opening gambit was to bring a bottle of vintage champagne home for them on Friday night, announcing at the same time that he had secured a good banking fraud case for hopefully late 2016 or early 2017. Wendy had consumed a whole glass of champagne before he was forced to mention it was for Tatiana. He noticed how she continued drinking and chatting with hardly a pause, although within a short time she had managed to prise from him that he had met Tatiana for a drink.

He admired the way she convincingly pretended that this was of no concern to her whatsoever, although after another couple of glasses she could not resist saying, "Poor little Tatiana, it looks like she's got herself into hot water, I hope she doesn't bring anyone down with her!"

The rest of the weekend passed without another reference to Tatiana, a fact that relieved David immensely.

On Sunday, he travelled north to Newcastle and stayed in his usual hotel, receiving a friendly greeting from the pretty young receptionist. He was beginning to like Newcastle. The hotel was comfortable with a good sized room overlooking the river and equally important, it was reasonably priced.

His evening was slightly disturbed when he received a call from Hugh's solicitor, Nick Mark. It was to inform him that, on Saturday night Nick had been out in Jesmond with his wife, when he had seen Walter Doyle arm in arm with Rosemary Petford-Williams going into the same restaurant. Having watched them together for approaching an hour, it looked to him like they were very close and probably having an affair.

Nick wanted to know whether David could make any use of the information. David thanked him but dismissed the idea. He could ask for Walter to be re-called to the witness box and put to him what Nick had seen. It might explain his apparent bias against Hugh. However, Walter would probably just deny it, saying he had taken her out as a friend for Hugh's sake. It would look to the jury to be a late and desperate attempt by the defence to discredit the prosecution witness. In any event, Hugh was about to give evidence and David was not sure how this news might affect him and the quality of the evidence he was about to give.

At 10:30am, Mr Justice Bright QC gave his ruling on the prosecution application to adduce Rosemary's statement. David told Sara to take a full note as he had already decided that, whatever was said in the judgment, it would probably form an arguable ground of appeal in the event of Hugh being convicted.

At 10:45am, the jury filed into court and, once they were seated, Jeremy announced that he had one final statement to read. He then read out the two-page statement from Rosemary Petford-Williams. David watched as most of the jury members looked towards Hugh when Jeremy read out that his wife thought he intended to kill Johns when he fired the rifle back in October 2014.

Once he had finished reading the statement, Jeremy announced that the prosecution case was now closed. David then stood and told the jury that he was going to call Hugh to give evidence.

David waited as the prison officers let Hugh out of the dock and he made his way towards the witness box, followed closely by one of the guards, a burly individual in his early forties with a short sleeved shirt displaying his tattoo laden arms.

No one else seemed to look at the guard though. All eyes in the court were focussing on Hugh. It was clear to all that he had trouble walking, although David was concerned he might be overdoing it when he appeared to stumble just before reaching the witness box.

Hugh was sworn and gave his name. David then dealt with a few background matters covering; Hugh's early life, his good character and his employment record.

"I'd like to ask you now about the rifle Mr Petford-Williams. We have heard from an expert that it is a Model 62A, 1890 Winchester pump action .22 rimfire rifle. Please tell the jury when you acquired it."

Hugh nodded, "Of course. It was probably about ten years or so ago now. I purchased it from an Antique dealer in Newcastle. It wasn't in working order and was over a hundred years old. I thought it was an antique and, as I was aware that antiques were exempt from the Firearms Acts, I kept it and did not apply for a Firearms Licence."

"We know that it was in working order the night Mr Johns died. How did it get into that state?"

"I've always had an interest in mechanical things. I decided to acquire parts for the rifle in order to make it work."

"Why?"

"I just wanted to see it in working order and use it for firing at targets I set up in my garden."

"Where did you acquire the parts from?"

"From a number of places. Sometimes I would see adverts in magazines, other times I saw parts in junk shops, places like that."

"So you were able to repair the rifle and put it in working order?"

"Yes."

"Did you not think then that you might need a firearms certificate?"

"No, I still considered that it was an antique."

"At some stage, you obtained ammunition for the rifle?"

"Yes, a friend obtained a hundred rounds for me."

"Can you tell us who that was?"

"No, I realise now it's an offence, I'm not going to get him into trouble."

"Again, did you consider that you needed a firearms certificate to possess the ammunition?"

"Certainly not. I thought that if the rifle was exempt, the ammunition would be."

"Mr Petford-Williams, I want to deal now with your home. We have heard when your interview was read out in court, that you told the police that you inherited the family home but due to the need to pay inheritance tax you had to convert it into four flats and sell off three of them.

We have also heard that you sold the three flats to; Dr Jeffries and Mrs Jeffries, Mr and Mrs Payne and finally William Johns. Please tell the court your dealings with them all, after you became neighbours?"

"I rarely saw the Jeffries and the Paynes and was never friends with any of them. The most I ever said was a quick 'Hello' to them. Johns was different. I met him in a local public house and we began chatting and found that we had a lot in common. He had been in the RAF and fought in the Falklands War. He was interested in military history, like me, and we would discuss various wars, campaigns and battles. I eventually invited him back to my home and he soon became a frequent visitor."

"How close was your friendship?"

"At first, very close." He looked down for a moment before continuing, "I confess that I don't make friends easily. I am always suspicious of the motives of people who want to be friends with complete strangers, but Johns never fell into that category. I never had any problems with him, at least not until I found him in bed with Rosemary!"

"Tell us what happened."

"It was in October 2014, I had just discovered that my niece, Sara," he looked at her for a second, "had been offered a training contract as a barrister in London."

David interrupted, "You mean a pupillage?"

Hugh looked slightly irritated at the interruption. An expression that was not missed by Jeremy.

"Yes, a pupillage or whatever you call a training contract for barristers!" He raised his eyes to the ceiling of the court room before continuing. "Anyway, Johns came round and joined Rosemary and I for a few glasses of wine."

"Are you close to your niece?"

"I regret not, I have seen very little of her over the years."

"So why celebrate her becoming a pupil barrister?"

Hugh paused for a few seconds, "I suppose the reality was we would have found something to 'celebrate' that night anyway. It was usual then to meet Johns for a drink."

"The court has heard that you suffer from diabetes. How long have you suffered with that condition?"

Hugh looked down at his feet as if embarrassed, "About five years now."

"What has been the effect on your health?"

"At first it was little problems but soon it began to have a major effect on my system. I found I had difficulty walking, finding it increasingly painful. Then I found that I could no longer maintain an erection for any period of time. Eventually, I found I could not even obtain an erection."

Hugh's embarrassment seemed to have completely disappeared as one of the older female jurors on the front row of the jury looked away as he said this. Hugh carried on, oblivious to her embarrassment, "Rosemary and I always had a regular and fulfilling sex life, but I regret that I became unable to perform and satisfy her."

"Did you have this condition in October 2014?"

"Yes. I had tried different things. I even tried a scrotal ring." He paused looking at the vacant expressions of some jurors, "It's a ring that is held in place around the scrotum and keeps the blood from flowing back from the penis. Supposedly it allows you to maintain a firm erection."

The female juror was now turning a deep shade of red. Hugh continued without noticing, "I even took Viagra, but it did not work and made me ill."

David had noticed the juror's expression and decided to move on just in case Hugh was going to regale them with any other experiments he had carried out.

"On this occasion, in October 2014, did you leave Rosemary and Mr Johns together?"

"I did, I went to my club to meet a few friends for a drink. I would frequently visit my club. I would walk there for the exercise, even though the walk became increasingly painful."

"Did you believe anything would happen between Mr Johns and Rosemary?"

"Certainly not! She was my wife and he was my friend."

"What were they like when you left your home?"

"They seemed very happy. They were chatting and laughing."

"Was there anything unusual in this?"

"No, they always got on very well. Rosemary liked Johns a lot."

"What happened?"

"I went to the club and met Walter and Tim and had a few double whiskies with them. I then walked home."

"How far away was the club from your home?"

"It was about five hundred yards."

"How long would that take you to walk."

"I am a little slow, so I suppose about eight to ten minutes."

David looked over at the jury and noted that all were listening intently now. He turned back and asked, "What happened when you got home?"

"I walked into the flat and immediately became aware of Rosemary giggling. It was obvious they were both in the downstairs bedroom. I heard some weird grunting sound from Johns. I knew what was happening. I felt terribly betrayed by both of them and I was angry. I wondered whether to quickly break in on them but then I had a different idea. I decided to go upstairs and get my rifle and come down and scare both of them. I went upstairs to my bedroom, as quickly as I could, got my rifle from the rear of the wardrobe, loaded it and went back downstairs."

"Did you say anything to them at this stage?"

"Not until I kicked the bedroom door in downstairs. They were having sexual intercourse when I burst in. I could see his naked backside going up and down between her legs and I could hear her moaning. I shouted at them both to stop and I called him a bastard."

"What did they do?"

"He got off her, took one look at me and laughed! He looked at the rifle and said, something like, 'Finally, Hugh, something you can get up!' Rosemary then laughed as well. I have never felt so hurt in my life. I confess I saw red. I aimed the rifle just three inches away from his head to his right and fired twice into the pillow. He stopped laughing immediately!"

Hugh could not resist smiling. David quickly asked, "We have all heard your wife's statement read out. Did you intend to hurt him?"

Hugh was silent for a second, adopting a look of real betrayal, he then answered sharply, "Of course not. If I wanted to hurt him I would have shot at his arms, legs or torso. If I had wanted to kill him, I would have shot at his head or heart. I wanted to scare him and I did. They both shut up."

"How did this situation end?"

"Rosemary begged me to leave the room and go to the kitchen so we could talk. I eventually agreed and we all went to the kitchen. She insisted we open some more wine and all have a drink together. We did."

"Did you discuss what had just happened?"

"Yes. It was a difficult conversation!"

"What was said?"

"I remember that Rosemary was affectionate. She touched my hand and told me how much she loved me. Johns was quiet throughout it all. She told me how much she wished we could continue to have a fulfilling sex life but it simply wasn't possible anymore. She told me that Johns was just a friend and that it was only sex for both of them and was not a threat to our relationship. She said she would like it to continue, but only with my permission."

"Did you give your permission?"

"Not immediately, but after a few days I relented."

"Whose idea was it to tie the pink silk ribbon round the bedroom door handle?"

"That was Rosemary's."

"How often did this happen?"

"Every couple of weeks."

"How did you feel about this?"

"I didn't like it. What man would? But I had to think of Rosemary's needs and I decided I would prefer to know who she was having sexual relations with rather than her going off with some stranger."

"Were you able to deal with this new arrangement?"

"I didn't like it but I had to learn to deal with it."

"We have heard from the witness, Timothy Granger, that in February you went to the club and appeared to be really upset. He states you said something about Mr Johns to the effect, 'I'd like to shoot that bastard and I would too, if it wasn't for the fact Rosemary likes him so much!'

Did you say that?"

"Yes I did."

"Did you mean it?"

"No it was just talk, I was upset and annoyed, I knew they would be in the house having sex at that time as I had tied the ribbon on the door handle of the spare room. I was annoyed, but I didn't mean anything by it."

David looked down at Hugh's proof of evidence that he held in front of him. He decided to move on to the day of Johns' shooting.

"Mr Petford-Williams let us move on to 18th June of this year. We know that you were with Mr Johns in your home that day. Why was that?"

"As I have said, we both had an interest in military history. It was the two hundredth anniversary of the Battle of Waterloo, it seemed a perfect time to meet up and have a toast to Wellington's victory."

"What time did you meet that night?"

"It was probably about 6:30pm."

"What did you consume?"

"We all drank red wine. I bought some half decent litre bottles of Bulgarian Cabernet Sauvignon. I didn't consider it appropriate to drink French wine that day!"

David wondered for a moment what half decent Bulgarian wine would come in litre bottles but let it pass and asked, "How were you all that evening, were there any arguments?"

"Disagreements, not arguments. We disagreed on why Napoleon lost the battle."

David smiled, "Sorry, I meant to ask whether you and Mr Johns fell out over anything?"

"No, not at all. It was a convivial evening. We all drank a great deal but that wasn't unusual."

"We know that you went to your club that night. Why was that?"

"I always like to go to my club if I can. I like to take some exercise and the short walk takes a lot of effort for me and I assume must be good for my system."

"Did you place a red silk ribbon on the spare bedroom door?"

"No, I did not, I wasn't going for long. They knew the rules."

David hesitated a second before asking the next question, he was not too happy with some of Hugh's answers, nor the tone he was adopting.

"At what time did you go to the club?"

"It was about 9pm."

"So at your usual pace you would have arrived there some time around 9:10pm?"

"Something like that."

Mr Granger and Mr Doyle suggest that you seemed tense that night. Were you tense?"

"No more than usual. It was probably the drink. I may have been affected by it because I'd probably had a bit more than I usually do before going to the club."

"We have heard that you arrived and had a couple of drinks with your friends, Tim and Walter."

"Yes, that's right."

"Mr Granger gave evidence that, after you had a couple of drinks, you said, 'I have to get back you never know what those two might get up to in my absence and I might need to put a stop to it!' Did you say that or anything like it?"

"I did."

"Why did you say it?"

"It was a personal joke. Tim and Walter did not know that often when I left the flat, Johns and Rosemary would be having sexual intercourse. This night, because I had not tied the ribbon onto the door handle, I did not expect them to be doing anything. I was really joking to myself."

"Do you recall what time you left the club?"

"Yes, it probably was around 9:45pm."

"So, you would have reached home around 9:55pm?"

"About that."

"When did you realise that Mr Johns and your wife were in the spare bedroom?"

"As soon as I opened the front door.

"Did you say anything?"

"I can't recall, I may have said something."

"Your neighbours state they heard words to the effect, 'I'm going to kill you, you bastard.' Did you say that?"

"I may have done but I don't recall saying it."

"Could anyone else have said it or anything like it?"

Hugh gave a firm, "No!" in response.

"Can you recall saying anything?"

"No, not really. I just remember going upstairs to collect my rifle. I had scared Johns the first time in October, I wanted to scare him again."

"Did you load the rifle?"

"Yes, there was already a magazine with bullets in it, I just put the magazine in and cocked the rifle which put a bullet in the chamber. I then made my way downstairs."

"What happened then?"

"It was an accident. I had my finger covering the trigger. I had the rifle in one hand pointing in front of me. I came down the stairs and stumbled. I grabbed at the rifle and pulled the trigger accidentally. It must have been pointing at the lavatory door and the bullet went through and hit Johns."

"Did you know he was in the lavatory?"

"No, I did not."

"When did you realise he was?"

"It was when the blood started to come out from under the door. At first, it was a trickle, then it started to flow quickly."

"What did you do?"

"I kicked the door open and saw Johns there on the floor, bleeding badly from a wound in his neck. I shouted out for Rosemary to get a towel to stop the bleeding."

"Did she do that?"

"Yes."

"What did you do?"

"I ejected the bullets from the rifle, I didn't want any more accidents, and then I placed it against the stairs. I then went to the phone and dialled 999 and asked for the ambulance and the police."

"What did you do then?"

"I told Rosemary to put the towel to his neck and apply pressure to try and stop the bleeding. I then went outside to direct the ambulance to the address so they could help Johns as soon as possible."

"We have heard that the paramedics arrived first and then the police. Is that how you recall it?"

Hugh's demeanour clearly changed. "Yes, I directed the paramedics to Johns and they took over from Rosemary. The police then arrived.

"What did they do?"

"I was told to get on the 'fucking floor'. Before I had a chance to do anything, they pounced and applied a Taser to me. I have never felt such excruciating pain before."

David nodded as he asked, "The police officers say you were still carrying the rifle. Is there any truth in that?"

"Absolutely not. I had put the rifle by the stairs before the paramedics arrived."

"Did you do anything that the police may have construed as threatening?"

"No, I did not. I had no opportunity to do anything."

"Would you have if you could?"

"Certainly not. I called them!"

"You were arrested and taken to the police station where you were later interviewed?"

"Yes."

"We have heard those interviews read out. Were the contents true?"

"Yes, absolutely."

"Mr Petford-Williams, the prosecution has charged you with the offence of murder. It is alleged that you deliberately shot Mr Johns intending to either kill him, or at least to cause him really serious injury. Is there any truth in that allegation?"

"None whatsoever! Of course I was annoyed when I found that Johns and Rosemary had betrayed me and broken our agreement. I felt they were rubbing my face in it. However, Johns was my friend. Yes, I wanted to scare him but I never intended to hurt him. I never knew he was in the lavatory that day. I stumbled on the stairs and the rifle accidentally fired. It was a tragic accident."

He paused before adding, "It is something I will regret for the rest of my life."

CHAPTER 35

A TESTING TIME FOR HUGH

Jeremy stood up and looked directly at the jury rather than at Hugh, "Do you love your wife?"

Hugh looked surprised and clearly annoyed at what was a personal question, but he answered quickly, "Of course I do, but I don't see what that has to do with anything!"

Jeremy ignored the response and asked, "You and your wife have been together for many years."

"Yes."

"You cannot imagine a life without her?"

"No."

"This situation you found yourself in must have been intolerable?"

"It was difficult, as I explained."

"Had you got used to the idea that they would have sexual intercourse together, albeit with your permission?"

"Yes, I had."

"However, you couldn't stand the idea that they would have intercourse without your permission?"

"No, of course not."

"No doubt you were really angry that night when you found them having sexual intercourse without your permission?"

"I was."

"That's why you got the rifle?"

"It is."

"And that's why you killed him!"

Hugh paused, "No, as I have already said, it wasn't like that. I didn't intend to shoot him. I intended to scare him with the rifle."

Jeremy paused for a few seconds before continuing, "Let's look at that statement carefully. You knew this was a powerful gun?"

"No, I didn't. I didn't think it was that powerful."

"Really?"

"Yes, really."

"You had set up a target range in your garden?"

"Yes."

"You had put bales all around so that no shots would travel outside the range?"

"Yes, that was for safety against ricochets and the like."

"You made the bales doubly thick at the end of the range to prevent stray shots?"

"Yes."

"You must have realised how powerful the gun was if you thought it necessary to double up the bales of hay at the end of the range!"

Hugh was quiet for a second before answering. "It was a precaution, nothing more."

Jeremy took the rifle in his hands. "This is a powerful rifle, capable of killing vermin, small animals and, as we now know, it is capable of being fired through a thick English oak door and killing a human being!"

Hugh momentarily looked down at his shoes, "Yes."

"You knew this wasn't an antique didn't you?"

"No."

"You knew you should have a Firearms Certificate but you never even bothered to apply for one?"

"I didn't think I needed one."

"Come now, you are very proficient with firearms aren't you?"

"I wouldn't say so!"

"Please, Mr Petford-Williams, do not be so modest. You have told us you were able to convert this de-activated old rifle into a working one?"

"I don't think it was de-activated, it just didn't work."

"I'm sorry, what is the difference?"

"De-activated suggests it has been deliberately converted so it will not fire. That was not the case here. It was simply broken."

Jeremy smirked as he replied, "I accept your superior knowledge of firearms!"

Hugh suddenly realised where this was going. "I'm not an expert."

"You certainly know a great deal about rifles. You were able to 're-activate' or if you prefer, repair a broken rifle."

"I relied on a few magazines and obtained the necessary parts."

"Magazines? I presume these were firearms magazines?"

"I believe so."

"Where else would you find any reference to re-activating or fixing a firearm than in a firearm's magazine?"

"I don't know."

"Did you regularly buy firearms magazines?"

"I wouldn't say regularly."

Jeremy looked at a schedule of prosecution exhibits that the police had prepared. "I see that 57 firearms magazines were found at your home in the cellar."

"I don't know the number."

"It was a large number?"

"I suppose so, but they were obtained over several years."

"And those magazines contain references to the law on firearms don't they?"

"I have not studied them in great detail."

"Why buy them then? I suggest you have studied them and you have far more knowledge about firearms than you would have this jury believe."

"I deny that."

Jeremy looked towards the jury and was happy to see a few smiles. He turned back to Hugh, "Let's move on to that night in October when you accept that you discharged this rifle in the direction of Mr Johns."

"I never discharged it in his direction."

"Oh, but you did Mr Petford-Williams! On your own admission you placed two bullets into the pillow he was lying on. Indeed, according to your wife's statement, you deliberately fired at him!"

"I did not."

"Is your wife a liar?"

"No." He paused, "But she can make mistakes like everyone."

"She believed you deliberately aimed at Mr Johns."

"That's nonsense. If I had deliberately aimed at him, he would have died."

Jeremy waited for that statement to be considered by the jury before he added, "Like you did on 18th June of this year?"

Hugh was clearly getting annoyed at the questioning, "I have already told you several times that it was an accident."

"In October of last year, you discharged a rifle into the pillow that Mr Johns was lying on. You wanted to kill him, didn't you?"

Hugh was turning redder with each minute, "Mr Asquith, if I had wanted to kill him from that range I would not have missed once, never mind twice!"

"Very well, assuming for the moment you are telling the truth and you didn't intend to shoot him on that occasion, it was a terribly dangerous thing to do, wasn't it?"

"No, I knew I wouldn't hit him. I aimed carefully and missed by inches."

"What if he had moved his head suddenly?"

"I would still have missed."

Jeremy nodded before adding, "Of course, we will never know, will we and we cannot ask Mr Johns?"

"I aimed to hit the pillow, he was not going to move suddenly. I would not have fired if he did."

"You could never have known if he was going to move at the same time as you pulled the trigger could you?"

"I didn't intend to kill him and I didn't hit him, I simply intended to scare him and I did."

Jeremy picked the rifle up from the bench in front of him, "Where did you keep this rifle?"

Hugh was clearly having some difficulty being patient with the questioning and replied curtly, "As I've said already, I kept it upstairs in my bedroom, in the wardrobe."

"Did you keep it loaded?"

"Of course not."

"Why?"

Hugh raised his eyebrows and looked up towards the ceiling, "That would be ridiculously dangerous."

Jeremy smiled, "So it was obvious to you that loading this rifle and presumably carrying it around, could lead to an accidental discharge with potentially fatal consequences?"

"Of course."

"And, according to you, that is exactly what you did on 18th June of this year?"

Hugh was silent, so Jeremy continued, "You loaded a firearm, carried it downstairs knowing how dangerous this was, and fully aware that an accidental discharge could lead to fatal consequences?"

"Yes."

"And yet, knowing all that, you still went downstairs with this loaded firearm?"

"Yes."

"Let me ask you a few questions about that night. You have already said that the situation was intolerable. Sharing your wife in this intimate way?"

Hugh's complexion had changed back to the greyish white of a prison pallor but now he began to redden again slightly as he replied, "Yes, although I was not sharing her as such.

"That night you had not granted them permission to have sexual intercourse?"

"It wasn't like that."

"I'm sorry, I thought that was exactly what it was like. You would place the red ribbon on the door and that was the sign that you permitted them to have sexual intercourse?"

"Yes, but it was not really permission, it was more of a ..."

"More of a ...?"

"Being resigned to it."

Jeremy nodded before continuing, "I'm sorry, I am sure we all understand, it was a case of being resigned to it. Of course that presumably means you were incensed when you returned and discovered they had breached your agreement?"

"I was unhappy."

"You were more than unhappy. You told us you saw 'red' the first time this happened. Now that you had come to an arrangement with them and they still breached it, you must have seen 'red' again?"

"I did."

"On this occasion, it must have been worse than the first time, they had flagrantly breached your agreement?"

"It was worse, I was incensed."

"So you decided to kill Mr Johns?"

"No, I decided to scare him."

"But that had not worked the first time. Although no doubt he was scared when two bullets ripped into the pillow he was resting on, just inches away from his head, he had still breached his agreement with you. No doubt you wanted a more permanent solution this time?"

"That's not right. I wasn't thinking, I was seeing red, I was angry and annoyed. I went upstairs to get my rifle and then I stumbled on the stairs and discharged it accidentally."

"No, Mr Petford-Williams, that is not what happened. You went upstairs to get your rifle to kill Mr Johns, or at least to cause him a serious injury?"

"No, Mr Asquith. I did not."

"You even told him what you were going to do when you shouted, 'I'm going to kill you, you bastard', and then, as you had just threatened, you killed him."

"No, it was an accident."

Jeremy picked up the rifle, "An accident Mr Petford-Williams?"

"Yes, an accident."

"We have seen the firearms expert give evidence in this case. Because of your modifications, this rifle requires more pressure on the trigger to discharge a bullet than would normally be the case."

"Yes I know that."

"I suggest you could not accidentally discharge it by stumbling."

Hugh looked at the jury before answering impatiently, "But that is what happened."

"Let me ask you to take the rifle and demonstrate this accident to us."

David rose to his feet, "I do object to this request. Mr Asquith is asking Mr Petford-Williams to recreate an 'accident' and of course, by its very nature, he will not be able to recreate an accident, an unintended occurrence. In any event, the situation in this courtroom is wholly different to that occurring on the stairs in Mr Petford-Williams's home on the evening of 18th June 2015!"

Mr Justice Bright thought for a few seconds, "No I will allow the demonstration, I consider it is relevant although I have no doubt the jury will have your comments in mind Mr Brant."

David sat down, he had never expected his objection to succeed but at least he had been able to make his points to the jury before the demonstration was carried out. In any event, he might be unnecessarily concerned, he had warned Hugh that he might be asked to demonstrate what happened and Hugh had assured him he would be able to.

The usher passed the rifle to Hugh who pumped the mechanism causing the hammer to fall backwards and the trigger to move forwards.

Jeremy looked at the jury and then at Hugh, "Mr Petford-Williams, will you now place the rifle in your right hand in the position it was in as you say you came down the stairs that night and pull the trigger when it is convenient for you to do so?"

Hugh placed the rifle in his right hand and placed his finger on the trigger and then held the barrel in his left hand. Jeremy immediately asked, "Did you have your finger on the trigger as you descended the stairs?"

Hugh looked up, "Yes, it is the easiest way to carry it."

"And did you have your left hand under the barrel?"

Hugh hesitated, "I'm not sure."

"You told us earlier that, 'I had the rifle in one hand pointing in front of me.' Surely that would be the way you carried the rifle downstairs. No doubt you would have held the bannister coming down stairs in order to steady yourself?"

Hugh nodded, "I suppose so."

Hugh let go of the barrel and now had the rifle in his right hand.

Jeremy then asked, "Could you demonstrate how the accident occurred?"

Hugh pulled on the trigger but on his first try he failed to discharge the hammer. He steadied himself and this time succeeded.

Jeremy nodded, "I see you had difficulty recreating the 'accident'. I suggest that is because there was no 'accident'. It was a deliberate act of shooting after you had taken aim at the toilet door?"

"No that's not right. I'm a little nervous and as Mr Brant has said, it is not easy trying to recreate an accident."

"As we saw, Mr Petford-Williams, as we saw!"

Hugh ignored the comment as Jeremy asked him to give the rifle back to the usher. David expected him to say, 'We don't want any accidents do we', but he resisted the temptation.

Jeremy took the jury bundle in his hands and turned to page 7, the photograph of the rifle by the stairs.

"Would you look at page 7 of the jury bundle please?"

Everyone in court with access to a jury bundle turned to page 7.

"Mr Petford-Williams, this is where you say you placed the rifle after you discovered you had shot Mr Johns?"

"Yes."

"According to your evidence, you realised you had shot him when you saw a trickle of blood flowing under the bathroom door?"

"Yes."

"This soon became a stream of blood and you kicked the toilet door open?"

"Yes."

"You must have seen the terrible state that Mr Johns was in. No doubt it looked to you that he couldn't be saved?"

"Yes."

"You then ejected the bullets from your rifle and placed it by the stairs."

"Yes."

"If your intention was just to scare him, why did you need to put more than one bullet in the rifle?"

Hugh hesitated before answering, "I wasn't really thinking straight at the time."

"You told us earlier that you had a magazine with bullets already in it. How many bullets?"

"I don't know, I think ten."

"You shot one and then emptied the gun and eight more were found so presumably the magazine only contained nine bullets?"

"Yes, it must have been nine."

Jeremy shrugged and continued, "You have heard the evidence of Police Constables Savage and Rimmer. They state that you had the rifle in your hands when they came into the property. PC Savage used the Taser on you and then he placed the rifle there, as we see in the picture. That's what happened isn't it?"

"No."

"They're lying then?"

"Yes they are, no doubt covering up for Savage's unlawfully electrocuting me!"

"Mr Petford-Williams, I suggest to you that what happened that night was that you came home and were surprised to find your wife and your friend having sexual intercourse together, in breach of your agreement?"

"Yes, as I have already said."

"It was bad enough they were having sexual intercourse with your permission, but it was wholly unacceptable to you that they were doing so in breach of your agreement?"

"Yes, as I have already said."

"That so incensed you that you 'saw red' as you say and cried out that you were going to kill Mr Johns?"

"I don't recall saying that."

"You went upstairs, loaded your rifle and having heard him go into the toilet, you aimed at where his heart would be if he was sitting down on the lavatory seat and shot him. That is what happened that night, isn't it?"

Hugh looked directly at the jury, "No that's not right. I was surprised to see that they had breached the agreement. I was angry and I did get the rifle, but it was to scare him not to kill him. I stumbled on the stairs. It was an accident. If I had intended to kill him or seriously injure him, I wouldn't have phoned for an ambulance and the police. It was just a terrible accident."

Jeremy looked at the jury as he added, "No, Mr Petford-Williams, it was not an accident.

I suggest that the moment you pulled the trigger, you intended to kill or at least cause serious bodily injury to Mr Johns, and you succeeded. He died as a result of you deliberately shooting him"

"That's not how it happened."

"I further suggest that it was only then that you calmed down and realised the enormity of what you had done. On your own admission just a few seconds ago, you saw that he was dying and could not be helped. Your only thought at that stage was about yourself. You phoned for an ambulance and the police concocting your story that it was an accident, solely to protect yourself, which has been your aim ever since."

Jeremy sat down immediately, refusing to wait for any response from Hugh and turning his face away from him. Hugh did not answer but just stood facing the jury with a crimson coloured face and an angry expression.

CHAPTER 36

THE DEFENCE WITNESSES

Hugh spent almost the entire day in the witness box and the court adjourned just after 3:30pm as the other defence witnesses could not attend until the following day.

David had wanted to call the firearms expert, Dr Francis Macdonald, next, but was told he could not be there until 12pm on Tuesday afternoon, so, at 10:30am on Tuesday morning, he called his next witness, Dr Henry Willis, Hugh's General Practitioner.

The doctor took an affirmation and gave his name to the court and then David took him through his qualifications and experience. He had all the usual qualifications expected of a general practitioner, plus a few more, but, most importantly, he explained that he had spent twenty-five years working in a local practice in Jesmond. David looked towards the jury as he asked, "So, doctor, there can be no doubt you have considerable experience as a GP, dealing with general medical matters?"

Dr Willis cleared his throat noisily in response, "I suppose that's right."

David turned to him and smiled, "I understand that you have known Mr Hugh Petford-Williams throughout that twenty-five years?"

"That's right. When I joined the practice, Hugh was already registered as a patient there. I saw him quite early on and successfully treated a recurring condition that he had. It involved an irritating rash that would regularly occur and which had been treated at the surgery on a number of occasions. It continued to recur, particularly when he was stressed. I was aware of a new medication that had just come on the market, and I prescribed it. I can't recall what the medication was called now, and there have been so many since! However, it worked and, as a result, Hugh insisted that only I deal with him thereafter."

"How often have you seen Mr Petford-Williams over the years?"

"Well, Hugh wasn't a regular attendee of the surgery at first. As he got older, he attended more regularly until it was probably every month. However, I did meet Hugh quite frequently socially. We were both members of the same Golf Club until his diabetes took hold and made walking difficult for him. We are also both members of the same two clubs in Jesmond and we frequently met for meals and drinks. I have visited his home quite often and he has visited mine. So, in answer to your question, I have probably seen Hugh at least once a week throughout that period."

"You are aware of the charges he faces?"

"Yes, I am."

"In those circumstances, and with your knowledge of him, do you feel able to help us with an assessment of his character?"

"Yes, certainly. As I have said, I have known Hugh for twenty-five years now. Hugh will probably be the first to admit that he can at times appear surly and rude. It is not deliberate or intentional on his part but just part of his character. When people first meet him they often form the wrong impression about him.

Over the years, I have got to know him well and I can say he is a true friend. We still have arguments, sometimes heated and often on irrelevant matters, but I know that I can trust Hugh implicitly. I know what he is charged with and I am very surprised. I know that Hugh is not a man of violence. Ironically, he has an interest in military history. My experience has often been that those who are interested in that subject abhor violence themselves and Hugh is one such character. In short, he is a thoroughly decent man, kind-hearted and honest and a true friend."

David was almost taken aback by the answer. The doctor's proof of evidence, supplied by Hugh's Solicitor, had said very little about character, simply that he thought of Hugh as "a good, honest friend".

Realising he could not improve on this glowing reference, David moved on, "Doctor, you have treated Mr Petford-Williams over the years for a number of ailments, I only want to deal with one, namely, his diabetes. Can you assist us with his medical history and the consequences of that disease?"

Dr Willis looked towards the jury as he had earlier been instructed to do. "Yes, certainly. Hugh is overweight, he is clinically obese and has been for a number of years. He enjoys his food and alcohol and clearly eats and drinks far more than is good for him. Over the years, I have warned him about this. It is in my opinion clear that as a result of his diet, and in particular, his alcohol consumption, that he developed Type 2 diabetes. This was diagnosed about five years ago, in early 2010. At first, I recommended that he control the condition by diet, but later, when it was clear that this was not working, I prescribed metformin. Then, as there were worries about his liver, I prescribed, Sulfonylurea to control his blood sugar levels."

"Can you help us with the effects of diabetes on Mr Petford-Williams?"

"One well documented side effect is erectile dysfunction or impotence. This is usually due to the damage that diabetes 2 can cause to small blood vessels such as those found in the penis. Damage can also be caused to nerves causing a reduced blood flow and loss of sensation in sexual organs.

Hugh has suffered from these problems from quite early on after the diagnosis. Normally, this is not a problem and there are a number of medicines out there that can assist, such as Viagra. However, Hugh found he was unable to take Viagra and similar medicines because of unpleasant side effects. I know he has tried a number of other remedies, some of which I recommended and some which I did not! Unfortunately, none have worked and he remains impotent."

"What about his ability to move?"

"Again, a common feature of Diabetes 2 is that it affects a patient's gait. Diabetes can cause neuropathy, nerve disease and poor circulation. Hugh exhibits signs of both. This can lead to a weakening in the sensation in his legs and make him unsteady on his feet."

"So, if he was coming down the stairs, is it possible he might stumble from his condition?"

"Well, of course anyone might stumble coming downstairs, but, yes, his condition makes it more likely that it might happen to him."

"Yes, thank you Dr Willis, will you remain there, there may be a few questions from my Learned Friend for the prosecution."

Jeremy rose slowly to his feet and pleasantly greeted the doctor, "Thank you for attending court Dr Willis, I know your time is valuable so I shall try not to detain you for longer than necessary. Firstly, you are clearly not only the defendant's family doctor, but also his friend?"

"Yes, as I've said."

"You have watched the onset of his Diabetes 2 and seen the symptoms he has exhibited?"

"Yes."

"In the five years you have known him since he was first diagnosed with diabetes, have you ever seen him stumble, either on stairs or otherwise?"

"I have seen him have problems with his gait."

"Yes, no doubt, but have you ever seen him stumble on stairs?"

"No."

"Obviously, in his condition, there is a risk that he might stumble on the stairs?"

"Yes, of course."

"A risk he would be well aware of?"

"Yes."

"Would you agree that, in those circumstances, it would be the height of recklessness for him to walk downstairs holding a loaded rifle in one hand with his finger on the trigger?"

"I would think it the height of recklessness for anyone to do that!"

Jeremy grinned at the witness, "Yes, thank you doctor, let me move on."

Jeremy picked up the rifle in front of him. "Dr Willis, as his friend, were you aware that the defendant had this rifle at his home?"

"No, I wasn't."

"He never mentioned it to you, his close friend?"

"No, he didn't."

"But you visited his house, surely you saw the firing range?"

"I did visit his house and saw the range. I never really thought about it. But I didn't know he had that rifle."

"He was your patient so no doubt you discussed many personal details about his life with him?"

"Where they were relevant, yes."

"No doubt he discussed his wife with you and the problems about being impotent?"

"Obviously he did, as I was trying to help his medical condition."

"Did he tell you about the arrangement that he reached with Mr Johns and his wife whereby they could have sexual intercourse if he tied a ribbon around the door handle of the spare bedroom?"

"No, he did not."

"Did he ever discuss Mr Johns with you?"

"He mentioned him a few times and I met Mr Johns on one or two occasions."

"Did you discover what his feelings were towards Mr Johns?"

"He seemed to like him most of the time, although he did say to me once that Mr Johns could be irritating."

"Nothing more?"

"No."

Jeremy beamed at the witness, "Thank you, Dr Willis. That is all I wanted to ask."

David decided not to re-examine and simply thanked Dr Willis and called his next witness, Sir Reginald Spalding JP.

Sir Reginald was a local magistrate and had been for the last thirty years. He was in his late sixties and was almost entirely bald with just a few grey hairs appearing from below his ears and around his neck, above his collar line. He was a similar size and build to Hugh.

He was not a stranger to Newcastle Crown Court having sat there with a judge and other magistrates on a few occasions hearing appeals from other magistrates' decisions. He walked into court with great confidence and took the oath and gave his name without being asked.

He had been called by David as a character witness as he had known Hugh for thirty odd years and spoke highly of him. David had wondered whether to call him after the glowing reference given by Dr Willis, but, as Sir Reginald had hung around outside court from 9am, he decided to use him.

"Sir Reginald, I understand that you are a Magistrate and sit at the local Jesmond Magistrates Court?"

"That's right."

"And you have done so for the last thirty plus years?"

"I believe it is exactly thirty years this year."

"No doubt in that time you have seen all manner of criminal cases?"

"I most certainly have."

"I understand also that you know Hugh Petford-Williams, the defendant in this case?"

"Yes, I do."

"How long have you known him?"

"About thirty-two years. I knew him before I first sat as a Magistrate. Indeed, Hugh was one of the people who first encouraged me to sit as a Magistrate."

"In that time, how often have you met with Mr Petford-Williams?"

"Very frequently. We attend the same social events, charitable events and the like. I would say I saw him every couple of weeks until this incident."

"You are aware of the charges he is facing?"

"I am."

"Bearing that in mind, are you able to assist the court by giving us your opinion of his character?"

"Yes certainly, I consider Hugh is one of the few good people you meet in life. Although he can be a little opinionated at times and stubborn, he is an honest and trustworthy man."

"As you know, he has been charged with murder. Since you have known him, over the last thirty-two years, has he ever exhibited any signs of violence?"

"Not at all. He has raised his voice a number of times but I have never seen him act in a violent manner or even threaten violence."

David thanked him and sat down wondering whether Jeremy would even bother to question this witness. He was rather hopeful he would not and became slightly dismayed when Jeremy rose to his feet and asked, "Sir Reginald, you have just told us you have never seen the defendant act in a violent way or threaten violence to anyone."

"That's correct."

"Of course, I assume you have never seen him immediately after he has walked into his own home and found his wife in bed with a neighbour?"

"Good God no!"

Jeremy smiled at the jury, "Thank you, I have no further questions."

CHAPTER 37

THE DEFENCE EXPERT

Dr Macdonald arrived at court at 11:45am on the Tuesday. David had arranged to have a last minute conference with him before the court sat at 12pm and the Judge rose for 15 minutes to allow this. There was no new information that David could glean and so, at 12:00pm, he announced to the jury that his next witness was Dr Macdonald.

All heads in the courtroom turned towards the swing doors as the witness came in. David took one look and turned round to Sara who gave him a knowing look. Dr Macdonald was sweating heavily and looked very nervous. Not only did he look the exact opposite to the way he had appeared in conference in Jesmond a few months earlier, but completely different to the way he had looked just a few minutes before.

The usher gave him a cup of water after he had been sworn and given his name to the court. It was noticeable that the cup shook slightly in his hand. David momentarily looked down at his papers just to check that the witness had given evidence in court before. Yes, there it was a reference beneath his impressive qualifications. "I have conducted a large number of investigations into firearms matters for both the prosecution and the defence and have given evidence in court on many occasions." David noted it did not say how many times but assumed it was a significant number and wondered whether the current performance was simply an example of stage fright. After all, many great actors, such as Lawrence Olivier, had supposedly been sick with nerves before going out onto a stage before a live audience. Presumably the same could happen to an expert witness? He decided to deal with his evidence slowly and ease Dr Macdonald into it.

"Dr Macdonald …"

The witness turned to him with a confused expression on his face.

David started again, "Dr Macdonald, I understand that you are a firearms expert who has dealt with a large number of previous cases involving firearms and given evidence on a large number of occasions for both the prosecution and the defence?"

It was meant to be a statement but came across as more of an inquiry.

"Tha, Tha, That's right."

David paused before suggesting, "I understand you have had to rush here from another part of the country, please take your time to catch your breath before answering."

"Th, Th, Thank you."

David closed his eyes for a split second in frustration before continuing. Of course people have stutters but he did not expect an expert witness to suddenly develop one the moment he gave evidence.

"Dr Macdonald, I want to ask you about your qualifications, can you take us through them?"

"Ye, Ye, yes."

David smiled and led the witness through his extensive Curriculum Vitae, stopping him occasionally so he could explain the meaning of a qualification. Noticeably, after a few minutes, Dr Macdonald's stutter had disappeared and his confidence appeared to return.

Clearly, it was a form of stage fright, thought David, everything should be alright from now on. He decided to move on and ask questions about the rifle. "I understand that you were given an opportunity of examining the rifle before you wrote your report?"

Dr Macdonald nodded and produced his notes of the examination. "Ye, Ye, Yes, that's correct."

David momentarily paused, "Are you feeling alright?"

"I, I, I'm fine, thank you."

"Very well, can you tell the court about your examination?"

"Ye, Ye, Yes. I examined the rifle in th, th, the presence of the prosecution expert, Dr Br, Brown, at his laboratory."

David waited before asking the next question, hoping that Dr Macdonald might regain his confidence. "Did you conduct any test firing of the rifle?"

"Ye, yes, we did. We test fired some cartridges that had been seized from the defendant's home."

"Did you notice anything in particular about the cartridges?"

"Ye, yes they were rimfire cartridges. They were not very powerful as you would expect in a .22 rimfire weapon."

"Why is that?"

"In an ordinary cartridge the firing pin strikes the centre of the cartridge to fire the bullet. In a rimfire, as the name suggests, it strikes the rim. Hence the rim is weaker than in a normal cartridge and contains less propellant."

David smiled, the stutter had disappeared.

"Can you tell us about the rifle itself?"

"Ye, yes. It was a Model 62A, 1890 Winchester pump action .22 rimfire rifle. It had been modified slightly and some parts were not original."

"Did this affect the performance of the rifle?"

"Yes, it did make a difference to the trigger pull."

It seemed that Dr Macdonald had finally lost his stutter, "Can you assist as to what you mean by the trigger pull?"

"Yes, normally a Winchester 1890 model would need a trigger pull of about 2 ½ to 3 lbs weight. In other words, if you put the rifle's stock on the ground, you would need the equivalent of a 3 lb weight attached to the trigger to activate it. In this case, non-standard parts had been used to repair the rifle so a higher trigger pull was required of about 3 ½ lbs."

"Is that a great deal more?"

"No, Not really."

"Could you still accidentally pull a trigger with a 3 ½ lb trigger pull?"

"Oh, yes."

"I understand that you considered Dr Brown's report and the examination he carried out at the scene. Have you any observations to make?"

"Yes, I was surprised that he had used old methods to examine the scene and not used a more modern laser scanner to produce a 3D image that could be manipulated to examine the scene from different angles."

"Could this make any difference in this case?"

"It's feasible it could."

"Did you use a laser scanner to examine the scene?"

"No, I never examined the scene. By the time I was instructed the lavatory door had been repaired or replaced and the place cleaned. Such an examination at such a late stage would have yielded no useful results."

"Dr Brown told us that he did not use a laser scanner because of cost implications. Can you assist on that issue?"

"Yes, I am slightly surprised at that. Once you have access to such a scanner and the computers to input and analyse the data, the actual cost of the examination should not add much, if anything."

"In this case, Mr Petford-Williams states that he stumbled on the stairs and accidentally discharged the rifle. You have fully examined all the facts surrounding this case. Have you seen anything in your investigation that demonstrates that this could not be an accident?"

"No, certainly not."

David thanked the witness and sat down. This was the final witness in the case and he knew that Jeremy would try and make some inroads into his evidence. He almost exactly predicted the wording of Jeremy's first question in cross examination.

"Dr Macdonald, what you are saying is, that it is possible this was an accident?"

"Ye, ye, yes."

David looked up from his notes. It looked like the witness' nerves had come back.

"Of course, I suppose almost anything is possible, but what this jury has to decide is was this an accident or was it a deliberate shooting with Mr Petford-Williams intending to kill Mr Johns or at least cause him really serious injury."

"I understand that."

"Let us examine the 'accident scenario' for a moment. If this was an accident, it would be the height of recklessness for a man who is experienced with firearms, a man who regularly uses a firearm, a man who regularly buys firearms magazines, to walk downstairs with his finger on the trigger of a loaded rifle?"

Much to David's consternation, Dr Macdonald nodded enthusiastically, "Oh yes, I, I, I agree."

"Indeed, would it be fair to say that you would not expect such an experienced person to walk downstairs with his finger on the trigger of a loaded rifle?"

"Most certainly, I would not."

"So can we discount accident then?"

David was about to object when the witness answered, "I am not qualified to say, it is a matter for the jury and either scenario is equally possible."

David remained seated, satisfied with the answer. Jeremy stared at the witness for a few seconds before asking, "You are an expert in these matters?"

"I am an expert on firearms and their use. As I have said, it is quite possible this was an accident."

"But it's not likely is it?"

David looked up from his notes, expecting Dr Macdonald to give the same answer as before. Instead he was horrified to hear the witness say, "Oh no, I don't think it likely!"

CHAPTER 38

THE PROSECUTION CLOSING SPEECH

David did not re-examine Dr Macdonald for any length of time, the damage was already done. In common parlance the witness had "gone bent" and given evidence that he was not expected to give. It happened, but not often with expert witnesses! Especially when the questioning had been anticipated. David knew it had damaged Hugh's case, the only question was, by how much?

The rest of Tuesday was spent by the Judge and counsel, in the absence of the jury, discussing the legal directions the Judge was going to give. It was now Wednesday morning, and all the parties were in court as Jeremy turned towards the jury to address them.

"Ladies and gentlemen, you may think this is an unusual case with a number of strange features and conflicts of evidence. Fortunately, you do not need to reconcile every conflict of evidence. Some are wholly irrelevant to your verdict. For example, the use of the Taser by Police Constable Savage. You may think that Police Constable Savage was justified in the use of the Taser entering a flat where the defendant was still holding the rifle he had just used to shoot Mr Johns with and pointing it at the paramedics. Equally you may think that there was no justification for Police Constable Savage using that Taser as the defendant was no longer a threat. However, it really doesn't matter and I suggest you do not need to waste your time on that issue. Your determination of whether the Taser should or should not have been used will not help in your determination of whether the defendant committed the act of murder and I urge you to concentrate on the relevant issues in this case.

Also, it may well be that you feel some sympathy for the defendant. It cannot be easy suffering from diabetes and the associated conditions, even if, as appears to be the case from his own doctor's evidence, they were self-induced by a bad diet and a heavy drinking habit.

I suspect many of you feel sympathy for the predicament he was in. He was clearly deeply in love with his wife. What did his good friend, Mr Granger tell us? He told us that the defendant often said how much he loved his wife, Rosemary, as he said in his own words, 'He used to say she was his only love and he would do anything for her.'

Sadly, the defendant was unable to satisfy her sexual desires and he had to tolerate the fact that Mr Johns was fulfilling a function he no longer could in their marriage. It is natural to feel sympathy for him in that situation.

Of course though, that sympathy, understandable as it is, can play no part in the verdicts you must reach in this case. This case must be determined on the evidence alone. Feelings of sympathy, emotion or prejudice can play no part in your deliberations. You must look at the evidence in this case coldly and clinically and answer one question, has the prosecution proven its case so you are sure of the defendant's guilt?

Of course, whatever sympathy you may feel towards the defendant, never lose sight of the fact that, on that night, Mr Johns lost his life. Every human life has an infinite value. In his case he was a man who no doubt would otherwise have had many years of life ahead of him. A brave ex-RAF pilot who had seen combat defending the Falkland Islanders who had been invaded and overwhelmed by the forces of a tyrannical dictator."

David looked towards the jury wondering how many had noticed that having told them not to rely on sympathy and emotion, Jeremy was now playing on their sympathy and emotions towards the victim.

Jeremy continued unabated, "The prosecution say it was murder, the defence say it was a tragic accident, although, even on the defendant's own case, you might think he has admitted manslaughter by loading a firearm then carrying it downstairs with his finger on the trigger in his condition. He was aware that he was prone to stumbling, he knew there was a real risk he could accidentally discharge the firearm and that this could lead to fatal consequences. On his own evidence, you may think it clear that it was the height of recklessness. He took a wholly unnecessary risk with the lives of those around him. What did his own witness and close friend, Dr Willis say when I asked him, 'Would you agree that in those circumstances, it would be the height of recklessness for him to walk downstairs holding a loaded rifle in one hand with his finger on the trigger?'

He replied, "I would think it the height of recklessness for anyone to do that!"

However, the prosecution say that was not the case. This was not manslaughter, this was not a grossly negligent accident, this was murder!

Not cold-blooded but hot-blooded murder with passions rising, carried out by a man who could no longer satisfy his wife's needs and who was clearly jealous and angry that another man was carrying out that role.

We have heard how the defendant reluctantly came to some arrangement with them. The tying of the red ribbon around the door handle of the spare bedroom. However, in his own words, he found the situation 'intolerable'. How much more intolerable was it when they broke the rules and Mr Johns, as he saw it, flagrantly violated his hospitality that night, not caring at all whether the defendant walked in on him and Mrs Petford-Williams in the middle of a sexual act.

He has told us that he saw red. Did he think about the consequences of his actions when he went to the wardrobe, took out the Winchester 1890 firearm, carefully loaded it and went in search of his victim, or did he, in the intense heat of passion in that moment, want revenge?

No doubt my Learned Friend, Mr Brant, will remind you of the burden of proof in this case and I will not criticise him for that. Rightly it is a high one. No doubt he will suggest you cannot be sure of the defendant's intent that night. However, I suggest that you most certainly can. There are a number of important pieces of evidence that tell you exactly what his intent was.

You may think the starting point in this case is that incident in October 2014. The first time that the defendant found his beloved wife and Mr Johns in bed together making love, in his own house. How awful that must have been for him. What did he do? Did he barge in and remonstrate with them there and then? No, he paused, assessed the situation and planned his next move. He went upstairs, loaded his rifle and came downstairs, without stumbling!

He went into the spare bedroom and pointed the rifle at Mr Johns' head. What was his intent? He tells us it was to scare Mr Johns. Really? Can you believe that? Remember what he told you when he gave evidence. 'He got off her and laughed at me! He took one look at the rifle and said, something like, 'Finally Hugh, something you can get up!' Rosemary then laughed. I have never felt so hurt in my life. I confess I saw red.'

Who better to assess his intent than the person who knows him best and had known him almost all of his adult life. His wife Rosemary. What did she believe his intent was? You have heard her statement read to you, she clearly believed he intended to kill Mr Johns. You will recall her words, 'I was terrified. I thought that Hugh intended to kill William, but in his anger he had missed him.'

Was that why he fired two shots and not one? Because he missed on his first shot, pumped the rifle again and then missed again?

Of course, you will want to consider that Rosemary did not give her evidence live and the defence had no opportunity to cross-examine her. However, was she likely to have changed from her belief, clearly formed at the time those shots were fired, that her husband was so angry he wanted to kill Johns?

We know that matters calmed down. How often these courts see that happen. A person who has deadly intent one moment can carry on a remarkably cool conversation with their intended victim the next. Often you hear of cases where a momentary rage gives way to immediate remorse and a few minutes later, the person causing a serious injury is the one who phones for an ambulance. Human nature has many depths and you may think in our studies of it we never get further than the shallowest part.

It was after this October incident that they all came up with the idea of the red silk ribbon. A charming way of dealing with the difficulty of communication. After all, the defendant could hardly leave the house and shout out, 'You can have sex with my wife now!'

Of course though it must have made for great difficulties between them and, you may think, it was almost inevitable that we would end up in the position we are now in. If passions are aroused between two people, are they likely to ignore them just because there isn't a silk ribbon tied on the door handle of the spare room?

The defendant must have been aware of this and it must have eaten away at him. You may think that, after reaching this agreement, the defendant's true state of mind was revealed by his own friends and witnesses.

In relation to Mr Johns, Dr Willis gave evidence that the defendant, 'seemed to like him most of the time, although he did say to me once that Mr Johns could be irritating.'

The defendant was more candid with his closest friends. Mr Granger told us, 'I got the distinct impression that Hugh could not stand Johns.'

It went further than merely finding him irritating and not being able to stand him. You will recall Mr Granger's words, 'In February, Hugh came into the club and was really upset. He had clearly been drinking. He started complaining about Johns and said, 'I'd like to shoot that bastard and I would too, if it wasn't for the fact Rosemary likes him so much!'

Rosemary appears to have liked Mr Johns a little too much!

Now, Mr Granger, for the first time in this court, said that he had met Mr Johns and did not like him and said this to the defendant, who told him that, 'Johns was alright, once you got to know him'. You will no doubt want to be careful when you consider this evidence. It never appeared in Mr Granger's witness statement and may well have been an attempt to save his good friend. However, you heard from another of the defendant's friends who I suggest gave truthful evidence to you. Mr Doyle had no doubts about the defendant's feelings towards Mr Johns. He told us, 'I got the impression that he did not like Mr Johns. Something about him being too attentive towards Rosemary.'

Mr Doyle, a good friend of the defendants went further. He told us, 'I remember earlier this year he even said he would like to shoot him!'

When I asked him how the defendant appeared when he said this, he replied, 'Like he meant it!'

This evidence comes from two witnesses who are close to the defendant, who assessed that he wanted to shoot Mr Johns, a short time before he actually did.

So let us move on to the night of the fatal shooting. Large quantities of alcohol were consumed by the defendant, Mrs Petford Williams and the victim, Mr Johns in the defendant's home. The alcohol must have had an effect on all of them. We all know that people do things under the influence of drink that they would not dream of doing if they were sober. But please remember, as His Lordship will no doubt direct you, 'a drunken intent' is still an intent.

The defendant left his home to go to his club. He did not tie the ribbon round the door handle. It was clear to him that he was telling them he would not be long and they were not permitted to have sexual intercourse.

In the defendant's mind, Johns and Rosemary knew the rules, but they broke them, showing no respect for his feelings. He must have had some idea this was going to happen.

You will recall the evidence of his friends, Mr Granger and Mr Doyle that when he reached the club he was tense and both gave evidence that he said words to the effect, 'I have to get back, you never know what those two might get up to in my absence and I might need to put a stop to it!'

He returned to his home to find the agreement had been broken. Again, he did not immediately confront them. He went upstairs, he took the rifle, loaded it and carried it downstairs and a shot was fired into the toilet door. Was it really an accident, as the defendant says?"

Jeremy shook his head from side to side, "No, it was not. There are cogent reasons why this was not an accident and you can see them plainly in the evidence before you. Where was the bullet fired? Exactly at the point Mr Johns' heart would be if he had been seated on the toilet. Is that a remarkable coincidence that an accidental shot would hit that exact spot? No, even the defence's own firearms' expert, Dr Macdonald said this wasn't likely. There was other evidence as well that shows us this was no accident. You will recall the evidence of the neighbours. They heard words that could only have one intent. In a high pitched voice, undoubtedly demonstrating how worked up he was, the defendant shouted out, a few seconds before the shot was fired, 'I'm going to kill you, you bastard!'

What better evidence of his intent can we have than those words spoken from his own mouth seconds before he applied the pressure required to discharge this rifle."

Jeremy picked up the rifle and pulled the trigger and the hammer clicked loudly, making one or two jurors jump.

"As you heard from the two firearms experts, this rifle has been adapted by the defendant. He clearly has considerable knowledge about firearms, more than he has been willing to share with this court.

It requires a greater trigger pull than an ordinary rifle, making an accident far less likely. You will recall, when I asked the defendant in court to demonstrate this so-called accident, he failed to do so. No doubt you will want to make some allowance in a courtroom where he may have been nervous, but the reality, you may think, is that he could not pull the trigger because this rifle needed someone to hold it with both hands and take careful aim before they pulled the trigger. And that is what I suggest happened in this case.

The defendant had had enough. Even if the October shooting had only been to scare, he knew that it had not worked. He needed a more permanent solution to his problem, and that was to shoot and kill Mr Johns.

It is a sad case and emotions and sympathy do feature strongly, but when you put aside sympathy, emotion, prejudice and concentrate on the evidence, I suggest there is only one proper verdict, guilty of murder."

CHAPTER 39

THE DEFENCE CLOSING SPEECH

Mr Justice Bright turned to David as Jeremy was sitting down, "Would you like a short adjournment Mr Brant or would you like to make your speech now?"

Although a simple question, it was not an easy one for David to answer. Knowing that jurors usually had a limited attention span for speeches, it was often a good idea to have an adjournment for a few minutes before addressing them further. However, in this case, David had to accept that Jeremy had made a powerful speech against his client and he felt it essential to rebut it as quickly as possible.

"My Lord, I am happy to give my speech now."

There were no audible moans from the jurors which gave David some comfort that the decision was the right one.

He faced them all and looked through the assembled faces making eye contact with every one of them before he began.

"On 18th June of this year, just over four months ago now, William Johns died from a single shot fired from this rifle."

He pointed to the rifle on the desk in front of him.

"That rifle was held by Mr Petford-Williams and there is no dispute that it was his finger on the trigger and that he was responsible for firing the bullet.

However, that is clearly not the end of this matter. No one disputes the simple facts in this case. The issue, as you are well aware by now, is whether this was an accident as Mr Petford-Williams has claimed from the beginning, or whether, as the prosecution claims, it was a deliberate act, an aimed shot from that rifle intending to kill or at least cause a really serious injury?

My Learned Friend has addressed you on emotions, sympathy and prejudice. Let me say at the start I agree with him! They can play no part in your deliberations. Neither sympathy for Mr Petford-Williams, nor for Mr Johns. You must look solely at the evidence in this case.

A large number of witnesses, both for the prosecution and the defence, gave evidence before you. However, you will have noted that only one witness who gave evidence, was actually present in the house that night and that was Mr Petford-Williams. He didn't need to give evidence. He does not have to prove anything. As you heard from my Learned Friend for the prosecution, and as His Lordship will direct you in due course, the obligation to prove this case rests purely on the shoulders of the prosecution and it is a heavy burden. You cannot find Mr Petford-Williams guilty of any offence unless you are satisfied so that you are sure of his guilt.

No doubt you will want to consider Mr Petford-Williams' evidence carefully. Although he does not have the burden of proving anything in this case, the fact that he has given evidence before you does mean that the prosecution must prove he lied to you before you could convict him of any offence.

You saw Mr Petford-Williams give evidence and that evidence was skilfully tested by my Learned Friend in cross-examination. Was he caught out in a single lie? You may easily conclude that he was not.

Was there any part of his evidence you can be sure he lied to you about? Again, I suggest not.

When you do consider his evidence, please do consider that he appears before you as a man of good character. He has had no previous problems with the law prior to this case. That goes a long way to his credit. He is not some criminal reprobate who frequently appears before the courts, charged with offences of violence, who you might think was easily capable of yet another such act. He is not someone who has a string of offences for perjury or perverting the course of justice or even offences of dishonesty which might make you question what he said under oath. He has a previous unblemished record, an impeccable character.

Of course you are aware, because it has been admitted, that he pleaded guilty in these proceedings to possession of the rifle and ammunition, without possessing a firearms certificate. You have heard the basis of that plea. It is his case that he did not realise that he needed a firearms certificate for this rifle and ammunition.

He was aware that there is an exemption in law for firearms that are classed as 'antiques.' This firearm was in excess of 120 years old and clearly would count as an antique. However, the exemption only applies if the firearm is kept as a 'curiosity or ornament'. He did not know that, once he obtained ammunition, and fired it, it was no longer kept as such in law and accordingly, he had to plead guilty. As we all know, 'ignorance of the law' is no defence, but that offence is a technical one, known in law as an offence of 'strict liability.' It does not make him a hardened criminal who was intent on murder.

I ask you not to hold that conviction against him.

In this case, you are aware that he has never been convicted of any other offence. More importantly, you might think, you have also heard witnesses, from both the prosecution and defence, who have spoken highly of him.

The prosecution called Timothy Granger to give evidence. He told you that Mr Petford-Williams, 'is one of the most honest, kind, generous, decent people I have ever met. He would help out any friend in need.'

He went on to say that Mr Petford-Williams was not a violent man by nature, he is not the type of man to get angry and, as he put it, 'I doubt he would even shoot a rat, never mind a man.'

We called before you, Dr Henry Willis, who told you he could trust him 'implicitly.' He told you that he was not a man of violence, and, indeed, that he abhors it and 'he is a thoroughly decent man, kind-hearted, honest and a true friend.'

We also called before you the Magistrate, Sir Reginald Spalding JP, before you. A man who is used to dealing with criminals and judging people on an almost daily basis. He told you, 'Although he can be a little opinionated at times, he is an honest and trustworthy man.'

Please bear those excellent character references in mind when you consider the evidence he gave before you and the prosecution's suggestion that he was a man intent on murder, or, at least intent on causing really serious harm to his friend, Mr Johns that night.

Let us then turn to look at the prosecution case together and compare it with the defence case. The defence case is simple. This was a terrible tragic accident. Yes, Mr Petford-Williams had intended to scare Mr Johns by firing the rifle, but he did not intend to kill or seriously injure him, he did not intend to injure him in any way.

The prosecution say you can discern his intent from a number of pieces of evidence. In fact, when you look at it closely, we suggest you can do no such thing.

The starting point, the prosecution say, is the written statement of Rosemary, which you heard read out to you. The prosecution could not produce Rosemary to give evidence so I was never allowed to cross-examine and test her recollection of that night in October 2014. Her statement was read to you under the hearsay provisions contained in an Act of Parliament.

You may think in this case that it is deeply unsatisfactory that such a statement could be read without the opportunity of testing it. I would for example have liked to ask her how drunk was she that night? It is clear from that statement that she drinks a considerable amount and is prone to forgetfulness and blackouts and probably false recollections.

In any event, what does her statement amount to? Mr Johns had made a crude reference to Mr Petford-Williams' impotence. In return he had given Mr Johns a look of pure hatred and fired the rifle at Mr Johns. She believed from what she saw that he had intended to kill him but in his anger had missed him.

Of course though, her statement is equally consistent with Mr Petford-William's version of events that he just intended to scare Mr Johns. Of course he would put a look of hatred on his face and look like he intended to kill Mr Johns. If he didn't, he wouldn't have succeeded in scaring him. However, the fact that the shots were made from a short range and hit the pillow, tells us all we really need to know. Mr Petford-Williams had practised with this gun many times in his garden at targets set up many yards away. As he told you in evidence, if he had wanted to kill or seriously harm Mr Johns, even if he might have missed once, he would not have missed twice from point blank range.

The prosecution's case then relies upon his anger at finding the two of them in bed, in breach of his agreement with them.

Really!

The prosecution case is that he could handle them having sexual intercourse, but he formed a murderous intent when they had sex without his permission. As a case, it really defies common sense.

To unravel this case, we suggest you look at all the circumstances. He found them in bed together in October 2014. He decided to give them both a scare by shooting the gun into the pillow. You will have noticed an important fact about that occasion. The rifle was fired twice. He fired once, then pumped the rifle again putting another bullet into the firing chamber and fired that bullet into Mr John's pillow.

We suggest the most important fact in this case, and one the prosecution cannot explain, is that, on 18th June 2015, as both the prosecution and the defence agree, the rifle was only fired once. You will recall one witness thought it had been fired twice. That was the evidence of Dr Jeffries, but he must have been wrong. He probably heard something like a door slamming. It is clear this rifle was only fired once that night.

If he was intent on killing Mr Johns or seriously wounding him, surely he would have fired more than once? He had eight more bullets in the rifle's magazine.

Please remember, the bullet was fired through a door. It would have taken sometime before he realised he had hit Mr Johns. If he was intent on murder or causing him really serious harm, he would have fired again and probably again until he was sure he had hit his target.

But he didn't!

The rifle was fired once which is wholly consistent with an accidental discharge rather than a deliberate one.

You will note how the prosecution have conveniently ignored this fact. They talk of some immediate remorse. Is that likely in the case of someone who has formed the intent to kill or cause really serious harm that the intent dissolves and disappears after the first shot is fired?

The prosecution know they have this problem which is why they have tried to rely on other factors. They say you can discern his intent from the opinions he expressed about Mr Johns.

They rely on Mr Doyle's evidence. He told you that Mr Petford-Williams did not seem to like Mr Johns. After all, just a few short months before this incident, he told Mr Doyle, 'I'd shoot that bastard if it wasn't for the fact that Rosemary likes him so much!'

However, the reality is that, at the time this was said, Mr Doyle did not think he was being serious, despite what he told you in court. His statement reads, 'I thought little of the comment at the time.'

Mr Granger, another prosecution witness, also heard this comment but, as he told you, he also thought little of the comment at the time and thought it was said out of frustration and not a serious comment.

Mr Granger also told you that he had met Mr Johns and had not formed a favourable impression of him, thinking him pushy, but it was Mr Petford-Williams who came to Mr Johns' defence and said, he was alright once you got to know him. That is not consistent with some deep-rooted resentment towards him.

Now we get to the night of the incident. The 18th June, 2015, and the two hundredth anniversary of the Battle of Waterloo. Mr Petford-Williams had invited Mr Johns to his flat for a few drinks. Was he really likely to have done that if he could not stand him?

After a large amount to drink, Mr Petford-Williams went to his club and met his friends, Mr Granger and Mr Doyle. They have both given evidence that he looked a little 'tense'. He says he was not tense but he might have seemed that way because he had had a little more to drink that night than normal, before he arrived at his club. What reason did he have to be tense that night? He did not know that his wife and Mr Johns were going to breach their agreement with him and he had no reason to suspect that they would do so that night, when, to his knowledge, they had not done so since the agreement was reached in October 2014.

Both Mr Granger and Mr Doyle heard Mr Petford-Williams make the comment, 'I have to get back, you never know what those two might get up to when I'm away.' Mr Petford-Williams states there was nothing in the comment, and, as Mr Granger said, it was said in a jokey sort of way and he didn't take any real notice of it. Mr Doyle also clearly thought nothing of it at the time as is clear from his witness statement made a few days later.

Mr Petford-Williams arrived home and upon entering his flat, as he has freely admitted, he was angry to see that his wife and best friend had broken their agreement. It is common ground between the prosecution and defence that he went upstairs to get his rifle. The prosecution claim it was to kill Mr Johns. Mr Petford-Williams states it was to scare him. After all, it had worked the last time he had confronted them in bed together.

Was this a premeditated murder or was it an accident? We suggest everything points to an accident, or, at least, you cannot be sure on this evidence that it was premeditated murder.

Take for a moment the evidence of the neighbours that the prosecution rely on so heavily. What does it amount to? They heard Mr Petford-Williams shout words to the effect, "I'm going to kill you, you bastard." The prosecution say that is clear evidence of his intent but, actually, it's exactly the sort of thing he would say if he was intending to scare Mr Johns. In itself, it does not take the prosecution case any further.

Let's move on then to consider the expert evidence about what happened when he came downstairs. In reality, we suggest there was one important point emerging from all of the expert evidence you heard in this case.

No expert could rule out this was an accident.

You will recall the pathologist, Dr Roper's evidence, when I asked him whether this was an accident or a deliberate shot, he answered, 'both are equally consistent from my examination. You will have to look for other factors to answer that question.'

Even the prosecution's firearms' expert, Dr Christopher Brown, when asked by Mr Asquith, could not say which position Mr Petford-Williams was in when the shot was fired. He told you, 'No, they are all equally possible. I consider you would have to take into account factors other than just the ballistics to come to that determination.'

Admittedly, the defence expert when questioned by Mr Asquith did say it was more likely to have been an aimed shot rather than an accidental one. However, you will no doubt have noticed that this seemed to contradict his earlier evidence and it must be remembered, he had not seen or heard all of the evidence in this case in order to determine whether this was an accident or not. He had not, as an example, seen Mr Petford-Williams give evidence and be tested in cross examination. Nor did he hear Dr Willis' evidence that a person with Mr Petford-Williams' condition was more likely to stumble on the stairs.

In any event, we are not dealing with what an expert considers to be most likely. We do not deal with probabilities in criminal courts. We deal with the test of whether you are satisfied so that you are sure which is the same as the old test of 'beyond a reasonable doubt'. Importantly, no expert can rule out Mr Petford-Williams' emphatic claim that this was an accident.

What other evidence do you have to consider? You have the 999 call. Does a man who intends to kill, or intends to cause really serious harm, immediately phone for an ambulance? Of course not. He would surely have been more likely to pump the rifle again and put another shot through the door if that had been his intent.

You heard that 999 call played to you. Didn't Mr Petford-Williams sound genuinely concerned for Mr Johns' life? Didn't that sound more like someone who was genuinely worried about accidentally injuring a friend, rather than an example of immediate remorse, as the prosecution put it?

You will have noted that he gave his version of events straight away, before he had any knowledge of what evidence the prosecution would gather. He told the operator it was an accident, he did not mean to shoot Mr Johns and he was worried that Mr Johns might die.

We know as a result of his call, the paramedics came to his address. He did not bar their way or prevent them gaining access to his property. Quite the opposite, he encouraged them to enter the property to try and save Mr Johns' life. Again, that is not the action of a man who intended to kill or cause really serious bodily harm.

The paramedics also helped us on another issue. The claim by Police Constable Savage that Mr Petford-Williams was covering them with a rifle and was believed to be a continuing threat who needed to be 'Tasered'.

My Learned Friend has addressed you on the basis that this piece of evidence cannot assist you on the central issue of Mr Petford-Williams' intent. However, if you thought for one minute that he was pointing a loaded rifle at paramedics, you would undoubtedly consider him a man capable of any violence, including murder. The truth is the evidence from those officers about him holding a rifle, threatening the paramedics and the need to use a Taser on him was fabricated.

Mr Petford-Williams told you the truth about what happened. He ejected the cartridges from the rifle and then placed the rifle by the stairs before the paramedics arrived. His version was supported by the prosecution witness Mr Marshall, the paramedic who told you he saw the rifle propped up against the stairs the moment he went into the property. He also confirmed that the police officer swore at Mr Petford-Williams, which the officer denied, and then used the Taser on him when there was no reason whatsoever to use it.

Indeed, it is a noticeable feature of this case that when you look for support for Mr Petford-Williams' version of events, it frequently comes from prosecution witnesses. It is a clear sign he has been telling the truth throughout and this was simply a tragic accident and not a murder.

Finally, I want to say a few words about manslaughter. This is clearly the fall-back position of the prosecution. Mr Asquith, in his speech, claimed that Mr Petford-Williams has admitted manslaughter by his own words. In fact, he did not. Was it sensible to carry a loaded firearm downstairs in his condition? Of course not, but that is not what he is charged with and in itself it does not amount to manslaughter. It is his case that he did not know Mr Johns was in the lavatory when he came downstairs. He had no reason to, he believed he was in the spare bedroom still coupling with Rosemary. He did not anticipate hurting anyone when the rifle was accidentally discharged and he is no more guilty of manslaughter than he is of murder.

Of course, ultimately the decision is one for you after discussions between yourselves about the evidence, but we suggest that a close analysis of the evidence in this case leads to one clear conclusion, Mr Petford-Williams is not guilty of murder or manslaughter.

As he told the emergency services when he made that 999 call, just minutes after the incident and has maintained throughout, this was simply a tragic accident.

CHAPTER 40

THE JURY DELIBERATIONS

On Thursday afternoon at 12:30pm, the jurors retired to consider their verdicts. Mr Justice Bright had summed up the case to them on Wednesday afternoon and Thursday morning. He directed them on the law and reminded them of the important evidence in the case. Now he sent them out to their deliberating room with the court ushers.

The jurors entered their jury room and soon started their deliberations. Contrary to what Hugh had thought might be the case, only two were claiming unemployment benefits. Three had taken early retirement, there were three housewives and one house husband who would normally look after their own children and were all annoyed that they had to arrange childcare to assist with this trial. There were also four jurors who had welcomed the time off from their normal employment.

It was one of the latter who offered to be the foreman. She was Julie Coral, who worked in a local solicitors' firm as a bookkeeper. The firm did not conduct any criminal work, but this did not stop her from announcing, "I've probably got the most experience of trial work here and am best suited to deal with any issues that might arise in our discussions."

A few jurors looked at her with surprise but no one objected and, in any event, before anyone had an opportunity, she took a seat at the head of the table.

The others took seats around the table, sitting next to jurors they had spent the trial sitting next to. It was noticeable that the last seats to be taken were those on either side of Julie.

Barry Hughes took the seat on Julie's right. He was a 34-year-old store manager at a local furniture shop in Jesmond. She gave him a smile but he ignored her. He had wanted to sit next to Tracey Adams, a 25-year-old beautician, but the seat next to her had been quickly taken by the 23 year-old Scott Rogers, one of the benefit claimants that Hugh had feared might be determining his future.

Julie started the discussion, "I think that first we should look through the written directions the judge gave us on the law so we know what questions we should be asking ourselves."

Barry immediately chipped in, "Why? The reality is all we have to determine is whether this was an accident or not. The rest should fall into place once we've done that!"

There were a few murmurings of agreement around the table. Julie slightly reddened as she replied, "Obviously, that is the important question but the judge did give us a number of different options if this wasn't an accident. It could be murder or manslaughter depending on a number of factors."

Barry was dismissive in his reply, "Yes, but first we have to determine whether this was an accident or not!"

Again, there was a general murmuring of agreement. Realising that the majority in the room were against her proposal, Julie decided to try and take back control of the discussions, "I agree with Barry, we should firstly concentrate on whether we think this was an accident or not."

Roger Hurst, the 29-year-old house husband spoke up in response. "I think that Johns deserved what he got. Fancy having sex with someone's wife in his own house the moment he turns his back."

The room fell silent until Mary Peters, a 55-year-old ex-civil servant, spoke up, "Roger, even if we agreed with you, that's not the issue. We were told to put emotion aside and apply the Judges' directions on the law to the facts we find."

Jenny Powell, a 23-year-old housewife who liked Roger, added, "I can understand Roger's feelings.

I could never find the defendant guilty of murder, whatever he did."

Julie felt she had to intervene. "Jenny, I am sure we all have sympathy with that view, but we all took oaths to try the case according to the evidence and that is what we must do. Shall we start by dealing with whether we believe this was an accident or not?"

William Piper decided to add his opinion. He was 62 and a retired Postmaster. "Of course it wasn't an accident. He said he was going to kill the bastard, he went upstairs, got his rifle, loaded it, came downstairs and just managed to put a shot into the door where Johns' heart would be. How could that be an accident?"

Barry intervened, "I don't think that's altogether fair. We have heard he has diabetes and was prone to stumbling. It could easily have been an accident. How did he even know Johns was in the toilet?"

Jenny, feeling chastised after her earlier intervention, decided to try again, "I agree with Barry, I think it was an accident. If he was going to kill Mr Johns, he would have done it the first time he caught them in bed together. I think he was only intending to scare him."

William looked at them both as if they were mad, but he tried his best to reason with them, "Even the defendant's expert said it was more likely to be an aimed shot than an accidental one!"

Maria Harris was a 30-year-old housewife. She had said very little to anyone throughout the trial as she had more worrying concerns at home about numerous unpaid bills. She had thought her husband was paying them but had discovered, just before the trial, that he had a serious gambling habit and was using all his money to pay for that and as a result, the family was heavily in debt. She felt now that she ought to make some contribution to the discussion, "I wasn't impressed with the defence expert. He seemed so nervous and he seemed to contradict himself. Anyway, I thought it a good sign that the defendant's own niece represents him. She obviously knows him well and must believe he's innocent."

William stared at her, convinced now that he was in a room full of morons. "How can his niece representing him make any difference to the evidence in this case. Actually, I think she shouldn't have been representing her own uncle. Surely that was unprofessional?"

Julie decided it was time to take control again, "Shall we just concentrate on the evidence and not on the barristers. I would like to look through the photographs in the jury bundle again."

She looked up and felt distinctly uncomfortable at the icy stare that William was giving her.

CHAPTER 41

THE VERDICT

The jury was sent home on Thursday at 4:30pm and returned to court on Friday at 10:00am, when they were quickly sent out of court to consider their verdicts.

At 2:00pm, the Judge had them back into court and gave them a majority direction informing them they could now return a verdict on which at least ten of them were agreed.

At 3:12pm, they filed into court and took their seats. Hugh looked at their faces as they entered the courtroom. Some returned his gaze, others ignored him. Once they were all seated the clerk stood to ask them their verdicts.

"Would your foreman please stand?"

Julie rose from her seat, which was nearest the Judge and looked at the clerk of the court.

The clerk continued, "Would you answer my first question, yes or no? Have you reached a verdict of which at least ten of you agree?"

Julie nodded and answered at the same time, "We have. Sorry. Yes."

"On count one on this indictment do you find the defendant guilty or not guilty?"

Julie looked towards Hugh before answering, "We find the defendant not guilty of murder, but guilty of manslaughter."

Hugh grasped at the rail of the dock as the clerk asked, "And is that the verdict of you all or by a majority?"

Julie confirmed it was by a majority and when asked to give the breakdown she stated, "Ten agreed and two disagreed."

Mr Justice Bright QC waited a few moments for the parties in the courtroom to quieten down and then he addressed David and asked if he was ready to deal with the sentence.

David quickly replied, "I am My Lord and I should add that my client has asked that he be sentenced straight away."

The judge nodded and asked Jeremy to outline Hugh's antecedents.

Jeremy looked through some papers in front of him, "My Lord, as Your Lordship heard during the course of the trial, Mr Petford-Williams has no previous convictions, cautions or reprimands recorded against him and was hitherto a man of good character."

The judge nodded in agreement as Jeremy continued. "Has Your Lordship read the 'Victim Impact Statements' I have handed up from Mr Johns' former wife and from his mother?"

"I have, thank you," answered the Judge graciously.

"Does Your Lordship require me to read them out in court?"

"No, thank you. I have read them. They talk of a loving man who will be greatly missed by those who knew him. Nothing would be served by reading them out in detail, I shall consider the contents in sentencing the defendant."

Jeremy sat down and David rose to his feet, he took a quick look at Sara who had tears in her eyes. It was undoubtedly difficult for her. Cases like these were always emotional and it took a while to become hardened to them. In this case, it must be much worse that it was her uncle who was now being sentenced for manslaughter.

He turned back to face Mr Justice Bright, "My Lord, the courts have always acknowledged that sentencing in these types of manslaughter cases is a difficult exercise with so many options available. Of course, one has to consider that a life has been taken and Your Lordship will be very mindful of that fact in sentencing. However, balanced against that is the fact that the jury's verdict means that Mr Petford-Williams did not intend to kill, nor did he intend to cause really serious harm. The jury has clearly rejected his claim that this was an accident, but have found that he anticipated some potential injury but not a serious one from his actions, therefore he falls to be sentenced on the basis that the death of Mr Williams was an unforeseen and unintended result of his reckless act.

Your Lordship has heard that Mr Petford-Williams is a man of previous impeccable character. As you heard during the trial, people who know him personally speak highly of him and his charitable works in the community.

Your Lordship will have formed an impression of what occurred that night from the evidence that you have heard. Mr Petford-Williams has lived with a serious debilitating condition that has robbed him of an important function. He had come to terms with that and the fact that his wife had her own needs which he could no longer satisfy. It must have been horrible for him to have to deal with a situation whereby when he left the house he knew that the woman he loved, would be indulging her passions with another man.

However, he had formed a pact, an agreement, where he could tolerate that provided no one outside the three of them knew and provided that certain safeguards were in place so that he would not walk in on a distressing scene. Sadly, that night, the terms of that agreement were broken. When he left his home he had no intention of harming Mr Johns, when he returned he had no intention of harming Mr Johns, although tragically that is what happened.

Your Lordship will no doubt want to take these factors into account: A man's life was lost and an illegal firearm and ammunition was used, balanced against the previous impeccable character of Mr Petford-Williams, the lack of any real premeditation, the fact a single shot was fired through a door, the fact that the original situation was not of his making and the important facts that there was no intention to kill or to cause serious injury. Further, you will consider that, upon realising what had happened, he immediately phoned 999 and tried to save Mr John's life.

In all these circumstances. I ask you to be as lenient as you feel the justice of the case allows."

David sat down and heard a muffled sob next to him.

Mr Justice Bright looked at his papers for a few seconds and then addressed Hugh, "Mr Petford-Williams, you may remain seated whilst I address these remarks to you. This is a tragic case, tragic not just because a man lost his life but tragic for both you and your wife who have to live with the memory of what occurred that night.

The jury has convicted you on the evidence they heard, which means that they rejected your defence of accident. The prosecution case has been fought by you and has taken some time and expense to conduct. Your sentence cannot and will not be increased for that reason but it does not mean that you do not benefit from the powerful mitigation you could have by pleading guilty and showing genuine remorse for your actions that night.

I have listened carefully to everything eloquently advanced by your counsel on your behalf. No one could have said more for you. I have also listened carefully to the evidence in this case. It is difficult for anyone listening to the evidence not to feel some sympathy for the predicament you found yourself in and for the humiliating agreement that you felt you had to reach for the benefit of your wife. In sentencing you, I take into account your condition and the circumstances you found yourself in. However, none of that explains your possession of a lethal, illegal firearm and ammunition. It probably does not need to be said, but if you had not possessed that rifle and ammunition, Mr Johns would not be dead and you would not be here today facing this sentence.

I accept that you did not intend to cause Mr Johns any serious harm that night when you left the house nor when you returned, but within a short period of time of returning, upon your own admission in evidence, you 'saw red' and were annoyed that your agreement had been broken.

You made the journey upstairs to get that rifle which was kept in your wardrobe. A ludicrously dangerous way to keep a rifle as you had not even locked it away! You then compounded this by loading it. The jury has determined you did not intend to kill or cause really serious harm to Mr Johns, but their verdict also rejected your false protestations that this was simply an accident. I am firmly of the view that you deliberately fired that gun through the lavatory door. You probably expected to scare Mr Johns but you knew full well that your actions could cause some injury but nevertheless you took that appalling risk which ultimately led to Mr John's death.

Stand up please."

Hugh rose slowly to his feet gripping the bar in front of him.

"For the offence of manslaughter I pass the minimum sentence I can in the circumstances of this case, a sentence of eleven years' imprisonment. For the possession of the illegal firearm and ammunition I pass sentences of four years for each firearms offence to run concurrently with the eleven years I have passed for the manslaughter charge. That is a sentence of eleven years in all. You will serve half that time less any time already spent in custody.

You will also pay the court charge and the victim surcharge.

Take him down."

CHAPTER 42

THE SILK RIBBON

Sara was trying to steady herself as she and David took the only working lift down to the ground floor in order to gain access to the cells. David tried to be supportive but found the situation difficult.

It was one thing to console the client after a manslaughter verdict but having to console the junior barrister was altogether different. He decided never to accept another brief again where his junior had some personal relationship with the client.

Sara dabbed at her eyes thinking how unfair the verdict was. It had nothing to do with the fact that Hugh was her uncle. She would have felt the same way whoever the client was, after all she had seen very little of her uncle over the years. No, she felt distraught because she was convinced Hugh was not guilty. She did not believe for one moment that he deliberately shot through the door that day. She could sense it.

Ten minutes later David and Sara were seated in one of the interview rooms in the cell area as a beaming Hugh joined them.

"Excellent result Mr Brant and of course, Sara, I cannot thank you enough."

David looked at him quizzically, "Hugh, you were found guilty of manslaughter, you will have to serve five and a half years inside less the few months you have been on remand. I'm a little surprised you are so happy. I wanted to discuss a possible appeal with you."

Hugh stared at him, "Appeal! I've no intention of appealing."

"But there are grounds, I consider the Judge was wrong to allow the prosecution to place the evidence before the jury of what your wife said in her statement. She was not a compellable witness and it was inadmissible and at the same time, very damaging."

Hugh continued to smile. "I do thank you both for all your hard work, but I am content with the result."

Sara was astonished, "Why? Are you saying you deliberately shot him now?"

David cast her a quick look as if to say we do not ask questions like that at times like this, but she carried on, "I would like to know why you don't want to appeal when we have strong grounds?"

David interrupted, "Perhaps it would be best if I asked the questions, Sara?"

Hugh stopped him from continuing, "No, Mr Brant, I think my niece is entitled to know the answer, but, before I say any more, I would like to ask a few questions."

David nodded so Hugh continued, "Can the prosecution appeal this verdict?"

David replied, "Not as such. The prosecution cannot appeal a case except in extreme circumstances, for example, if someone had intimidated witnesses or members of the jury they might be able to argue it was a 'tainted verdict' and seek a retrial. Also if 'compelling evidence' is discovered in the future they could apply to retry you, but those are extreme examples which very rarely happen and I have no reason to think they will apply here."

Hugh nodded, "Thank you. As a matter of interest, can they appeal the sentence?"

"Only if the sentence was considered to be unduly lenient could they seek what is called an 'Attorney-General's Reference' and apply to the Court of Appeal to reconsider it, but, in this case, although it is on the low side, it is unlikely anyone would consider it 'unduly lenient' so it's not likely the prosecution will appeal it."

Hugh continued smiling, "Finally, now I am convicted of manslaughter, are the Prosecution likely to pursue anyone else for the shooting?"

Both David and Sara looked surprised at the question. It was Sara who could not help blurting out, "But you've always told us you shot Johns by accident!"

Hugh looked at her for a few seconds before answering, "I assume that everything I tell you is confidential and you cannot repeat it?"

Sara looked at David as he replied, "It is confidential, it is covered by legal professional privilege and we cannot waive that except in exceptional circumstances where someone's life might be at risk. I assume you are not going to tell us you are going to kill someone?"

"Good grief no! I've never hurt anyone in my life!"

David looked at him quizzically, "What about Mr Johns?"

"You never answered my last question, Mr Brant, is the prosecution likely to pursue anyone else for the shooting?"

David shook his head and adopted a surprised look, "It's highly unlikely, they consider you pulled the trigger, indeed, it was their case that you murdered him."

Hugh smiled again, "Good! Then I will tell you why I don't wish to appeal. It's very simple really. I love Rosemary and she loves me. I shall tell you what happened on the basis that you never repeat it."

They both agreed and Hugh continued, "We were all drinking that night and I did go out to the club. I did tie a ribbon to the door handle as I was going to be away for some time. I returned after about an hour which should have been long enough for them, but, just before I entered the flat, I heard a rifle shot. I quickly opened the door and saw Rosemary with the gun in her hands. It was Rosemary who had shouted out, "I'm going to kill you, you bastard."

I took it from her and saw a hole in the lavatory door and then saw the blood trickling from underneath. I kicked the door open and saw Johns collapsed on the toilet. I eased him to the floor and shouted to Rosemary to get a towel and apply it to his neck.

I asked her what had happened. She was in a terrible state. She told me she had persuaded Johns to go the spare bedroom and they had sexual intercourse. She told him she loved him and wanted the three of us to stay together forever. He apparently laughed at her and said the situation couldn't last and he was already getting bored with it. He told her he didn't love her and he didn't think she loved him. He told her it was just meaningless sex and he would be moving on soon. She was drunk and distraught and she went upstairs and got the rifle and loaded it. I had shown her in the past how to do it. Meantime, he went to the lavatory. She came down the stairs, heard he was in there and fired a single shot through the door from the stairs. She was apparently trying to reload when I appeared.

I don't believe she wanted to kill him, she was just distraught at the caddish things he had said.

I couldn't let her face a murder trial, so I quickly removed the ribbon from the door and took the rifle and went outside, through the kitchen. There I fired a shot into a target so I would have firearms' residue on my hands. That was the second shot that the witness said he heard. I couldn't find the discarded cartridge in the dark, which is why the police found it when they searched.

I then went inside, closing the kitchen door behind me, hoping no one would realise I had been outside. I ejected the remaining eight bullets and placed the rifle against the stairs. I then got Rosemary to wash her hands to try and remove any firearms residue from her just in case anyone checked her. I didn't think there was any time to change her clothes. I then phoned for an ambulance and the police and told them I had fired the shot by accident. Rosemary did wash her hands but in her intoxicated state she didn't dry them, which is why the paramedic noticed she had wet arms. Fortunately, no one seemed to notice that evidence or make anything of it.

You will see now why I cannot appeal. I'm content with a manslaughter verdict. In just over five years, I will be released and spend my remaining years with Rosemary. If I appealed and was acquitted there is every chance a competent police man might do some more digging and they might charge Rosemary. She wouldn't be able to handle it. She blurted out it was her fault and said she had shot him when the paramedics arrived. Fortunately, they did not hear all of what she said because she was so drunk. I have no doubt that if she was interrogated, even by that simpleton, Detective Sergeant Bull, she would admit the whole thing and probably spend the rest of her life in prison. I couldn't let that happen. This way, we will be together, forever, in just a few short years."

David wondered for a moment whether to mention what Nick Marks had seen concerning Rosemary and Walter Doyle. He decided to broach the subject carefully, "Hugh, would it make any difference to you if Rosemary wasn't going to wait for you?"

Hugh looked at him and adopted a smirk. "Oh, you mean her affair with Walter Doyle! Don't worry, Mr Brant, I'm well aware of that. I do have friends visit me in prison, including

Timothy Granger who came to see me before the trial. He told me about Walter Doyle and Rosemary. I'm not concerned. William Johns wasn't the first man Rosemary took as a lover. She has strayed in the past, but she has always come back to me and I have no doubt she will do so this time."

A short time later, David left the court with Sara. David noticed that she had tied her hair back with the silk ribbon from her brief. She explained she had lost her hair scrunchie. They said very little else to each other, although no doubt both were having the same thoughts. They soon separated, Sara going to stay with her parents and David returning to his hotel. He would stay in Newcastle for one last night and travel home on Saturday morning.

He went to his room and took the Petford-Williams' case papers out of his bag and placed them on the bed. He removed them from their lever arch files and put them in a pile. He then took the red silk ribbon that had come with the papers and tied them in a neat bow at the end.

He looked at the ribbon and grinned, momentarily amused by the number of uses one could make of a simple silk ribbon.

Books by John M. Burton

THE SILK BRIEF

The first book in the series, "The Silk Trials." David Brant QC is a Criminal Barrister, a "Silk", struggling against a lack of work and problems in his own chambers. He is briefed to act on behalf of a cocaine addict charged with murder. The case appears overwhelming and David has to use all his ability to deal with the wealth of forensic evidence presented against his client.

US LINK

http://amzn.to/1bz221C

UK LINK

http://amzn.to/16QwwZo

THE SILK HEAD

The second book in the series "The Silk Tales". David Brant QC receives a phone call from his wife asking him to represent a fireman charged with the murder of his lover. As the trial progresses, developments in David's Chambers bring unexpected romance and a significant shift in politics and power when the Head of Chambers falls seriously ill. Members of his chambers feel that only David is capable of leading them out of rough waters ahead, but with a full professional and personal life, David is not so sure whether he wants to take on the role of *The Silk Head*.

US LINK

http://amzn.to/1iTPQZn

UK LINK

http://amzn.to/1ilOOYn

THE SILK RETURNS

The Silk Tales volume 3

David Brant QC is now Head of Chambers at Temple Lane Chambers, Temple, London. Life is great for David, his practice is busy with good quality work and his love life exciting. He has a beautiful partner in Wendy Pritchard, a member of his chambers and that relationship, like his association with members of his chambers, appears to be strengthening day by day.

However, overnight, things change dramatically for him and his world is turned upside down. At least he can bury himself in his work when a new brief is returned to him from another silk. The case is from his least favourite solicitor but at least it appears to be relatively straightforward, with little evidence against his client, and an acquittal almost inevitable.

As the months pass, further evidence is served in the case and begins to mount up against his client. As the trial commences David has to deal with a prosecutor from his own chambers who is determined to score points against him personally and a co-defending counsel who likewise seems hell-bent on causing as many problems as he can for David's client. Will David's skill and wit be enough this time?

UK LINK

http://amzn.to/1Qj911Q

US LINK

http://amzn.to/1OteiV7

THE SILK RIBBON

The Silk Tales volume 4

David Brant QC is a barrister who practices as a Queen's Counsel at Temple Lane Chambers, Temple, London. He is in love with a bright and talented barrister from his chambers, Wendy, whose true feelings about him have been difficult to pin down. Just when he thinks he has the answer, a seductive Russian woman seeks to attract his attention, for reasons he can only guess at.

His case load has been declining since the return of his Head of Chambers, who is now taking all the quality silk work that David had formerly enjoyed. As a result, David is delighted when he is instructed in an interesting murder case. A middle class man has shot and killed his wife's lover. The prosecution say it was murder, frustration caused by his own impotency, but the defence claim it was all a tragic accident. The case appears to David to be straightforward, but, as the trial date approaches, the prosecution evidence mounts up and David finds himself against a highly competent prosecution silk, with a trick or two up his sleeve.

Will David be able to save his well-to-do client from the almost inevitable conviction for murder and a life sentence in prison? And what path will his personal life take when the beautiful Russian asks him out for a drink?

UK LINK

http://amzn.to/22ExByC

USA LINK

http://amzn.to/1TTWQMY

THE SILK'S CHILD

This is the fifth volume in the series, the Silk Tales, dealing with the continuing story of Queen's Counsel (the Silk), David Brant QC.

Their romantic Valentine's weekend away in a five-star hotel, is interrupted by an unexpected and life-changing announcement by David's fiancé, Wendy. David has to look at his life afresh and seek further casework to pay for the expected increase in his family's costs.

The first case that comes along is on one of the most difficult and emotionally charged cases of his career. Rachel Wilson is charged with child cruelty and causing the death of her own baby by starvation.

The evidence against Rachel, particularly the expert evidence appears overwhelming and once the case starts, David quickly notices how the jurors react to his client, with ill-disguised loathing. It does not help that the trial is being presided over by his least favourite judge, HHJ Tanner QC, his former pupil-master.

David will need all his skill to conduct the trial and fight through the emotion and prejudice at a time when his own life is turned upside down by a frightening development.

Will he be able to turn the case around and secure an acquittal for an unsympathetic and abusive client who seems to deliberately demonstrate a lack of redeeming qualities?

UK

https://goo.gl/YmQZ4p

USA

https://goo.gl/Ek30mx

PARRICIDE

A courtroom drama set in Ancient Rome and based on the first murder trial conducted by the famous Roman Advocate, Marcus Tullius Cicero. He is instructed to represent a man charged with killing his own father. Cicero soon discovers that the case is not a simple one and closely involves an important associate of the murderous Roman dictator, Sulla.

UK LINK

http://amzn.to/14vAYvY

US LINK

http://amzn.to/1fprzul

THE MYTH OF SPARTA

A novel telling the story of the Spartans from the battle of the 300 at Thermopylae against the might of the Persian Empire, to the battle of Sphacteria against the Athenians and their allies. As one reviewer stated, the book is, "a highly enjoyable way to revisit one of the most significant periods of western history"

UK LINK

http://amzn.to/1gO3MSI

US LINK

http://amzn.to/1bz2pcw

THE RETURN OF THE SPARTANS

Continuing the tale of the Spartans from Sphacteria, dealing with their wars and the political machinations of their enemies, breathing life into a fascinating period of history.

UK LINK

http://amzn.to/1aVDYmS

US LINK

http://amzn.to/18iQCfr

THE TRIAL OF ADMIRAL BYNG

Pour Encourager Les Autres

BOOK ONE OF THE HISTORICAL TRIALS SERIES

"The Trial of Admiral Byng" is a fictionalised retelling of the true story of the famous British Admiral Byng, who fought at the battle of Minorca in 1756 and was later court-martialled for his role in that battle. The book takes us through the siege of Minorca as well as the battle and then to the trial where Byng has to defend himself against serious allegations of cowardice, knowing that if he is found guilty there is only one penalty available to the court, his death.

UK LINK

http://goo.gl/cMMXFY

US LINK

http://goo.gl/AaVNOZ

TREACHERY – THE PRINCES IN THE TOWER

'Treachery - the Princes in the Tower' tells the story of a knight, Sir Thomas Clark who is instructed by King Henry VII to discover what happened to the Princes in the Tower. His quest takes him upon many journeys meeting many of the important personages of the day who give him conflicting accounts of what happened. However, through his perseverance he gets ever closer to discovering what really happened to the Princes, with startling consequences.

UK LINK

http://amzn.to/1VPW0kC

US LINK

http://amzn.to/1VUyUJf

Printed in Great Britain
by Amazon